AGE OF CAMELOT

The Legend Comes to Life

By Crystal Wolfe

Cover Art by Crystal Wolfe
Cover Design by Crystal Wolfe
Interior Design by Crystal Wolfe
Typography by Crystal Wolfe
Edited by Crystal Wolfe

March 24th, 2026
FIRST EDITION

ISBN-13:
978-1-954258-13-6

Library of Congress Control Number:
2026932453

United Publications
New York, NY

AGE OF CAMELOT

Dedication

This book is dedicated to all the dreamers who feel connected to, and want to know more about what might have happened in the legend of the Age of Camelot.

Table of Contents

Explanation of Symbols:

~ ~ ~ means a change in time
* * * means a change in character
~ *** ~ means change in character and time

Note: Sections of the book that are italicized are scenes from the past.

Introduction

I wrote this book about the characters of Camelot, and what might have happened to them, because I have always been fascinated by this time period. I researched this historical time for this book, and I researched it throughout my life, to pen with this pseudo "historical fiction" fantasy romance based on what I uncovered over the period of my lifetime.

Each chapter in this novel is told from a different character's perspective. It's also the first spinoff of The Creation Series. This book can stand alone, but there's a few characters from the series that are referenced, as some characters in that series are descendants of Morgan le Fay, Merlin, and Arthur.

I hope this novel will sweep you away, that you will feel yourself pulled into another world, another time. I hope it will be an escape into a romance that takes your breath away and stirs your spirit and moves your heart. I hope it provides answers to some of the mysteries from the *Age of Camelot*.

Prologue
The Golden Age of Camelot

There came a time in Britain when the land seemed blessed by fate itself. This was the Golden Age of Camelot.

The white towers of the city gleamed across the countryside like beacons of hope. Travelers spoke of its wonders in every village and kingdom. Merchants came from distant lands, and poets sang songs of the king who ruled with both justice and mercy.

That king was King Arthur.

Arthur sat upon the throne not as a tyrant but as a guardian of the realm. His crown was heavy, yet he wore it with humility. Beside him ruled his beloved queen, Queen Guinevere, whose wisdom and grace won the hearts of the people.

But Camelot's true strength did not lie only in its king. It lay in the brotherhood of warriors who gathered around the legendary Round Table.

At that table sat the greatest knights the world had ever seen Among them was the noble Sir Lancelot, unmatched in courage and skill with a blade. There was also Sir Gawain, fierce and loyal, whose strength was said to grow with the rising sun. Others included brave Sir Kay, wise Sir Percival, the mysterious Bedivere, who wielded his power and might with the magic of runes, and the noble knight Sir Galahad, whose purity of heart would one day shape the destiny of the kingdom.

Presiding quietly over them all was the great wizard Merlin, whose counsel guided the king through the dangers of power. His magic was the guiding force of Camelot; it's foundation and its protection.

Under Arthur's rule, roads once haunted by bandits became safe again. Farmers tilled their fields without fear of war. Villages rebuilt themselves, and churches rang their bells across peaceful valleys.

The knights of Camelot rode across the countryside, not to conquer kingdoms but to defend the weak. They fought dragons, giants, and cruel warlords who preyed upon the innocent. Wherever injustice rose, a knight bearing the emblem of Camelot soon appeared.

Stories of their deeds spread far and wide. Children pretended to be knights of the Round Table in village streets. Bards wrote poems and songs extolling their noble deeds. They sang their names in royal courts.

For a brief and shining time, Camelot seemed invincible. Within Camelot's great hall, the nights were filled with laughter. Long tables overflowed with food and wine. Musicians played harps while dancers spun across polished stone floors. Torches flickered against the high vaulted ceilings.

At the Round Table the knights gathered not as rivals but as brothers. They shared tales of adventure and tested one another's courage with friendly contests of strength and skill.

Arthur often laughed among them like any other knight. This closeness made the brotherhood strong. It was said that no army in the world could defeat warriors who trusted one another so completely.

During this golden age, many of the greatest legends of Camelot were born. Sir Lancelot rescued captives from dark fortresses and defeated tyrants who terrorized entire regions. The Three Enchanter Knights faced magical enemies and mysterious challengers who tested the honor of the Round Table. And throughout it all, the quiet wisdom of Merlin guided the kingdom like a hidden star, obscured by mist, yet the driving force behind it all.

Even in these glorious years, Merlin sometimes stood alone upon Camelot's towers, staring toward distant hills. For he alone could see what others could not.

The future.

He saw that this golden age would not, could not last forever. Love would turn to betrayal. Brotherhood would fracture. War would return to Britain. But on those bright days, none of that darkness had yet come to pass.

Camelot shone like a dream made real. And for a brief moment and shining moment in history, the world believed that such a kingdom might last forever.

It was an enchanted kingdom, in an enchanted time, and it is their stories we tell of here in this book you hold in your hands.

This is the story of how Camelot came to be. The backstory, and what happened to all the key characters that were an integral part of this fairy tale, this legend, once fact and history, from so very long ago.

I tell their tales in the *Age of Camelot*...enjoy.

Chapter One
Igraine

The castle rose from the sea as though carved from the bones of the earth itself—its granite walls anchored to a jagged cliff of stone, waves forever breaking at its heels. At high tide, the ocean wrapped it in a shimmering moat without shore or mercy, turning it into a lonely island. Only at low tide did a narrow causeway reveal itself, slick with salt and seaweed, a fleeting path between land and legend.

Its towers climbed like watchful sentinels into the wind, their banners snapping in the sharp, briny air. Gulls circled the battlements, their cries weaving through the boom and crash of restless water. The outer walls were weathered silver by centuries of storms, etched with salt and scarred by the memory of siege and thunder. Narrow windows glowed amber at dusk, lanternlight flickering against the vast blue-gray expanse.

The drawbridge did not cross a river but the sea itself, lowered only when the tides and the will of its keepers allowed. Below, hidden caverns tunneled deep into the rock, where the ocean whispered secrets against the stone.

On calmer days, the water reflected the castle in perfect symmetry, doubling its grandeur in a mirror of shifting light. But when storms gathered, waves climbed the cliffs in furious assault, cloaking the fortress in spray and shadow.

From afar, it seemed less a structure built by human hands and more a natural extension of the coastline—unyielding, solitary, eternal. A stronghold not only against armies, but against time, tide, and the endless hunger of the sea. A castle to protect, one of several Lady Igraine called home.

But Castle Tintagel was her favorite. The sunrise over the water painted the sky in purples, pinks, oranges and blues. It was so beautiful it took her breath away. It often did. It was such a different home than the one she was raised in.

She lived a privileged life—and she knew it. She took nothing for granted, for she'd been born into a simple life. Her father had run an orchard of fruits. They'd lived off the land, and sold what they could.

They sold pears, plums, peaches, damsons, and apples. She remembered the apples especially—all the diverse types, with their subtle hints of flavors, and all the delicious things they had made of them—apple pies, apple fritters, apple cakes, meat marinated in apple sauce, apple juice, apple jam, apple honey, apple so ripe off the branches of their trees that the juice squirted and foamed at their mouth with every bite.

They'd been the most delectable of apples. It was one of the things she missed from her poor upbringing, though she didn't miss much else.

Her parents were long dead now. She'd been grateful to Gorlois, the Duke of Cornwall, for plucking her out of poverty and obscurity, bringing into the courts of the Castle Tintagel as a Lady, as his wife. At first, her heart hadn't been sure—but all and all, he'd given her a good life, and together they had three beautiful daughters and a son that she loved completely and utterly, as every mother should.

Gorlois had provided for her and their children, and she was grateful. He was a couple decades older than she. A strong, brute of a man. Tall, with thick black hair and a muscular build. He could be rough, but over the years, she'd softened him. He loved her, of that she was certain.

And did she love him?

Not in the mad, usual way. Not with lust, or passion. He'd felt that for her. He'd taken one look at her in her family's orchards, with her skirts billowing about her, and her long, dark hair flowing in the wind, and fallen madly in love.

But she?

Hers was a deeper, wiser love. A love of gratitude and steadfastness. A love that had come in time, for the father he was to their children, and the good treatment of her, and those he governed.

He wasn't perfect. He had a temper, and was known to throw things about and break things on occasion. But he'd never gotten physical, and in the end, if she patiently waited out the storm, he was just as quick to forget his anger too. Overall, she was the beauty that had tamed the beast.

Her son was Gormand Cador, the eldest, who was destined to become the Duke of Cornwall one day. She loved her daughters too: Elaine, Morguese, and Morgana, the youngest. All of her daughters were showing signs of the Gift. Especially Morgana. She would be a powerful sorcerous one day, if she let her. It ran in their family, through the women of the line.

Igraine's mother had had it. She and her father had renounced it; after seeing the ruin it left for those who wielded the power out of greed and spite. It was a sad story.

Igraine's mother had lost her family early on from the plague, when she was only eight or nine. She alone remained. Thus, no one had taught her how to properly use—and control—the magic within her. One day her foster mother made her angry, as parents want to do to their teenagers, who are just growing into themselves.

But not knowing the power she held within her, her rage soon turned into a violent storm that swept through the small village, killing everyone but her. Again, she was the lone survivor—only this time, she was the cause of the deaths.

Vowing to never use her magic again, to remain calm and self-controlled always, this story was told to Igraine from the time she was a small child. It was a warning, a cautionary tale.

Igraine's mother too was grateful. Grateful to find a man who loved her, gave her children, and provided a simple life of fruits, sweet off the vine. Even after sharing with him her terrifying past, which she regrated with all her heart.

It was better than she'd come from. And she raised Igraine with that same powerful sense gratitude, and that fear of the destruction that magic could cause, if left unchecked.

Magic should never be used to control, to dominate, or to alter the course of destiny and time. Igraine knew that evil had come from her family line in the Celtic and Franc regions.

Some of the magic lay dormant in Igraine. She had renounced it. She did not practice it. But she believed in it.

If the magic could be used for good, if good could come from it, then perhaps...but fear stayed her hand from using the power within herself. Fear that the power would haunt her, and call her, and trick her–as it had so many others.

She was afraid of the harm that magic could do. And she often made a silent prayer that magic would never wreak such harm again, from her bloodline.

She played with her children in the courtyard, keeping an eye especially on the little one, Morgana. She would have to be careful with that one. She would have to guide her well, as her mother had done with her. For surely, she would beautiful, and surely, she would be innately powerful, and she would need to know the dangers of magic, to not repeat the same mistakes as her ancestors.

Uther Pendragon was succeeding his brother, Ambrosius, to the throne, and had invited his nobles and their wives to the ceremony, with a feast and dancing afterwards, so Igraine and Gorlois were preparing to leave Cornwall to attend.

Lady Igraine lovingly gathered her daughters and son about her to say goodbye when it was time. After all, the King's court was no place for children. The Court often had local dignitaries that came for dinner—to dance and meet all the ladies of the court for a dalliance, whether or not they were already wed.

Tomorrow night, King Uther Pendragon, the Great King who'd killed the dragon would be crowned. She was curious what he would be like. What kind of a man could kill a dragon? He must be a great beast himself to do so.

Gorlois and Igraine put on their cloaks and he whisked her off onto the carriage that would take them to the grand castle ruled by Uther Pendragon. "Are you nervous?" Gorlois asked her quizzically, for her hand shook as he lifted her onto the carriage.

There were butterflies in her stomach—she had no idea why. It was if she felt in her spirit that destiny awaited her at the King's Court. A destiny not of her making, yet as inevitable as the sun's rise each dawn.

"I'll be fine dear, I'm just a little chilled," she told her husband, to assuage his concerns. He wrapped his arms about her when they sat in the carriage, and for a horrible moment she felt like a caged bird. His arms felt like a trap. She couldn't breathe and had a sudden urge to throw herself from the carriage, and away from him.

Whatever has gotten into me? she asked herself, forcing herself to tenderly caress his arm as he held her. Yet she couldn't shake the feeling of being at the heels of fate.

When they arrived at the Castle, very late, they ate a quick meal and went to their designated suite in the West Wing, going right to sleep.

Igraine rose to behold the sunrise over mountain views, and sighed at the beauty that lay before her. She thoroughly enjoyed visiting all the castles in Britain. They were all so majestic and magnificent in their own unique ways.

Gorlois had business to attend to during the day, so Lady Igraine was free to do as she pleased. She had a maid servant draw her a hot bath, and soaked in it for what felt like ages.

She could see the heat rising from the water the servants had heated for her use. It was such a far cry from how she grew up, and she felt again that intense gratitude for Gorlois bringing into this charmed life.

She dressed with great care for the ceremony, wearing a red and gold satin gown with threads of real gold that seemed to make her dress glow. The red seemed to shine.

Igraine's maid servant brushed her long dark hair, that reached her buttocks, and carefully curled it into long romantic tendrils smooth and silky. Igraine's green eyes blazed like cat's eyes against the brightness of the red.

She was beautiful. She knew it. She was aware of her beauty, not in a vain way. But in the way of a kitten suddenly discovering its likeness in the mirror, and with a curious realization discovering it was a cat.

Her beauty didn't mean anything to her. Like a pretty set of plates from France, they were a nice token, but she would be fine with or without them. Just as she would be herself, regardless of how she looked.

But she was smart of enough to know that to a man, looks mattered. She didn't like it much, but it was a fact. Sometimes it worried her that if Gorlois had fallen in love with her for her looks, did that mean if she lost her looks, he wouldn't love her anymore?

She shook the thought form her mind. They had four beautiful children that bonded them together for life. Gorlois came up to the suite in the afternoon only moments before the ceremony was scheduled to start.

Straight after ceremony, the group would head into the dining hall for drinks and dinner and then dancing that would likely last until the wee hours of the morning. The ceremony was sure to be the stuff of legend.

Because Gorlois was so late, they didn't sit where they were supposed to, in the second row. They got a seat in a middle row instead, and Lady Igraine could barely see a thing.

She had heard so much about the great warrior who had slayed the dragon, from her husband, when he helped him to win battles that belonged to Uther Pendragon, and his older brother. But she couldn't see him through the throng of people.

She caught a glimpse of a man in bright red wearing a golden crown walking down the aisle, but looked forward to dinner when she would hopefully get a better view of him.

~ ~ ~

After the ceremony, everyone went into the dining hall and began to drink. Uther Pendragon made a grand entrance, carefully later than everyone else, but not late enough that he should offend their appetites.

He was tall, and athletically trim. He had suave medium brown hair that strategically fell across his left eye. He was handsome. Devilishly so. And young. He was dressed well, in red. Igraine's heart suddenly skipped a beat. Her heart had never done such a thing before. She had always been too sensible to involve herself in petty gossip, and certainly far too faithful to ever consider an affair.

Yet when Uther Pendragon's eyes found hers across the table, a magnetic pull made her lightheaded. The magic within her surged towards him like a wave beating the shore. Suddenly time stood still. The magic was there between them, the magic Lady Igraine did not want, or seek.

She forced herself to turn away, staring down at her empty plate. As soon as the King was seated, the servants began to serve them. She determined to concentrate on the quality and deliciousness of the feast.

Yet Lady Igraine could barely eat. *I love my husband,* she reminded herself. And regardless of how she might feel, she would be loyal. It was her nature. She was grateful to her husband and owed him a great debt. She would not betray him for an affair, even with a King.

It wouldn't be worth it, she told herself. But her heart pulled relentlessly at her will.

It exercised every last ounce of her self-control not to look up from her plate again. She felt King Uther's eyes on her through the whole dinner.

"Who is that beautiful creature down there?" Uther asked to the person next to him, pointing.

"Why that's Lady Igraine, Lord Gorlois' wife," the man replied, staring at the King curiously, but not daring to ask why he asked.

Besides, his eyes said it all.

After dinner, and before the music and dancing had begun, Uther cornered her, in a shadowed corner of the hall. "You're stunning–you've bewitched me!" he said in a rush of passion.

She pushed him away. "I'm a married woman, your highnance."

"So?" he asked.

"So, I'm not that kind of woman. I'm a Lady, and true to my Lord."

"That only makes me want you more."

Lady Igraine was finding him rude and very pushy. "I'm going to go now, your highnance."

"You mean you won't stay to dance?"

"No. Now if you'll excuse me."

She put down her face, staring at his hands that gripped her arms. He reluctantly released her.

"I want you," he said bluntly.

"Well, I'm sorry, your highnance–you can't have me."

She was attracted to him in spite of herself, but his conversation left a lot to be desired. She decidedly didn't like the King. Gorlois was so smart and strategic. She excused herself, and slipped up to their chambers for a quiet night of sewing before bed. She was making a cape for little Morgana.

Lord Gorlois came looking for her. "Don't you feel like dancing, my love?"

"No, my dear," she told him. "I'm tired tonight."

"And yet, I find you sewing."

"That's different dear."

"Come dance with me."

"Not tonight, darling."

"Then I shall just have to stay up here with you—and give you a reason to be tired." Lady Igraine smiled, and set down the little cape.

Lord Gorlois made love to her, falling right to sleep afterwards. It was over in a handful of minutes, leaving her unsatisfied and restless.

She sighed. Her mind drifted to Uther Pendragon. "I wonder—STOP!" she ordered herself.

Lord Gorlois snored loudly. She sighed again, turned the light off, and went to sleep.

~ ~ ~

The next day, she stayed confined to her chambers while the duke went about his duties. She could get away with hiding during the day. But the nightly feast was required by all members of the court to attend.

She was barely out of her chambers and into the public arena, when Uther accosted her at the door to the dining hall. "My lady," he whispered, taking her hand, and kissing it.

She pulled her hand from his lips quickly. "Please, my Lord, do not make such a public display."

"I am the King. No one would dare to say anything."

"But–it isn't right."

"Then come away with me–to my quarters, where I can express my affections more intimately."

"Absolutely not!"

"Do you deny the King his fancy?"

"Indeed, I do."

"Why do you play coy, my Lady?" asked Uther, feigning anger.

"Because I *am* a lady–and I am not *your* lady."

Gorlois came into the dining hall just then, with the King all over his wife. His face darkened. His eyes glared. Finally, the King released his hold.

Gorlois took his wife's arm and they went back up to their bedroom.

After getting away from him, she went back up to her bedroom with Gorlois. He was furious. "How dare the King behave so brazenly with my wife!"

"We must leave here now, Gorlois."

"Why? Is there more?" Gorlois' face had turned red with fury.

Lady Igraine bit her upper lip, trying to decide what to do. Finally, deciding there was no other way to convince him, she told him the truth. "It wasn't the first time he acted that way with me, Gorlois."

"What did he do?" her husband demanded, concern creasing his brow.

"He *wants* me," she finally got out.

"Wants? Like...desires you?"

"Yes."

"How do you know."

"He's made it pretty clear, my love. He's propositioning me—demanding I give into his whims."

"My God. Is that why you came upstairs early last night and stayed in the room all day?"

She nodded. "And again, when you happened upon us, he was even more forceful. He, he, he asked me to come to his private chambers."

"What a bastard!"

"We must go, Gorlois—"

"I agree. Quickly and quietly. If he's angry, he can be damned—trying to have my wife right under my nose! King or no, he's a damn scoundrel is what he is!"

"Dear please."

"I'm sorry. I'll take you to the Tintagel Castle, and we'll send for the children. It's the safest place. He won't be able to reach you there."

"But what if he doesn't let this go—"

"We'll cross that bridge when we come to it. You pack our things now, and I'll make sure the carriage is ready for our departure."

He was as good as his word, but just as Lady Igraine feared, the King was angry at their leaving without the proper goodbyes and protocol. Angry enough to start a war with her husband.

~ ~ ~

She found herself thinking of Uther more and more as the days went by in the Tintagel Castle. Gorlois has placed her at the incomparable Tintagel Castle, while he prepared to defend his territory from Dimilioc.

Even though Uther Pendragon was older than she, he had lived such a charmed life. Princes and Kings were often spoiled which made them perpetually immature ego maniacs, while she had come from poverty, and was born an old soul.

Could a man like him ever mature? She didn't know. She wondered. She wanted to stop thinking of him—but passion was something Gorlois could not offer her.

He could be rough, in a clumsy way. In truth, sometimes when they made love, she was repulsed by him... his hairy back, his red, wild hair.

The King was immature—but passionate and quick-witted. Her husband was the only man Igraine had ever been with. And she wondered how different love-making could be with a man who was different in body and soul.

She didn't want to wonder—to ponder such things, and she did everything she could to force the unwanted thoughts from her mind. Yet in secret, in the deepest corners of her mind and heart, she wanted him too. In spite of herself, and her goodness.

She wouldn't dare act on impulse. Desire did not compare to the steadfast, faithful love of her husband. But she was a beautiful young woman yet who couldn't help but wish for a little more in life, and from her marriage.

She continued on with her routine. She took care of her duties. She cared for her children. She performed all she was supposed to as the wife of a Duke—including making love with him on a regular basis, though sometimes his heaviness and sweat made her almost gag. It never lasted long, and for that, she was grateful. She was always looking for what she could be grateful for.

And sometimes, though he could be cruel; she took it on the cuff. She stayed quiet and strong for her husband. A rock. She secretly wondered if the King still wanted her, or had moved on to any of the other ladies of the court he could have on a whim.

Then the day came that a war started—over her. A scroll was delivered to Tintagel that ordered her husband to the front lines, and she knew that Uther still wanted her. Though she was honestly concerned for the safety of her husband, a small part of her found pleasure in the King's desire for her.

But if he came to her, she would surely rebuff him. She would be careful not to let on a single hint of her infatuation with him. He was handsome and athletic and young to be sure, but she had four children with Duke Gorlois.

What of them?

No, it would be selfish and stupid to give in to her flesh. Even if her husband never knew—she would know. And it would haunt her for the rest of her life.

She would not be able to live with the guilt. So, she would stay strong, and as much as the King wanted her—he could not, would not have her.

Yet the stronger she was against the idea—the more she thought of him. She even dreamed of him at night, dreamed that he was thinking of her, talking about her, and devising a plan to be with her.

Chapter Two
Uther Pendragon

Incensed at their departing without leave, Uther determined to lay siege to Gorlois' castles. Weeks of battles later, nothing had been conquered and he was more frustrated than ever.

"I have to have her!" Uther told his friend, Ulfin.

"Calm down, Arthur," he told him harshly.

"Is that any way to speak to your King?" he demanded, angrily.

"No, but it's how I need to speak to my crazy friend—to knock a little sense into his head!"

Uther laughed. "You're right as always, Ulfin."

"You're too impulsive and impetuous when it comes to women, Uther. I'm always telling you that. A woman like Lady Igraine—she's going to want a mature man. She's married with three daughters and a son."

"But I'm still older than her—and I'm the King of All Britain!"

"I know that, Uther. And as your friend, I know who you really are. But no doubt you've only showed this side to her. How can you expect her to want you when you're going to war with her husband? What do you want? An affair? Because she's not the type. She's a lady."

"That makes me want her more!"

"So, you want her husband to die on the front lines—like David with Bathseba?"

Uther looked away sheepishly. "Well..."

"Do you want to marry her or just go to bed with her?"

"I want to marry her!"

"Well, then I don't know if trying to kill her husband has you off to a good start."

"I'm not trying to kill him—just keep him safely away while I devise a plan to get Igraine."

"What do you expect to happen with this war you've declared on her husband, Uther? Gorlois was wise to put Igraine in Castle Tintagel. It's his most protective fortress. It will be impossible to take Tintagel. It's surrounded by the water on all sides; and there's no other way into it, except that provided by a narrow rocky passage—and there, his warriors stationed there could forbid all entry, even if you took up your stand with the whole of Britain behind you."

"I've listened to your warnings and worries, Ulfin, I've heard you out, and I'm still going to force Gorlois on the front lines. He may not die. He's a great swordsman."

"Then what? You think Igraine will immediately fall into your arms—and into your bed, while her husband is off at war?"

"Well, no..."

"Look, I think we need professional help."

Uther bulked and turned up his nose. "What do you mean?"

"Merlin."

"Oh, of course!" Uther exclaimed, looking relieved.

"He will know what magic can help us. I think I heard that wizards can change shape and forms into animals and other people—maybe he can make you look like Gorlois so that we can sneak into the castle and you can get this out of your system with Lady Igraine. And hopefully, she won't ever realize what happened."

"What are you saying—that I just have her for one night?"

Ulfin rolled his eyes. "That's all it usually takes to get a woman out of your system."

Uther glared at him. "That's not true—and Igraine is different."

"Indeed! She's married," Ulfin laughed. "But you're my best friend so I want to help you. We can even ask Merlin to disguise me as Gorlois' right-hand man, and I'll come with you to make sure you don't get into any trouble."

"Really? You'd come along?"

"Of course. I know you. You'll be too distracted fantasizing about Igraine to pay attention to any danger."

"That sounds great!"

"I just want you to be a little careful of Merlin."

"Why would you say that? He's my greatest ally and advisor."

"Yes, and I know he's got...a lot of skills, but I don't completely trust him. He's too invested in your affairs. I'm afraid he's trying to control your destiny."

"That's your opinion, Ulfin, not gospel. He's the greatest wizard of all-time, certainly the greatest wizard of our day, and I'm fortunate to have him on my side."

"I agree. Let's just try to be careful of him. Mark my words, he'll bring the downfall of this kingdom."

"He speaks prophesies about our destiny—he doesn't *control* our destiny," Uther insisted.

"We'll see," answered Ulfin. "Time and history shall tell. But what about the battles you waged with Gorlois? Didn't you two become friends."

"We were comrades in arms—that's all. We really weren't friends."

"And Lady Igraine is far more alluring than the old brute, aye?"

"I suppose so. Let's go to Merlin now and see what he can do for us."

So, they set off to find Merlin. As the King swept away with a whirl of his red cape, lined in white fur, Ulfin hurried after him, keeping his worry to himself. There was an ominous feeling that plagued at him, chewing at the corners of his mind like a mouse chewing at the bread that led to a trap. Something Merlin had prophesied was about to come to pass, he could feel it, and whatever it was, he was sure it would lead to the ruin of his friend.

He liked Merlin, in theory at least. He knew he was a great wizard. He was jovial and humorous enough as well. But the wizard's prophesies worried him. He was too involved in Uther's life. He was powerless to do anything but watch their fates come to pass, but he felt uneasy with Merlin's hand in it...

~ *** ~

Uther and Ulfin stood in the deep woods, where an oak tree stood tall and proud. He began to look for something on the tree, touching it in different places.

"Whatever are you doing?" Ulfin asked him.

"Summoning Merlin," he answered him, still looking on the tree for something. "Ah! There it is!"

Uther found a knob and put his right hand on it, pulling it from underneath.

"I don't know what you expected that to do—" Ulfin began. And in a puff of smoke, Merlin suddenly appeared before them.

"You were saying?" Uther asked him, with a smug smile.

Ulfin gulped. "Yes, um, nevermind!" The truth was, he was a little afraid of the old wizard.

"Merlin, how good it is to see you!" Uther gushed. "You're the only one who can help us!" Merlin was used to his passionate nature—he would have referred to it as dramatics.

"What is it, my King?" he asked patiently.

"It's Lady Igraine—I must have her! I have sent her husband, Duke Gorlois, to the front lines. But Ulfin doesn't think she'll sleep with me when he's gone. What can you do to help?"

"I was preparing for this my friend."

"You were? You knew this was going to happen?"

"Indeed. Lady Igraine is integral to your future, and the future of your Kingdom."

"So, we will wed?"

"All in good time, my King. One thing at a time. Before I help you, I must have your word on something. Ulfin—would you mind excusing us for a moment?"

Ulfin quickly nodded, and began to walk through the woods alone, eager to get away from the intense energy of the old wizard he found so unsettling.

"What do you want that you didn't want Ulfin to hear about, Merlin?" Uther asked curiously.

"Oh, he will hear all about it later, but it is a private matter between us."

"Okay—so, out with it. What do you want?"

"I want any son you have with Igraine."

"A son?"

"Yes."

"How do you know I will have a child with Igraine?"

"I just know."

"But my son will be destined to be king one day."

"Precisely—and that's why your child could never be raised by you and Igraine. He would always be in danger. By allowing me to take care of the child, he shall be protected."

"So, you want the child to protect them?"

"Exactly!"

"Will he know who their parents are?"

"Of course—he will be told when the time is right."

Uther thought for a moment. "So, it would be like giving the child up for adoption for their own good—in order to spare their life so that they can eventually rule the kingdom in peace?"

"Yes, Uther. You are very clever, you understood right away."

"And who better to appoint as a guardian to the child, then the greatest wizard of all-time?" Uther nodded to himself, "Yes, Merlin, I agree to your terms. Although no child shall come of Igraine and I, if I don't have her! What do you have in mind to help me?"

"For this, my friend, you shall need a disguise."

"Well, surely, I can't change overnight to look like Gorlois? He's a big beast of a man!"

"Of course not! My magic shall disguise you to look like Gorlois—just for one night of passion with Igraine."

"But I want to marry her as well!"

"You shall. But first things first. Your time with her is very important."

"Why?"

"That you shall know in time, my King. Something very special will come from your night together. Now leave me for a few hours to prepare. And prepare yourself—bathe and put on a fresh pair of clothes and cologne. Get ready to see her."

"Good idea," Uther agreed. "I'll leave you to your wizardry, and be back when the clock chimes thrice. That shall give me time to prepare for the journey to Lady Igraine. I will come with the carriage, and we shall leave immediately."

~ ~ ~

When Ulfin and Uther returned, Merlin was ready for the enchantment. He had memorized the spell that would change Uther's appearance from the King of Britain to the Duke of Cornwall, and that would change Ulfin's appearance into that of Gorlois' friend, Jordan.

But there was a catch.

The spell would only last for 24 hours. Just enough time to get to Igraine, make love to her, and return home.

They watched in wonder as Merlin worked his magic. When Uther looked in his small, hand-held mirror, he did a double take. It was not himself he saw—but the Duke of Cornwall, Gorlois. His body *felt* the same, yet he looked totally different. It was a strange sensation—to see yourself as something different than who you really were, and how you really felt.

He saw Ulfin do the same thing as he looked in the mirror and saw one of Gorlois' best friends, Britaelis. "Well," Ulfin said trepidatiously, "I suppose we should be off."

"Wait," said Merlin. "Not quite so fast."

They watched in amazement as Merlin transformed himself into another of Gorlois' friends.

"What are you doing?" Uther sputtered out. "I'm coming with you," Merlin declared. "This is too important to leave to you two to your own devises. If anything goes wrong you shall need my help."

"That's true," the King nodded. He was surprised by Merlin joining them, but gratified by it all the same. He was right—they might need him and his magic. Magic tended to come in handy.

~ *** ~

So, we set off together, traveling as fast as possible to Castle Tintagel. I was nervous, and glad to have my friends with me. Ulfin made me laugh, regaling me with stories of our adventures and quests gone awry to get my mind off the matter at hand.

Even though we were thoroughly disguised we still had to be careful. No news would have come to the people there about Gorlois and his friends winning the war and returning to the castle, so an astute guard might be suspicious.

When Gorlois returned, the less people to have seen us the better. Because if we were seen then he would know we had been there. And if Igraine mentioned anything to him about that night he had returned and made love to her—then there would be hell to pay with both Igraine and Gorlois.

So that's why, even though I was disguised as Gorlois, and this was his Castle, I didn't want anyone in the Kingdom to see me. It was good to have my friends with me. We had been on countless adventures and travels together. Their help was needed and necessary right now, while my mind was elsewhere.

I was imagining Lady Igraine with her clothes off. I imagined taking them off myself, slowly, piece-by-piece. I imagined making love to her slowly, then getting harder and passionate as the night wore on. It was all I could think about.

So, when we arrived, with Merlin and Ulfin on either side of me, after we got through the gates, we bent under passageways, avoiding people when and where we could.

We finally stopped ducking and dodging in a quiet alcove. "Where shall you two be while I'm with Igraine?"

"We'll be guarding the door," said Ulfin instantly.

Merlin shook his head. "No, Ulfin will be guarding the door, I have business elsewhere."

"Business elsewhere?" I demanded. "What does that mean?"

"That is my business," Merlin answered mysteriously. "I will meet you boys at noon here tomorrow."

Ulfin and I shrugged. What else could we do? Merlin was a free agent, and we were lucky he'd joined us on this mission at all.

I arrived at Lady Igraine's bedroom door by dinnertime. Lady Igraine was getting ready to come down to eat.

I knocked on her door. "Come in," she said. I entered. Her breath caught when she saw me. I began to sweat. *Did she know? Did she see through my disguise?*

She ran into my arms, throwing herself about my shoulders. "My dear Gorlois! Have you returned home? Has the dreadful King come to his senses?"

I grimaced.

"What is it my dear," she continued. "Are you injured?"

"No, my love, it isn't that. I'm just so happy to be back here with you—in your arms." She smiled sweetly, looking up at me.

And without further words or thought, I lifted her up and twirled her around. "Why, what's gotten into you?" she laughed.

I moved in for a hot and sensual kiss. "Wow," she whispered, her body breaking out in goosebumps. "You really did miss me!"

I lifted her beautiful feminine body, all curves, unto the bed, and kissed her again, moving on top of her. My hands felt down her corset, starting to lift at her skirts.

Pulling her skirts up, I gripped her buttocks in my hands and squeezed them hard. She gasped in pain, and I smiled coyly, spanking her. She looked at me in surprise.

I lifted her from the bed, and began to slowly undress her. Now I went slower, to build the anticipation–that and removing all her clothes took some care and time. The corset–with all the strings–took quite a while to untie. I was growing impatient.

"What about dinner?" she questioned. "Aren't you hungry?"

"Hungry for you," I answered her. "Afterwards we will have dinner brought up to us."

"Whatever has gotten into you?" she looked at me quizzically, as if she knew something was different. That comforted me somehow. I continued to undress her, as if I was unwrapping a present, the gift I'd wanted and waited for and search the world for all my life.

Finally, she stood before me, completely naked. Her body was pure perfection. She was a dramatic hourglass. Her breasts and behind were full and firm. Her waist small and tiny, like a slim green stem lifting the bloom of a full, white rose.

I felt both lust and love burning in my heart and mind for her. Equally strong. I did not fight either feeling. I embraced them.

For she was everything I'd ever looked for in a woman. Everything I'd dreamed of. She was a vision of grace and beauty, and I knew that I loved her then, and that I always would.

Now I slowly removed my clothes, wishing she could see my real body and form. *All in good time,* I thought to myself. *As Merlin said, one thing at a time.*

Gorlois had nothing on me. No part of his body was as good as mine was. When I made love to her as Uther, as myself, it would be so much better.

Still, at least my body felt the same, so I could move like myself. Gorlois' heaviness and ugliness didn't affect my usual motions. I started slowly making loving to her then as her body warmed up to me, I began to thrust faster and harder. She cried out in pleasure with my movements. I felt certain Gorlois had never made love to her so well.

Hours passed. If I only had one night, I would make love to her all night. I would make our time together last. I refused to waste a moment of my time not touching her.

As I lay with my beauty, and she moaned in pleasure, I released myself into her. I felt her wetness all over me too. As our sweet nectars mixed together, I felt as if we were One, in a way I had never been with the other women I'd lain with. I'd never desired a woman more. And ours was not a desired that could ever be satiated.

We continued making love through the night until finally falling asleep in each other's arms by morning light. I would have to leave by the early afternoon to get home before I lost the form of Gorlois I wore like a cape about my neck. But for this moment, we slept in each other's arms.

I knew I didn't want her just for tonight. I wanted her for a lifetime. And I wanted to make love to her as Uther Pendragon, as myself, as the King of All Britain. I wanted her to want *me* too—to choose me, body and soul, forever.

I felt as if I had searched for her all my life. It didn't matter that she was born to be mine. And I was born to be hers. Love would conquer all—one way or another.

Merlin was right. Something special had come from our night of passion. An epic love that the poets would write about. A love I felt certain would stand the test of time—and whatever other tests the gods threw at us along the way. We would conquer them all with a love that was born of passion, and tempered by a love that was true.

~ *** ~

Merlin had slipped into a cave not far from the Castle. The cave was going to be his home away from home after Gorlois died, and Uther and Igraine were married. Unbeknownst to either one of them, Igraine would become pregnant with Uther's child from their night of passion, which Merlin himself had foretold to be the greatest King that Britain would ever know: *King Arthur.*

Arthur was the one Merlin had been waiting for all his life. Now his birth was imminent—Merlin would make sure of that.

Merlin spoke many spells in the cave, ensuring that destiny would unfold smoothly. Arthur would become the King his father never could be. Arthur would be the friend Merlin had always hoped for, and the son he'd never had, but always hoped for.

Fate was imminent. Merlin was at the cusp of what he'd been waiting for through many long centuries.

Let Uther have Igraine: Merlin wanted Arthur.

Lady Igraine would carry Arthur through to full-term at Castle Tintagel, until he was born at the castle. Then the baby would be whisked away for safe keeping, away and hidden from all those who would do him harm—and that included his own father.

Uther Pendragon was witty and bright, and he would mature over time, with the love of a good woman. But he would never be what Arthur was from birth.

Merlin recited spells through night to ensure that Gorlois would be dead by morning... and that sometime in the night, the seed of Arthur would take root in Lady Igraine's womb. Uther Pendragon and Lady Igraine were the couple destined to be the parents of this great King.

But they were not destined to raise him. Merlin would place him carefully in the care of one of the Lords, then come to him at the perfect time. Arthur would pluck the Sword from the Stone, as if it was nothing, when countless men of great height and strength and experience could not, and then he would guide and raise the lad to become a King that Britain could be proud of.

Merlin was practically salivating thinking of the moment when he and Arthur would come together, and never be apart. Arthur would be a student worthy of Merlin's time and care. He would be both smarter and wiser than his father. And he would have the solid goodness of his mother.

Yes, Arthur would be a worthy student, like a son, and Merlin's best friend. Once they came together, they would not ever be apart—until the end.

~ *** ~

Chapter Three
Gorlois

I had been one of Uther's most powerful allies in the war against the Saxons. Indeed, I was responsible for his victory. I had devised a strategy and tactic to defeat them. Is *this* how he treated those who helped him?

I thought of my beautiful wife safely protected at Tintagel. It was such a beautiful castle. Our pottery, glass, plates, and cups were of the finest quality, for ours was a wealthy kingdom.

We drank wine imported from the eastern Mediterranean, using food vessels from Gaul and North Africa to gather exotic spices and foods. Our stain glass window the topmost point of the castle was inscribed with a mixture of Celtic, Latin, and Greek words, names and symbols. It was my favorite castle in my territory.

I had considered Uther Pendragon a friend, now he was going to war with me to sleep with my wife? My how fast the seasons change.

I had been the vassal of Uther's brother, Abrosius. My arrival at the Battle of Kaerconan ensured the defeat of Hengist. And when Hengist's sons, Octa Ossa, rebelled, I helped Uther to defeat them at York.

And how was I repaid? By him trying to sleep with my wife? By him waging war on me and my men? The King was bastard I tell you! A bastard!

"All right men, get in line!" I ordered. I remembered how I had met the King. We had been comrades in the Battle at York. My mind drifted back to when...

~ ~ ~

Uther and I stood together at the front lines, looking fierce in their warrior array of armor from head-to-toe, with shields and two-edge swords.

Uther put a hand on my shoulder. "Thanks for coming Gorlois," he told me.

"Don't thank me until after we've won," I replied, my jaw set. I was determined to win this battle for my King, and his brother, Uther.

"So, what's the plan?" he asked me. "Cornelius said you had some ingenious plan that was going to bring us to victory?"

"I do."

"And?"

"And it's a trick. It's a trick that will work. Just wait. It's meant to be a surprise."

The wind came howling off the western sea, driving rain like spears against the shields of Britain. Along the black cliffs below Tintagel, beacon fires burned–not as signals of welcome, but of war.

The Saxons had landed.

At their head stood Octa and Ossa–grim sons of Hengist, iron-bound and wolf-eyed. Their longships clawed the shoreline like dark teeth, and their warriors poured onto British soil with axes raised and banners snapping in the gale.

Far above the crashing surf, the banners of the Dragon stirred. King Uther Pendragon sat astride his warhorse, red cloak whipping behind him, the golden dragon standard blazing against the storm.

I was right there with him—broad-shouldered, ruddy complexion and red hair that I hated, iron-helmed, his armor etched with the knotwork of Dumnonia.

"They mean to take the western cliffs," Uther said, voice like distant thunder.

I didn't look at him. My gaze was fixed on the beach below.

"Then they will drown in Cornish blood before they climb them."

The horns of war sounded. Cornish spearmen formed ranks along the narrow ascent from the shore—shields locked, spears angled downward like a forest of thorns.

The Saxons charged uphill, roaring in their harsh tongue. Axes struck shields. Wood splintered. Men shouted, cried out in pain.

Octa himself broke through the first rank, his axe splitting a Briton's helm. Ossa followed close behind, cutting a brutal path toward the heights.

Uther spurred forward. "For Britain!" The Dragon advanced.

When the left flank faltered under Saxon pressure, I rode straight into the breach. "Close ranks!" I roared.

I dismounted in the thick of fighting—preferring steel at arm's reach. My sword moved in controlled arcs, not wild fury, but disciplined precision.

A Saxon fell. Then another.

I planted my shield into the earth and rallied the Cornish around it. "Here stands Cornwall! Here stands Britain!"

The men steadied. The line did not break.

On the upper ridge, Uther and Octa met blade to blade.

Octa swung heavy and brutal towards Uther. Uther moved with surprising grace for a man armored in mail. He was young and athletic. Steel rang. Octa's axe bit into Uther's shield–nearly tearing it apart, but Uther twisted, drove his sword beneath Octa's arm, and blood darkened Saxon leather.

Octa staggered.

Seeing their leader wounded, Saxon morale wavered.

At that moment, I signaled for his great surprise I'd hinted to Cornelius about. Hidden behind the cliffs, Cornish cavalry descended in a flanking charge–hooves pounding like war drums. This was his secret strategy that I hoped would win us the war.

They crashed into Ossa's exposed side.

The Saxons, trapped between cliff and sea, realized too late that the narrow shore had become their grave. Ossa fought like a beast cornered, but he could not rally the men against horse and spear.

The tide turned. The sea swallowed retreating longships. The beach and ocean ran red.

As dawn broke, the storm cleared. Saxon bodies lay strewn along the rocks.

Uther stood overlooking the carnage, dragon banner rising behind him. I approached, helm under his arm in honor of Uther, "The western shore holds," I told him proudly.

Uther nodded. "Because Cornwall stood. I couldn't have done it without you."

For a moment, just a moment, there was unity.

Two great lords. One Britain. Neither of us knowing that love, not war, would soon drive us to ruin.

~ ~ ~

Gorlois recalled how his loyalty helped keep Britain unified under Uther during a fragile period. Gorlois helped save Britain... And was being destroyed by the very king he helped defend.

Gorlois had supported Uther as a faithful vassal. He allowed Uther to fight the Saxons at the great Castle Tintagel. He brought Cornish troops to reinforce Uther's army. They had increased their manpower threefold. This alliance helped Uther repel Saxon advances in several brutal campaigns.

By holding the southwest, Gorlois prevented Saxons from gaining total control of Britain's western regions. At this time, Britain was fragmented. Many regional kings acted independently.

After the death of King Aurelius Ambrosus, Gorlois turned his allegiance to his younger brother, set to inherit the throne. By recognizing Uther as the High King, it helped to maintain unity among the English rulers. It also strengthened resistance against Saxon tactic to divide England, and thus conquer it. This unity was crucial against Octa and Ossa's coordinated invasions.

Octa and Ossa, as sons of Hengist, were leaders of renewed Saxon invasions after earlier conflicts. Cornwall's landscape of natural cliffs, hard-to-invade terrain, and strong defensible sites like Tintagel made it a strategic ally. Warfare was mainly small-scale raids, making fortified hill forts key. Gorlois' extra troops and coastal defense were critical to the victory of the dragon.

And now we had come to this... like so many great men before us, we were outdone not by steel and war, but by the love of a good and beautiful woman.

Then for a moment, his mind drifted back to the first time he had seen her...

~ *** ~

She'd been picking apples out of her parent's orchard. The sunlight had shone down on her dark hair, lighting her hair and face in a strange glow, like the halo and holy light of an angel.

Her long hair was blowing in the wind, like a beacon, her skirt blowing seductively all about her curvaceous form. A storm was coming any minute. The wind had picked up quickly.

The sun became obscured by the darkening clouds. Just as it started to pour, I ran to the lady and wrapped my arms about her, in a mad dash to keep her safe.

She shoved me off her, screaming in the whining winds, words I couldn't hear. I was already in love, and she was terrified of me...

~ ~ ~

It took some time to convince her that I wasn't a madman, after scaring her at first sight. It took even longer for me to convince her to marry me.

Her parents were more willing to give me a chance than she was. Of course, I hadn't scared them to death right off the bat either.

Slowly, but surely, I convinced Igraine to marry me. I courted her arduously, showering her with gifts and attention. After she'd finally agreed to marry me, we made love under that very same apple tree where I had first seen her.

It was taboo to have sex before wedlock, and usually Igraine was poised and refined, but she had a wild side that I unleashed the first time we made love.

The following week we were wed in my castle, and less than a year later, our first child was born.

Cador was first. A son as the firstborn was surely a good omen.

Then Elaine, with her long, black hair. As my first daughter, she was my favorite.

Then Morguese, then Morgana.

All my beautiful daughters had their mother's long dark hair. Cador had bright orange hair and a ruddy complexion like me. Poor boy.

Those were the best days of my life. I was quite a bit older than Igraine, a couple decades older, so having a wife and children later in life was a gift for me.

I loved those kids as if they were a part of my very body and soul. I loved Igraine, as she owned my heart. Without her, my heart would fail to beat.

I loved my family so much–more than anything. I was so grateful to Igraine for giving me a chance. I knew she'd always felt indebted to me because I was the one with the status and the money. But in truth, it I was who was lucky to have shared my life with her.

~ ~ ~

Now here I was, on the front lines, when I needn't be. I had a wife and three daughters and a son at home to take care of. My mind was thinking of them when five men charged at me with their swords drawn.

My whole body was in armor...only my neck was uncovered. They must have seen that too. I saw the sword coming towards my face. I felt it hit my neck.

I knew the image of Igraine would be my last, and that image of her would carry me into my next life. But still I fought valiantly, hoping for my time with the wife and children I loved more than anything...

~ *** ~

The wind had changed.

Gorlois of Cornwall had known war his whole life—Saxon steel, Irish raiders, rival Briton kings—but this wind was different. It was carried not by salt and iron... but betrayal.

He stood upon the heights of Tintagel, watching waves shatter themselves against the rocks far below. Uther Pendragon had once stood beside him in battle. Now the Dragon banner approached Cornwall not as allies—but as threat.

King Uther was not with him—he'd set his men to fight this needless war...this war of lust and desire from a spoiled King.

He had seen it first in Uther's eyes at court. Not the fire of war. Not the burden of Kingship. Something much darker.

Uther's gaze lingered too long upon Igraine. Igraine—his wife, his heart, the jewel of Cornwall.

Gorlois was not a fool. Kings desired. Kings took. But he had believed Uther better than that. He had bled for him. Held the western shore against Octa and Ossa. He had watched men die beneath the Dragon standard. And now that same Dragon marched against him.

He left court without permission. Some called it insult. Some called it rebellion. He called it survival. He called it love for a wife he was unwilling to share.

The battle was the fort Dimilioc. Something in him knew it would be his last, and greatest fight. For it would be a fight for his Kingdom, his family, and his life.

His best friend, Britaelis, stood beside him as the first distant horns echoed inland. "Will he truly make war upon you?" he asked.

Gorlois did not answer at once. "Yes," he finally answered him.

Gorlois and his men rode hard down to the fortress. King Uther Pendragon's knights did not come in secrecy. They came with banners. With knights. With engines of war.

They besieged Gorlois' holdings inland first—drawing him away from center of the fort. It was strategy, not fury. Gorlois rode out to meet the Dragon's men in open field.

They fought valiantly all day. Night had fallen by the time the clash began to wind down. The knights on both sides were growing weary.

Torchlight flickered across steel. Rain fell—as it had on the western shore when they had fought side-by-side. Gorlois cut through a rank of royal soldiers with terrible precision.

He did not shout. Did not curse. He fought as a man betrayed fights: silent and unstoppable.

But Uther's numbers were greater. And worse—his purpose was personal. A spear struck Gorlois' horse. He fell hard to the mud.

Before he could rise, blades surrounded him. He saw the Dragon banner through rain-blurred vision.

Steel descended. The world narrowed. As Gorlois lay dying on the field... he had a vision.

Something stirred in the air. Far away, at Tintagel's gates, a rider approached under cover of darkness.

He bore Gorlois' face. His voice. His armor.

Igraine received him, believing her husband returned from battle.

But it was not Gorlois. It was Uther—cloaked in illusion by the sorcery of Merlin.

Merlin had woven glamour thick as sea-mist. And while Gorlois' blood cooled in the mud...

If legend grants him one final thought, perhaps it was this: not of jealousy, not of rage, but of Cornwall. Of the cliffs holding fast. Of the shore where he and Uther once stood united against the Saxons.

He had defended Britain from invaders. He had defended his king. He could not defend his own house.

The sea roared below Tintagel. And the old world shifted. The rain was warm. That was the first strange thing.

Gorlois lay on his back in the churned earth, breath ragged, with the sudden realization that the warmth he felt was from the iron taste of blood thick in his mouth, and pouring down his body.

The clash of battle had receded into distant thunder.

Of course, he had known he would die one day. He had not expected to die looking up at the Dragon banner.

Through blurred vision he saw it—red cloth snapping above the melee. King Uther Pendragon's coat of arms.

His king. His betrayer.

Another spear wound burned beneath his ribs. He pressed his palm against it and felt warmth pouring out of him.

Yet something else stirred—something colder than the rain. For a heartbeat, the noise of battle dimmed—as if the world inhaled. Gorlois' breath hitched. *Tintagel.*

The thought came not as memory, but as warning. He saw it in his mind—the black cliffs, the narrow bridge, the tower where Igraine waited.

And then—a flicker. A sensation like being watched from two places at once. His chest tightened. "No..." he rasped.

He had stood beside kings long enough to recognize ambition. But this was different. This was design.

He had seen the old man at court—quiet, sharp-eyed, wrapped in shadow. *Merlin.*

A counselor who spoke rarely, but when he did, men fates were shifted. Gorlois had dismissed him once as a court mystic.

Now, dying in the mud, he felt something tear across the fabric of the night. As if a door had opened. As if another version of himself had risen. A cold certainty spread through him. If he lay here dying—then who stood at Tintagel?

His heart pounded in terror greater than battle had ever stirred. Not for himself. For her.

The rain seemed to fall upward for an instant. The torches guttered blue. Finally, Gorlois understood.

Uther was not merely waging war. He was using his death. The siege inland... the draw away from Tintagel... the timing.

It was too precise. Too perfect. "Wizardry..." he breathed. Not as an accusation, but as recognition.

He tried to rise. His body refused. Blood pooled beneath him, warm and endless. He gripped the earth instead.

"*Igraine...*" he whispered. The name felt like a shield too late raised. Somewhere far beyond the battlefield, thunder rolled over the sea cliffs. And in that thunder, Gorlois felt the spell settle into place.

A deception walking in his skin. Speaking with his voice. Entering his hall. Entering *her* chambers.

He closed his eyes. Not in surrender. In fury.

If there are moments when the veil thins between life and whatever waits beyond—then perhaps Gorlois saw more than the mud and the rain. Perhaps he saw a child not yet born. A boy who would carry both Dragon and Cornwall in his blood. A king forged from betrayal.

If so, then his final words may not have been curse—but a warning, a hope, a cry.

"Let him be greater," he murmured in the dark. "Let him be greater than all of us. Let him be the best Britain has to offer this world," he said the words like a blessing, as a prayer.

The rain ceased. The Dragon banner lowered. One of Uther's men brought down his sword, cutting off Duke Gorlois' head in one quick, smooth motion. And far away, at Tintagel, the old world ended...and another age began.

~ *** ~

Chapter Four
Cador

Everyone in Tintagel thought that the Duke had returned to the castle, including Igraine. While Uther, disguised as the Duke, ravished Igraine, Gorlois was killed in the fighting at the siege of the other castle. On the very same night.

Uther claimed that he didn't want Gorlois' death, but no one believed the King's sincerity. With Gorlois' death, the castle surrendered to Uther, and he married the newly widowed Duchess soon after her husband was killed. That made Igraine Queen of Logres, or Queen of all Britain.

~ *** ~

I wanted vengeance for what King Uther Pendragon had done to my father. I wanted to take revenge on his son, Arthur. On that, Morgana and I were aligned.

I was twelve when our father was so cruelly taken from us—set out on the front lines of a battle the king waged to have sex with his wife, our mother.

Then to have mother turn around and marry him was beyond me. Elaine and I were quite enraged and let her have it. Morgana said we drove her away. But I couldn't stand the sight of that man—Uther.

I was dubbed the Duke of Cornwall to replace my father, a few years later on my sixteenth birthday. As the eldest, with three younger sisters, I grew up fast.

The great hall of Tintagel was heavy with the smell of salt and wet stone. Outside, the Atlantic crashed violently against the cliffs below the fortress, the waves striking the black rocks like war drums. The sound carried through the narrow windows and into the hall where the lords of Cornwall had gathered.

Banners hung from the rafters—black falcons on crimson fields, the sigil of the House of Gorlois. But the mood in the hall was not celebratory. It was tense. Somber.

~ *** ~

At the far end of the chamber stood the high stone chair of the Duke of Cornwall. The seat of Gorlois. Empty.

Before it stood a boy. Sixteen-years-old. Cador.

He wore a dark tunic trimmed with silver thread, and a sword hung awkwardly at his side—new, ceremonial, far too polished for battle. His red hair fell across his brow, and though he tried to stand like a man, the grief in his eyes betrayed him.

The hall was silent except for the sea. Beside him stood the Archbishop of Cornwall, old and stooped, holding a golden circlet in trembling hands. The duke's crown.

The same crown that had rested on Gorlois's head. Behind the archbishop stood the royal guests. King Uther Pendragon. And beside him—Queen Igraine.

Cador did not look at them. Not once. He stared straight ahead. At the empty chair. His father's chair.

Images burned like a wild fire in his mind...

The messenger arriving breathless from the battlefield. The blood-stained cloak. The terrible words. *The Duke of Cornwall has fallen.*

And worse still—his father's body returned in two pieces. His body and his head. The hall doors slammed in the wind. Cador's jaw tightened. The archbishop raised his voice.

"Lords of Cornwall, we gather today to confirm the rightful heir of this duchy."

The nobles shifted uneasily. Some glanced toward Uther. Some toward Igraine. Everyone knew what had happened. Gorlois had died in a war that began because the king desired another man's wife.

Cador had not forgotten. Cador would never forget.

The archbishop continued. "By blood and by right, Cador, son of Gorlois and Lady Igraine, stands before you as the next Duke of Cornwall."

Murmurs rippled through the hall. One of the older knights stepped forward. Sir Brestieas, who had fought beside Gorlois for twenty years. He knelt before Cador without hesitation. "My duke," he said.

One-by-one, the other lords followed. Armor clanked. Knees struck stone.

"My duke."

"My duke."

"My duke."

Cador felt the weight of their loyalty pressing down on him. He had trained with swords. He had hunted in the forests. But ruling a duchy? That had always belonged to his father. He knew he wasn't ready.

The archbishop stepped closer. “Do you swear,” he asked, “to protect the people of Cornwall, to defend its lands, and to honor the memory of those who ruled before you?”

Cador’s throat tightened. He thought of Gorlois riding out in armor. Laughing. Strong. Unconquerable. Now reduced to bones beneath the earth.

“I swear,” Cador said, his voice strong, belying how he really felt.

The archbishop lifted the circlet. The golden band caught the torchlight as it rose above the boy’s head.

Behind them, Uther watched quietly. Igraine’s face was pale. As the crown touched Cador’s hair, something inside him hardened to stone.

The archbishop spoke the final words. “Rise, Cador of Cornwall. Duke of this land.”

Cador stood taller now. The crown felt heavier than iron. The hall erupted into cheers.

“DUKE OF CORNWALL!”

“LONG LIVE CADOR!”

But Cador did not smile. Slowly—very slowly—his eyes lifted. For the first time, he looked directly at Uther Pendragon.

The King who had sent his father to war. The King who had taken his mother. The King who now stood inside his father’s hall as if he belonged there.

Their eyes met across the chamber. The roar of the crowd faded in Cador’s ears. For a moment the two of them simply stared at one another.

Boy Duke.

High King.

Then Cador turned away. He walked towards the great stone chair. His father's chair.

He sat down. The hall cheered again. But deep in his chest, Cador made a silent vow.

He would rule Cornwall well. He would protect his people. He would never forget the day his father died. And he would get vengeance on the King who had caused it.

~ *** ~

My main job was to care after my territory and all the people in it. I consider revenge my part=time job, and Morgana was my partners in crime. Morgeuse was a gentler sort—like our mother had been when she was a young mother taking care of us. Elaine started with Morgana and I—on our quest for revenge, but Morgeuse's reverent prayers must have taken their hold in her.

Morguese wanted no part in our attempts to hurt Uther, and subsequently, Arthur, the ruler of his enchanted kingdom they called Camelot. The baby was sent away and missing, or I would have killed him when he was young and defenseless—easier to kill.

Eventually Arthur, grew up, and grew too strong to kill easily, as he was under Merlin's protection. Camelot was a joke, as far as I was concerned. King Arthur was hailed at Britain's greatest King, but I knew the filth that he was born of. He was a bastard on the throne, if there ever had been.

And I ruled over my own Kingdoms better than Camelot and his "Knights of the Round Table." They dreamed of a land of fairness and equality, where average peasants could rise from the ranks and decide on occupations of their choosing.

How on God's green earth could a land like that ever survive? It was ridiculous. My father had taught me how to lead—with an iron fist and a golden heart, and that's how I led my people in my land.

I was proud of the job I did. I was proud of my bloodline and where I came from. And I was not a bastard on the throne, like Arthur was.

He had no *right* to rule over any kingdom. I'd heard through the grapevine that he had practically been a slave to Sir Ector while he was raising him. That's what a serf like him deserved.

The damn Sword in the Stone. Morgana had only managed to steal the sheath from Arthur—but the sword, Excalibur, had stayed steadily in his grip.

He had been a small, scrawny lad, only fourteen when he took the sword from the stone, and the wizard Merlin had dropped his pupil, Morgana, like a bad case of the bubonic plague, immediately turning his time and attention to child-rearing of that little prince.

Morgana was twenty then, and betrothed to King Urien, so she would have had to stop seeing Merlin anyways. But still. He resented his sister being dropped by the wizard so unceremoniously.

She deserved more respect. She'd become a great sorcerous, who planned and plotted to use her magic for revenge, the same way I planned to—only with my money and power.

What about what Arthur's father had done to our father? How could he justify it? Or did he even know? I'd heard he didn't even know who his parents were until the day he plucked the sword from the stone, thanks to Merlin.

Well, then one way or another–we would have to make sure that Arthur found out. I smiled to myself. This would be a fun cat and mouse game. I was the cat–and Arthur was the mouse I was planned on torturing... while waiting for him to grow up.

Chapter Five
Morguese

We grieved when our father died. We grieved—my sisters, brother and I. Our pain was palpable. I felt like I had lost a limb myself when he died in battle, his head severed.

But for the man who killed our father to then marry her—after impregnating her on the very night my father was killed by his trickery—was too much. It was all just too much suffering to bare.

My brother, Gormand Ricutas Cador, who we all called Cador, was twelve when our father died. Elaine was ten, I was eight, and Morgana was only six. The poor dear could barely even understand what was going on.

Morgana felt things deeply; she loved the hardest—with every last ounce of her being. When father died, that's when everything went wrong with her.

I couldn't blame her for how she'd changed, knowing what she went through—what we all went through, after father died.

It was too much for my sisters and my brother and I handle on our own. Our brother and Elaine, being the oldest, and more aware of what was going on, were hard on our mother for her choices after father's passing.

And for mother's part, she seemed to fall in love swiftly with the man who had, by all accounts, been the cause of her husband's death. We couldn't stand to see it. The way she fawned over him.

He clearly wanted her for himself. Like a toy. He sought to erase all traces of Duke Gorlois from her life, and that evidently included the children she had had with him.

So, Mother and her new husband—the King of all England, went to live somewhere else after the birth of their son, Arthur, while Cador, Elaine, Morgana and I all stayed behind at Castle Tintagel. My sisters and were waiting until we came of age and could be sold off by our stepfather, to some man we didn't know or love.

King Pendragon did not want his precious son to know of our existence. Oh, but we knew about his. Morgana in particular was enraged that Mother married him and a child with him. As she grew up, without a mother or father's care, her mind and heart hardened in a way that I found frightening.

She made up some story in her mind about how Mother had manipulated the King for our benefit, and that this was all part of a masterplan for revenge. She was hellbent on getting even with the King and his son someday—as if her very life depended upon it.

His precious son, Arthur, had replaced us, she believed. And Uther, who had so quickly and easily replaced our father, she was determined to believe our mother had just used to him to become Queen.

I wished Morgana was right, but I knew different. Our mother was romantic, and romance was something our father had never really been able to offer her. As much as that hurt, I knew it was true.

I knew she had fallen in love with Uther. For real.

It was painful and disappointing. But I understood it. I understood Mother, better than my other siblings ever had, and probably ever would.

She wasn't perfect, but everything she did came from her heart. She was good and sincere. She had been loyal to our father when he was alive, but after his passing... it didn't take long for Mother to give in to the romantic overtures of the dashing King of all England.

Morgana might have blamed her if she knew the truth. That's why she'd concocted that story of revenge. She needed to believe it. It was her way of being loyal to and stay loving of our mother.

But I accepted the truth—accepted my mother as she was—flawed yet infinitely good and kind. Well-meaning and genuine, though misguided by the King, he'd swept her away, and into a life grander than a Duke could have ever offered her.

She married up with our father, and now she was at the very top: the Queen. And I understood that the reason she'd gotten there—the reason she'd captured the hearts of these two great men, was because of her innocence.

She wasn't manipulative. She was truly pure at heart.

That's why they'd both fallen in love with her and had to have her. It was something she wasn't sure if her dear sister, Morgana, could ever comprehend.

Morgan was strategic and naturally magical and manipulative. She was jaded and cynical.

She couldn't believe in true love, love at first sight, soul mates, or even a love that grew with time. There were only ambition and vengeance for her because love had proven to be so painful. Rather than let the pain go, to let love in, she would choose the darker path of vengeance, leading to endless suffering.

For Morgana was not the only daughter of Igraine gifted in magic. I had the gift of Sight. And Elaine had the gift of Illusion.

These gifts were sure to serve them well. But I already knew Morgana's role in the fall of some future, enchanted kingdom, and the regret she would have to face in the end, for all her wrongdoing.

I took after their mother the most. I was the nurturer of our little clan. I tried to stay strong for her siblings, but I was feeling more than a little lost myself. With the death of father, and the virtual abandonment of mother, I felt like my compass was broken, and I wasn't sure where to go, or how to go on, from here.

At sixteen, my brother was set to become the new Duke of Cornwall. I was twelve. We were to attend the grand ceremony, like little soldiers, obedient and compliant to King Pendragon's wishes...

After the ceremony, I felt a calling on my soul. I asked mother to send me to the convent in France—the special monastery on an island near the West Pyrenes Mountains. I wanted to consider becoming a nun. Mother agreed. For we surely needed one holy and religious sister in the family to pray for all our souls.

~ ~ ~

The convent bells had just begun their evening toll when Morgeuse knelt before the small stone altar. The chapel smelled faintly of sandalwood incense and lavender oil. Candlelight flickered against the pale walls, throwing trembling shadows over the wooden crucifix.

At twelve-years-old, Morgeuse already knew the peace she felt here was unlike anything in the halls of Tintagel. She folded her hands tightly.

"Holy Mother," she whispered softly, "I wish only to serve, to pray for others—my family, and this world."

Behind her, the sisters moved quietly through the chapel, their long robes brushing the floor like whispers. Sister Agnes had allowed her to stay for the afternoon again, though everyone knew Morgeuse was a princess and not truly one of them.

Yet when she knelt here, she did not feel like a princess. She felt whole. She felt loved. She felt peace. She felt safe.

Outside the convent walls lay the world that had destroyed her family. Her father, Gorlois, Duke of Cornwall, had died on the battlefield. Uther Pendragon's war had taken him—killed on the front lines while the King pursued Lady Igraine with a hunger that had torn Cornwall—and their family—apart.

Now Igraine was Queen. And Morgeuse and her siblings lived under Uther's rule. Living in isolation in the convent, becoming a nun meant freedom.

A cold wind rattled the chapel door. Footsteps followed. Heavy footsteps. The door opened with a hard groan. Morgeuse turned slowly to see who entered in.

Queen Igraine stood in the doorway, cloaked in deep teal velvet. Behind her were two knights in Pendragon colors. And beside her, stood the man Morgeuse had begun to dread seeing.

King Lot of Orkney. Tall. Broad. Dark-hair and thick-bearded. A warrior king. A close ally of Uther Pendragon. The kind of man who belonged in battlefields and feasting halls—not in a quiet chapel where candles burned before saints.

She wished her mother had not brought him. "Morgeuse," Igraine said. Her tone was not cruel. But it was firm.

Morgeuse stood slowly. "Yes, my lady."

Igraine's eyes swept the chapel. For a moment something like guilt flickered across her face. "You should not linger here so long."

Morgeuse lowered her gaze. "I wished to pray."

Lot laughed softly behind them. "Pray?" he said. "What a child!"

Morgeuse's hands tightened in her sleeves to keep from grimacing. Igraine stepped closer. "You will have time to pray in your life, Morgeuse," she said gently. "But you must remember your duty."

"My duty," Morgeuse repeated quietly.

Igraine nodded. "The kingdoms need peace."

Morgeuse felt her stomach twist. She already knew what was coming. Rumors had drifted through the convent's irons gates for weeks.

Lot stepped forward now, examining her the way men examined horses before buying them. "She is young and inexperienced. I would prefer one more worldly. But she will do," he nodded.

Morgeuse felt her cheeks burn in protest. She bit her tongue to keep from speaking. Igraine ignored King Lot's remark.

"You will be married to King Lot," the Queen said. "The alliance will strengthen both our lands." The words settled like ice in Morgeuse's heart. A chill of dread swept over her body. She looked past Igraine toward the altar. The candles flickered. The sisters had all departed to the evening mass.

"My lady...mother..." Morgeuse said softly. Igraine waited patiently. Morgeuse swallowed, and said, "I wished to take vows."

Silence filled the chapel. Even Lot stopped moving, shocked into stillness. "You wished–what?" he asked.

Morgeuse lifted her eyes. "To serve God. Here. In the convent."

Lot burst into laughter. "Pendragon blood hidden under a nun's veil?" he said. "That is a waste."

Morgeuse bit her lip not to tell him that she did not have Pendragon blood. She had Cornwall blood. From her real father.

Igraine did not laugh. But her face hardened. "That cannot happen, my child."

Morgeuse's heart pounded. "But mother–"

"You are a daughter of Cornwall and Pendragon," Igraine said. "You are not free to choose such a life. Our kingdom needs you. Britain needs you."

Morgeuse felt tears sting her eyes. "My father–"

"Your father is dead," Igraine said quietly. The words struck like a blade. "And now the world we live in must be repaired. I need you to do this. Uther needs you to do this—the King."

Morgeuse's voice trembled. "I could serve God. My prayers could repair some of the damage, heal some of what was lost..."

Igraine stepped closer. "No, you will serve your kingdom. That is the best thing you can do help your family. You are sixteen now. It is time to do your duty."

Morgeuse looked at the altar again in longing, as the quiet candles flickering gently across the grey stone. She stared with longing at the peace she would never have, at the life she would never know.

Lot crossed the room and placed a heavy hand on her shoulder. "You will be queen of Orkney," he said. "You should be proud. It is an honor. Many young maidens would kill for such a title." His grip felt like a boulder, like the heavy burden of a crown she did not seek, or desire.

Morgeuse lowered her head. She thought to herself, *But I am not one of them, as much as I would like to be. I cannot be a nun.*

She knew obedience. It had been expected of her all her life. Her older sister Elaine fought it. Her younger sister Morgana rebelled and sought vengeance. They had disappeared. And until Uther and his knights could find them and drag them back to Cornwall to be married off like cattle, it was up Morgeuse to bring healing and peace to the lands. Not in quiet servitude and prayer as a nun—which was more natural to her spirit, but by becoming a Queen in an unknown Kingdom.

Slowly, she bent her knees and knelt once more before the altar. For a moment no one spoke. Her whisper was almost too soft to hear. "Forgive me."

Then she stood. Igraine watched her carefully. "Will you do this?" the Queen asked her pointedly.

Morgeuse folded her hands. "Yes, my lady."

Lot smiled. But Morgeuse did not look at him. She took one last glance at the candles. At the holy chapel that had felt like home. Then she walked toward the door. Toward the life she had not chosen, fearing that she was leaving the last of her peace behind...

~ ~ ~

Of all my siblings, I knew Uther liked me the most. He didn't like any of us much, really. But I was the only one who had never given him trouble. He took special care with me to come with mother and I to pick out my wedding dress, and I found that I liked Uther Pendragon, in spite of what had happened in the past. It had been eight years since father's death. And I sought peace, not revenge.

My time and education in the nunnery had helped me to process what had happened in a healthy way, and forgive the transgressions of those who shared my blood. I was not one to judge.

It was clear that Uther truly loved my mother—and that she loved him. It still hurt a little, deep in my heart, remembering how my father had once looked at my mother with a similar love light in his eyes.

Yet ultimately, I loved my mother. I wanted her to be happy. And Uther made her happy, so I tried to be good to him, and treat him with the respect due him as the King, and as my stepfather.

We grew as close as we'd ever been in the days before my wedding. So close, he asked if I would be comfortable with him giving me away. Mother was there when he asked me, and we both cried, telling him that was so sweet.

Though a bit difficult, I choked down any negative feelings and agreed to have him walk me down the aisle and give me away to King Lot.

Mother was overjoyed. Indeed, she had never looked happier. Even Uther looked pleased, and proud as a peacock–not just that he had won me over, but I could tell he had begun to think of me as the daughter he'd never had.

As difficult situations went, I was making the best of things. Mother was grateful, Uther was proud, and the rest of my siblings were furious with me. But they knew how I'd wanted to be a nun, so they couldn't be too tough on me, even though I knew they would have liked to have been.

My only request was to be married in a quiet ceremony at the chapel in the monastery in the mountains where I had been educated and had hoped to say my vows. King Lot agreed.

Cador was there. But I was disappointed that my sisters did not come. Still, the nuns were my true sisters. For if Morgana and Elaine continued on their path of vengeance, I doubted I would be with them in eternity. As much as I loved them, and would keep them in my prayers, I knew they were lost in another land full of magic and hedonism.

As King Lot took my hand in marriage, I felt some deep part of my soul die forever. Yet a new Morgeuse was birthed.

I would have to become stronger to be a good Queen of Orkney. As I said my vows allowed, I silently prayed for God to give me strength, to change my very nature, to become the best wife and mother and Queen I could be, forgetting all that was behind me, to focus on the life before me.

~ *** ~

Chapter Six
Elaine

In the distant western seas lay the Land of Maidens, a place sailors spoke of in half-whispers. Some said it was a kingdom founded by women who had turned away from the quarrels of Kings. Others claimed it was enchanted—that no man entered it without being changed in some way.

To many wandering knights, however, it became known for another reason. They went there seeking adventure. Few expected to *be* the adventure...

The afternoon sun glowed over the green hills as a lone knight rode along the narrow road that wound through orchards heavy with fruit. His armor bore the dust of long travel, and his shield hung loosely at his side.

Sir Aldric had heard the rumors: a land ruled by women who challenged knights for sport, wisdom, and sometimes their pride. He had not truly believed them. Until the arrow struck the ground before his horse.

The animal reared, snorting. Aldric looked up sharply. From the trees emerged half a dozen women clad in light armor of silver and green. Their bows were lowered but ready, their expressions confident rather than hostile.

One stepped forward.

She carried no helmet, and her dark hair fell in loose waves across her shoulders. Her eyes were bright with amusement. "Well," she said lightly, "another knight has wandered into our gardens."

Sir Aldric straightened in the saddle. “And who might you be?” The woman placed a hand over her heart with theatrical grace.

“Lady Elaine, captain of the orchard gardens... and presently your host.”

Aldric glanced around at the archers surrounding him. “You call this hospitality?”

“Oh, we are very hospitable,” Elaine said with a small smile. “But first we must see if you are worthy of it.” The other women laughed softly.

Aldric swung down from his horse, resting his hand on his sword. “And how do I prove that?”

Elaine drew a slim blade—not aggressively, but as though beginning a game. “You must duel me.”

“And if I win?”

“Then you are free to leave.”

“And if I lose?”

Her smile deepened. “Then you may stay as our guest.”

~ ~ ~

The duel did not last long.

Elaine moved like wind through tall grasses—swift, precise, and laughing as Aldric struggled to keep pace. Within a few minutes, she twisted his blade aside and tapped his shoulder with her own.

“Yield,” she said.

Aldric lowered his sword, breathing hard. “I suppose I must.”

The archers cheered. Elaine stepped closer, studying him with curious eyes. “You fought well,” she said. “Most knights do not last half as long.”

"Comforting," Aldric replied dryly.

She sheathed her blade. "Come," she said, gesturing toward the hills. "You are our prisoner now."

"And what becomes of prisoners here?"

Elaine tilted her head thoughtfully. "That depends on the knight... and the maiden."

~ ~ ~

That evening, music drifted through the courtyards of the Land of Maidens. Lanterns hung from the trees, and the air smelled of honey wine and flowers. For there, it was always spring: warm with heat, rich with ripe fruit, and fragrant with flowers.

Aldric sat beside Elaine beneath a flowering archway.

"You capture many knights this way?" he asked.

"Only those who wander in," she said with a shrug.

"And what happens to them?"

"Most stay a while," she replied. "They train, feast, tell stories of the outside world."

"And then?"

"Eventually they return home... usually with a very different opinion of our land."

Her eyes met his in the soft lantern light. "You do not seem like a cruel captor," Aldric said.

"Cruel?" She laughed quietly. "Hardly."

The music from the courtyard slowed into a gentle melody.

Elaine leaned a little closer.

"Our land was not built for cruelty," she said. "It was built for freedom... and for choosing our own paths."

Aldric studied her face. "And what path have you chosen tonight?"

For a moment she did not answer. Then she reached for his hand.

"That," she said softly, "depends on whether my prisoner wishes to remain a little longer."

Aldric smiled. "I think," he said, "I might."

"What else was this land of yours made for?" he asked, with a glint in his eyes.

"For love–free and untamed."

The sound of the maidens singing was the background of Sir Aldric as he hesitated no more. Leaning in for a kiss, he felt as if time itself was stayed here–by love, by passion, by bliss.

Elaine and the knight made love through the night, until the dawn. For weeks and months on end all they did was eat and make love. Sir Aldric was no longer a captive, but a willing prisoner of the hedonistic delights Elaine and Morgana enjoyed in the Land of Maidens, before their inevitable bitter end–of wives to Kings in unfamiliar lands.

~ ~ ~

Mist lay low across the valley like a pale veil, drifting slowly over the emerald fields of the Land of Maidens. The air there carried the scent of wildflowers and heather, with the distant hush of waterfalls, where no sound of war or steel had ever broken its beauty and peace. Marble towers rose among groves of apple and hawthorn, their windows open to the sun, their banners pale and delicate as swan feathers.

Elaine walked slowly along the white stone path that curved beside a clear pool. A statue in the center sprayed water. It was a statue of a beautiful naked woman carrying a basket of roses. The water mirrored the sky so perfectly it seemed as though another world lay beneath its surface. She knelt beside it, trailing her fingers through the water. Behind her came the soft rustle of silk.

"You always look as though you are searching for something in the water," Morgana said.

Elaine did not turn at first. Morgana's voice carried a cool music—beautiful, but edged with something sharper beneath.

"Perhaps I am," Elaine replied gently. "Reflections sometimes show truths that the waking world hides."

Morgana stepped beside her. The dark-haired sorceress wore deep green robes embroidered with silver ivy, and the breeze lifted the long strands of her black hair like a shadowed banner. Her eyes moved across the peaceful land with a faint expression of disbelief.

"So, this is the place they hide themselves," Morgana murmured. "A kingdom of women untouched by kings and wars."

"And by the ambitions of men," Elaine added softly.

Morgana gave a short laugh. "Ambition is hardly a thing men invented."

Elaine finally rose, brushing her hands together. Her gown was pale blue, the color of the pool, and her expression was serene in a way that made Morgana uneasy.

"You do not like it here," Elaine observed.

"It is too peaceful," Morgana replied. "A place that has never known danger cannot understand power."

Elaine looked out towards the distant orchards where young women practiced archery in quiet rows. "Peace is not weakness, Morgana."

"No," Morgana said slowly. "But it is fragile."

They walked together along the path as swans glided over the pool. The towers of the maidens gleamed in the afternoon sun; their laughter drifted faintly from a nearby courtyard.

"This land was founded so that women could learn freely," Elaine said. "Magic, healing, scholarship. No lord commanding us. No court whispering behind our backs of witchcraft."

Morgana's gaze sharpened slightly. "There is much fear and prejudice in Britain against witchcraft," she agreed. "This land is a welcome reprieve."

"Yes," Elaine agreed.

"Yet it is also intended to be a Land of Maidens. The knights who wander in are supposed to be used for their bodies for our pleasure, not to capture our hearts."

Elaine eyed her sister wearily. "And yet you loved a knight," Morgana continued, watching her closely. "Don't deny it."

Elaine did not answer for a moment. Instead, she looked towards the distant mountains where clouds gathered like pale ships. "We cannot always choose who we love," Elaine said at last.

"No," Morgana agreed quietly. "Our mother and King Uther Pendragon showed us that, eh?"

Elaine sighed. They stopped beside a small stone bridge where water ran beneath in silver ribbons.

"You and I are different, Elaine," Morgana said. "You have changed. Love has changed you. You value love. I do not. You seek harmony now. I seek truth. I seek knowledge that leads to justice."

"But is not your view of justice merely vengeance?" Elaine asked.

Morgana glared, "You once thought just as I do."

"I have changed, dear sister. I cannot be what I once did. I cannot seek vengeance anymore." She turned to her curiously. "But I would like to know about the truth that you seek..."

Morgana's eyes turned toward the horizon—toward lands far beyond the gentle scene. "The truth of magic and its power," she answered somberly. "Of what this world becomes when those who hold the throne are unworthy of it."

Elaine studied her carefully. "You speak of Arthur."

Morgana did not deny it.

The wind stirred the apple trees around them, scattering white blossoms across the bridge like falling snow. "This land endures because it stands apart from that struggle," Elaine said. "But the world beyond it cannot remain untouched forever."

Morgana watched the blossoms fall into the stream. "Nothing remains untouched forever," she said softly.

Morgana turned to her sister softly. "I also demand to know the truth about your plans. Are you thinking of going back? Are you thinking of becoming a Queen to the King of a man you do not know or love?"

Elaine sighed. "My dear sister, that is our destiny. I must ask that you come with me, and that we do our duty. This country yearns for peace, for the end of the battles and bloodshed that has plagued Britain for far too long. Shall you come with me, Morgana? Shall you do your duty beside your sisters and brother?

For a long moment they stood in silence as the peaceful valley stretched around them—bright, quiet, a wall of safety in a cutthroat world. While far away, beyond the hills and seas, the creation of Camelot would soon begin.

~ ~ ~

The bells of Galor rang from every tower, their bronze voices rolling across the harbor and the green hills beyond. Ships bobbed in the bright water like white-winged birds, their sails furled in celebration, and the streets below the castle walls were crowded with people who had come to see their King wed.

Inside the great hall, banners of deep crimson and gold hung between the pillars. Torches flickered against polished stone, though sunlight streamed through the high windows, turning the hall warm and bright.

At the far end stood King Nentres, dressed in a mantle of dark blue velvet trimmed with ermine. Though a seasoned warrior and ruler, there was an unusual softness in his expression that day—an anticipation he could not hide.

The doors of the hall opened slowly.

A hush fell over the crowd.

Elaine entered.

She walked with calm grace down the long aisle of polished stone, her gown flowing like pale moonlight. Silver embroidery traced the edges of the fabric in delicate patterns of vines and lilies; a design taught to her in the Land of Maidens. It was a land where women shaped beauty with patience and skill.

Her radiant amber hair had been braided with small white blossoms gathered from Galor's hills that morning. For a moment the king simply watched her approach, as if the hall, the nobles, and the Kingdom itself had fallen away in the breathless majesty of her beauty.

But standing not far from him, half hidden among the guests, another woman watched as well.

Morgana.

Her dark emerald eyes followed Elaine's every step. She had returned from the Land of Maidens with Elaine only weeks before, though she had little interest in weddings or celebrations.

Morgana leaned against a stone pillar, her black cloak blending with the shadows. She knew that as the youngest sister, her call to duty would be next. Morguese, the gentlest, was the first of them to be trapped in the net of matrimony. Elaine, the eldest and bravest was the second. Morgana, the youngest, and the truest rebel of the group, and the most resistant to duty, would be the last.

"Strange," she murmured quietly beside her sister, Morguese "After wandering enchanted valleys, with countless adventures, and the learning of ancient magic, she chooses a crown."

Morguese shook her head. "You ought to know better, Morgana. None of us have a choice."

The woman beside her was the softest of the sisters. Morgana knew she had longed to be a nun and redeem their family line. Wheras, Cador, Elaine, and she had vowed revenge of Uther and their half-brother, Arthur, Morguese longed for unity and peace.

"A crown is not always a chain," her sister told her sagely. "It is our duty. And we may make something good of it by bettering the Kingdoms we rule."

Morgana said nothing, though her gaze remained sharp. She knew that Elaine held her own pain and burden. She had fallen in love in the Land of Maidens.

She was not likely to ever see Sir Aldric again. And even if she did, she would not be able to express the love she held inside. Knowing her sister, Elaine, as she did, she knew her sister would try to love King Nentres, but would always hold a special place in her heart for the knight.

At the center of the hall, Elaine reached the dais. King Nentres stepped forward, taking her hands. "They told me stories of your journeys," he said softly, his voice meant only for her. "Of the trials in the Land of Maidens...the riddles, the enchanted forests, the lake spirits that guard their shores. They also told me of the love of knight... that were captured and chose to stay... for a time."

Elaine frowned, looking worried.

"I only met to say–I forgive you, Elaine. For whatever happened there, I forgive you. And I want you to know, that even though you do not love me now, I already love you, and I shall be dedicated to you, and to our marriage."

She looked up at him gratefully. "Thank you, my King." She hesitated, then added. "I learned a lot there."

"What did you learn, my queen?" he asked her.

Her light blue eyes met his. "That peace is something worth protecting."

They understood each other, and the ceremony went on.

The old bishop of Galor stepped forward, raising a silver-bound book. "My King," he said, "do you take this woman, Elaine of noble heart and wisdom, to be your Queen and partner in the rule of this fair land?"

"I do," Nentres said without hesitation.

The bishop turned to Elaine. "And do you take Nentres, King of Galor, to stand beside him in loyalty and truth?"

Elaine glanced briefly through the hall. Her gaze passed over the watching nobles... the cheering people beyond the doors and finally rested on Morgana. For a moment the two women looked at one another. Morgana's expression was unreadable–neither warm nor hostile, simply thoughtful, as if measuring the strange turning paths of fate.

Then Elaine turned back to the bishop. “I do.”

The rings were brought forth, simple bands of pure gold. When Nentres slid the ring onto her finger, the hall erupted in cheers.

Trumpets sounded from the balcony. Outside, bells began to ring.

“Long live King Nentres!” the crowd shouted.

“Long live Queen Elaine!”

King Nentres drew her close, kissing her as the celebration thundered around them. But near the pillar, Morgana merely folded her arms and watched.

“A Queen now,” she said quietly to herself.

Beyond the castle windows, the sea glimmered under the afternoon sun, bright and calm. For Elaine, the adventures of the Land of Maidens had ended. For Morgana... the greater games of Kingdom’s rise and falls had only just begun.

~ ~ ~

Warm sunset colors of orange, rose, and violet spilled through the tall windows of the eastern tower, turning the white stone walls soft with gold. Outside, the gardens of Galor stirred with the sound of birds and the distant murmur of the sea. The castle was walking slowly after the long celebrations of Queen Elaine’s wedding.

Inside the quiet chamber, two sisters sat across from one another. Elaine had removed her crown and set it upon a small table beside her. Without it, she looked almost the same as she had in the Land of Maidens—

calm, luminous, her shiny autumn hair loose around her shoulders. Yet there was something new in her bearing now: the quiet dignity and bearing of a Queen.

Across the room stood Morgana. She leaned against the window frame, her dark hair catching the pale sunlight. She had never liked the noise of court life, and the castle still seemed too crowded with nobles and courtiers lingering after the wedding feast.

For a while neither of them spoke. At last Morgana broke the silence.

"You wear it well," she said. "You look beautiful." That was Morgana's way of trying to be kind, but she sounded sad.

Elaine looked up. "The crown?" she seemed distracted, in her own world.

"Yes."

Morgana crossed the room slowly, glancing at the small golden circlet resting on the table.

"Most people shrink beneath such things," she continued. "Power frightens them."

Elaine smiled faintly. "I do not see it as power."

"I know. You see it as a burden—as a duty, as a loss of freedom—which it is."

Morgana sat down across from her sister, folding her hands on the table. "When we walked together in the Land of Maidens," Morgana said, "you spoke of freedom. Of living beyond kings and courts."

"I remember."

"And now you live inside one."

Elaine's gaze drifted toward the window where the sea glimmered beyond the gardens.

"The world beyond the Land of Maidens still needs kindness," she said quietly. "Peace cannot live only in hidden valleys. Sometimes it is braver to face the world."

Morgana studied her carefully. "You truly believe a Kingdom can be ruled with kindness alone?"

"No," Elaine answered gently. "Of course, not. But it may begin there."

A faint smile touched Morgana's lips. "You always were the hopeful one."

"And you always doubted."

"I don't doubt," Morgana said. "I observe."

She leaned back in her chair, her dark eyes thoughtful. "Kings rise and fall. Alliances break. Knights swear loyalty one year and betray it the next. Power changes people."

Elaine reached across the table and took Morgana's hand. "Not everyone."

For a moment Morgana did not pull away. "You were always the bravest of us," Morgana said quietly. "Even when we were children."

Elaine laughed softly, remembering. "You once turned my practice harp into a nest of frogs."

"They sang better than you did."

Elaine shook her head, smiling. The tension between them eased for a moment as memories surfaced—childhood halls, quiet lessons, long afternoons before politics and rivalries had shaped the world around them.

But Morgana's gaze eventually returned to the crown. "Tell me something honestly, sister," she said.

Elaine waited.

"If the day comes when this kingdom forces you to choose between kindness and power... what shall you do?"

The question hung in the air like a distant storm. Elaine thought for a long moment. Then she answered softly. "I shall choose what keeps the most people safe."

Morgana studied her face, searching for doubt or weakness. Instead, she saw only calm resolve. Finally, Morgana stood. "Perhaps Galor shall prosper under you," she said.

"You sound surprised."

"I am."

Elaine rose as well. "You're leaving?" she asked.

"For now."

Morgana moved toward the door, her cloak brushing the stone floor. But before she left, she paused. "You know," Morgana said without turning, "of all the rulers in Britain... you may be the only one I would hesitate to challenge."

Elaine smiled gently. "I hope you never feel the need."

Morgana glanced back, one eyebrow raised. "With our family?" she said. "One never knows."

Then she disappeared down the spiral stairway, leaving the chamber quiet once more.

Elaine stood beside the table for a long time afterward. Finally, she picked up the crown and placed it carefully upon her head.

Outside, the sea wind stirred the gardens, and the bells of Galor rang softly tolled. She remembered the wedding ceremony and feast less than an before... knowing that tonight King Nentres would expect to consummate their marriage. She shuddered in spite of herself, determined to do my duty.

Her blood would bring about the unity of their two Kingdoms. But her heart would always be divided between the man she truly loved, Sir Aldric, and the love of duty and honor that she had been born into because of who her parents were, trapped in a caste system of royalty that would turn her into little more than a puppet on a string.

She would lose herself in duty, in honor, in doing what was right, in becoming a good Queen to people who were not her own.

Chapter Seven
Urien

Morgana had no trouble cheating on her husband, once she learned that he had been the one to cut the head off of her father. Her sexual appetites were unmatched.

She offered her husband but one son, Owain. His crest was of the ravens, which was Morgana's special pets and messengers to her lovers.

She continued on with her practice of magic and visited the Land of Maidens, doing as she pleased with any man she pleased, biding her time for the moment she would strike out at her husband like a snake, and get rid of him and the horrible duty of a crown forever.

She wanted only to be the Lady of Avalon. She wanted to live with girls and women as her family. She wanted to treat men as women have been treated for years: as toys, as objects and play things to make love to and then discard. The weight of a crown, the duty, the obligations, the endless ceremonies, the court manners, did not suit her.

She was cut out for the forests, trees, water, and magic. She was cut out for loveless sex and hungry vengeance.

Of course, her husband did not know she knew the truth. She was an excellent liar. And every time she made love to him, she worked especially hard for his pleasure, relishing the day she turned the knife in his chest, and cut his head off his shoulders. She pretended to be an excellent wife, so that he would never suspect what was coming.

But she could not be held in a cage for long. And for her, being the wife of a king, was being held captive in a cage. She loved going out to battles with her husband. She was a great warrior Queen. She was one of the best warriors her husband had. That was her release, her relief.

Killing eased her bloodthirsty mind. But one kill she waited for, and was looking forward to the most. That of her husband, the King.

~ ~ ~

Dawn broke red over the hills of Rhegard, in the Solway Firth, staining the mist like spilled wine. King Urien stood at the crest of a rocky ridge overlooking the valley below. His cloak snapped sharply in the cold wind, and beneath him his warhorse pawed the earth impatiently.

"Urien" meant cold. But he was only cold on the battlefields.

Across the valley stretched the army of the Saxons. Hundreds of shields formed a dark wall across the fields. Their banners–black wolves with red serpents entangled around them–snapped above ranks of spear-men and axe warriors. The enemy had come in the night, marching hard across the borderlands to seize the river crossing that guarded the heart of Rheged.

But they had not expected Urien to meet them here. Beside the king, his captains waited. "They outnumber us," one muttered.

Urien's sharp gray eyes never left the enemy line. "Only if we fight them as they expect," he said calmly.

Below, the Saxon war horns began to blow—low and brutal sounds that rolled across the valley. Urien turned in his saddle.

"Signal the riders," he ordered.

A trumpet answered from the hills behind them. Down the slopes of Rheged thundered Urien's cavalry—two hundred armored horsemen descending like an iron storm. Their lances lowered, their shields painted with the red dragon of the north.

But Urien did not lead them forward. Instead, he raised his hand. "Hold."

The riders halted halfway down the hill, hidden partly by the morning fog. Below, the Saxon commander mistook the movement.

Thinking the Britons had panicked, he roared an order. The Saxon shield wall surged forward, charging uphill to crush what they believed was a retreating enemy.

Urien smiled grimly. "Now."

The trumpet sounded again. But the charge did not come from the hill. It came from the woods.

From both sides of the valley, hidden warriors of Rheged burst from the trees—spearmen and archers who had waited silently since midnight. His wife Morgana led them. The hidden army was also filled with women from the Land of Maidens, eager to use their skills. Arrows screamed through the air, striking the exposed Saxon flanks.

The shield wall faltered instantly. Before the Saxons could reform—Urien drew his sword. "For Rheged!"

His cavalry exploded down the hillside. Hooves thundered like a landslide. Lances smashed into the confused Saxon line just as the ambushed warriors closed from the sides.

Urien's blade flashed as he plunged straight into the chaos. A Saxon man bearing a giant battle axe rushed towards him, roaring. Urien leaned from the saddle and cut downward, his sword splitting the man's shield and sending him crashing into the mud.

Another enemy grabbed his bridle, trying to drag him from the horse. Urien struck him with the pommel of his sword, breaking the man's jaw.

Around him the battle roared—steel clashing, horses screaming, shields shattering. But the Saxon formation was already collapsing.

Trapped between the cavalry charge and the ambushers, their lines broke apart into scattered knots of desperate fighters. Urien spurred deeper into the fray.

Ahead he saw the Saxon war-chief rallying his men. The chieftain raised a massive axe and shouted in fury. Urien rode straight for him. The two leaders collided in a burst of sparks and steel.

The Saxon swung his axe in a brutal arc. Urien twisted aside in the saddle and slashed across the man's chest, cutting through leather and bone.

The war-chief staggered back, falling beneath the hooves of the charging cavalry. The Saxon banner of a red serpent entangled around a black wolf toppled into the mud.

For a moment the battlefield froze. Then the Saxon army broke. They fled across the valley in panic as Urien's warriors roared in triumph. By midday the field belonged to Rheged.

Urien dismounted beside the river crossing, wiping blood from his blade. One of his captains approached, still breathless.

"The Saxons are in full retreat, my King."

Urien looked across the valley where the enemy banners had once stood. "They will return," he said quietly. "They always do."

"But today they learned something," the captain answered proudly.

Urien slid his sword back into its scabbard, and waited for the captain to continue.

"That Rheged does not yield its land... and that its King and Queen do not wait behind walls, while others fight for their Kingdom."

Behind him, the warriors of Rheged raised their voices in victory, the sound echoing across the hills where the Saxons had believed they would conquer.

~ ~ ~

Night had settled heavily over the fortress of Rheged. Torches burned along the stone walls, their light wavering in the cold wind that crept down from the northern hills. Inside the King's private chamber, the fire in the hearth had burned low, leaving the room half in shadow.

King Urien stood beside the window, unfastening the leather straps of his armor. The day had been long—training with knights, reviewing border disputes, hearing petitions from farmers whose lands had been raided by Picts.

War never truly ended. But tonight, he felt strangely content. He was happy to be home with the wife he loved.

Behind him, Morgana stood in the shadows. She had dismissed the servants. Her dark hair fell loosely around her shoulders, all the way down to her ankles. Her black gown trailing across the stone floor like spilled ink. In her hand she held a goblet of wine, though she had not drunk from it.

Urien did not yet see the dagger hidden in her other hand. "You are quiet tonight," he said gently, setting his sword aside.

Morgana did not answer at first. Her eyes rested on the back of his neck.

A warrior's neck. Strong. Scarred.

The man who had killed thousands in battle. The man who had loved her faithfully for years. A man she had never loved.

"You fought well today," she said finally.

Urien smiled faintly. "You watched?"

"Of course."

He turned, pleased. Urien had always admired Morgana's fierce mind. Unlike many Queens, she did not hide from matters of war.

He stepped toward her. "You look troubled," he said, genuinely concerned about her.

Morgana tilted her head slightly, with a wry smile. "Do I?"

He studied her face. "Yes." He couldn't quite place or understand her strange expression.

He reached for the goblet in her hand and took a small drink. Morgana's fingers tightened slightly around the hidden dagger.

"You should rest," he said. "You worry too much."

She stared at him. Worry. The word almost made her laugh. He knew nothing of what lived inside her. Nothing of the memories that burned in her mind like brands of iron...

She was haunted by the battlefield where her father had been slain. Her father's corpse had been returned to his family in Tintagel in two pieces—his body and head. Gorlois, Duke of Cornwall. The man Uther Pendragon had sent to the front lines. The man whose head had been cut from his body while Uther slipped into Tintagel disguised by Merlin's magic to lie with her mother.

To steal Morgana's mother. To steal her kingdom. To destroy her father.

Urien set the goblet down. "You are very pale," he said softly. He stepped closer and caressed her cheek. Morgana's eyes burned with an emerald green flame.

He had always been kind to her. That was the tragedy.

"I loved my father," she said quietly.

Urien frowned slightly. "I know."

"They cut off his head," she continued.

The King hesitated. "Yes."

Her voice dropped lower. "They left his body in the mud like a dog."

Urien's expression softened. "That was war."

Morgana's eyes flashed. "War?" The word came out like poison.

Urien straightened slightly. "Morgana—"

"Did you think I didn't know? Did you think I wouldn't be told?"

He suddenly couldn't breathe. *Did she know?* He was silent now. He knew there was nothing he could say.

"Yes, my King, my husband—I know it was you who cut the head off my father. Because of you, they brought him back to us in two pieces."

There was no use denying it. "I'm sorry," he whispered, preparing himself for what was next.

"You are a warrior King," she said. "You understand such things. As you said yourself—this is war."

Her hand moved. The dagger slid forward. Urien's eyes widened just as the blade plunged into his chest. The sound he made was not a shout. It was a breath. A shocked breath.

He staggered backwards. "Morgana..."

Blood spread across his tunic. His hand closed around the dagger still buried in his chest. "Why?" His voice broke. Not with anger—with heartbreak.

Morgana watched him with a terrible calm. "Because this is how Kings die—you taught me that lesson when I was but six-years-old."

Urien sank to one knee, struggling to breathe. "I love you," he whispered.

For a moment something flickered across Morgana's face. Then it vanished. She stepped forward and pulled the dagger free.

Urien collapsed onto the stone floor. He tried to rise. Even wounded, the great warrior fought for life.

"Morgana... please... I can forgive you... if you can forgive me."

She did not answer. Instead, she walked slowly across the chamber floor, and lifted Urien's sword from where he had placed it.

The blade glinted in the firelight. Urien looked up at her. Now he understood. It was not just about betrayal. She had a purpose.

His voice was barely a breath. "Your father..."

Morgana's eyes were cold. "Yes."

She stepped behind him. Urien closed his eyes. Perhaps he thought of the battles he had won. Perhaps of the Kingdom he would never see again. Or perhaps only of the woman he had loved.

The sword rose. And fell. Steel flashed. The chamber echoed with the terrible sound.

When it was finished, Morgana stood alone in the dim firelight. Urien's body lay sprawled across the stone floor. His head lay several feet away.

Just as Gorlois's had once lain in the mud of the battlefield. Morgana stared down at the blood pooling around her feet.

Her voice was soft. "Now we are even."

She turned from their bed chambers; she walked down the castle halls. She walked out of the castle, went to the stables, took out her horse, and climbed him bare back. She told the guards to open the gates. She and her horse galloped away from the bounds of Solway Firth, as she promised to herself in the storm and rain that she would never return.

~ *** ~

Chapter Eight
Vivienne

The Lady of the Lake was not bound by the rules of land or court. Where others rode roads and followed seasons, Vivienne moved between moments—appearing when she chose, vanishing when she must, always with a purpose that few would ever know.

She moved like the water itself—fluid, elusive, and hard to pin down. She sensed when to leave, and when to stay. She sensed her destiny, and followed it with out pause or hesitation.

Tonight, she knew was a special night. A storm had nearly swallowed the shore. Waves crashed like war drums against the rocks, and the sky tore itself open with lightning.

She swam steadily to a hidden land. The wild waves carried her swiftly there. She watched and waited for the ordained moment that had been prophesied many years ago...

Waves crashed against the jagged rocks along the coast of France, sending white spray into the wind. Far above the shore stood a small fortress belonging to King Ban of Benoic. Torches burned in its windows, but their light could not push back the darkness gathering over the water.

Inside the stone chamber, a Queen labored in agony. Her dark hair clung to her face as she gripped the bed linens. The midwives whispered prayers while the wind rattled the shutters.

"Where is the King?" one of the women asked nervously.

"Still in battle," another replied. "King Claudas invaded his lands. Ban rode out three days ago."

Another cry tore through the chamber. The queen gasped for breath as the midwife leaned close. "My lady... the child is coming."

Clarine's eyes filled with tears. "Ban..." she whispered weakly.

But the king was miles away on the battlefield, steel clashing under the same storm-dark sky.

The child was born moments later. A small cry filled the chamber.

"A boy," the midwife said softly. "It's a good omen." She made the sign of the cross superstitiously.

She wrapped the infant in cloth and placed him in the queen's trembling arms. Elaine looked down at the tiny face. His eyes had just begun to open.

"My son..." she murmured. But her strength was fading quickly.

Outside, thunder rolled across the sea. The midwives exchanged frightened looks. "My lady," one said gently, "you must rest."

Queen Elaine barely heard them. She touched the child's cheek with shaking fingers. "Tell Ban... his son... will be brave... and strong."

Her breath grew shallow. Then, slowly, it stopped. The midwives lowered their heads in silence. The newborn cried louder, unaware that his mother was already gone.

Far away, steel rang against steel as King Ban fought desperately against the army of Claudas. He did not yet know he had a son. Nor that his queen had died.

~ ~ ~

Before dawn, the fortress fell. Claudas' forces poured through the gates while servants fled in terror. One loyal nursemaid seized the infant prince and ran toward the coast, hoping to escape by sea.

But the storm had grown violent. Rain lashed the shore as waves smashed against the rocks. The nursemaid slipped on the wet stones. The child tumbled from her arms and slid toward the roaring water.

"No!" she screamed.

The infant disappeared beneath the dark waves. The sea swallowed him whole, like the mouth of a whale.

For a moment, there was only the sound of the storm. Then the water began to glow. From the depths rose a figure clothed in silver mist.

It was Vivienne, the Lady of the Lake.

Her long hair flowed golden white like the cascading of water, bathed in a gold light, and her eyes held the quiet knowledge of the ages. She cradled the infant easily in her arms, the sea parting around her. The child stopped crying.

Vivienne looked down at him with curiosity. "So," she whispered, "you are the child Merlin spoke of."

The storm seemed to calm slightly around her. "The son of Ban," she said softly. "The knight who shall one day surpass them all."

The baby reached up and grasped her finger. Vivienne smiled faintly, her heart already filling with a mother's fierce and tender love. "You shall not die here tonight, my son," she whispered.

She turned toward the horizon. Far beyond the mortal shores lay Avalon—the hidden island of magic. Mist gathered across the sea, swirling around her like a living veil. As she stepped forward, the water hardened beneath her feet like glass.

"You shall grow where swords cannot reach you," she said to the child. "And I will teach you the deeper magic of the world."

The infant did not cry. Sapphire blue eyes watched her closely.

"Ah," Vivienne murmured, lifting the child into her arms. "So, you are the one they shall call Lancelot."

The mist closed around them. When it cleared, the shore was empty. Only the restless sea remained.

Lightning flashed again, but she was already gone—drawn beneath the surface, into a realm untouched by storm or sorrow. There, in her hidden world, she would raise him—not merely as a knight, but as something finer, sharper... and perhaps more dangerous.

~ ~ ~

I was the beautiful, illustrious Lady of the Lake. I could win the heart of a man in moments... and kill him in mere moments more. And I often did. Merely for the sport of it.

No man could resist me. As a siren of the waters, a cousin of the muses, it was easy for me to lure men to my bed, and just as easy it was to take their life.

Did I love any of the men I bedded? I liked the challenged. I enjoyed the conquest if it was someone wealthy or famous. But no, love did not really factor into my life. I think it would have taken all the fun out of it.

I did not love these men... but I did love the boy, Lancelot. He was an orphaned prince who I had taken in and was raising. I also worked closely with my proteges Bors and Lionel, but I raised Lancelot like my own son, in the enchanted land of Avalon.

I didn't like to speak or think much of love, but if there was anything or anyone I cared for, it was him.

I taught the boy what I could of the siren's art of romance and charm. As a handsome French boy, his good looks certainly helped.

I knew that his future depended upon how lovable he would become to the fairer sex—irresistible, as all sirens are. I cut his hair in a princely fashion to attract the ladies of good-breeding. I showered him colognes and special oils, and dressed the boy in all the latest fashions.

"Someday you will meet a woman who will change your life," I told him proudly. "She will be of high rank. She will make you. Your handsomeness shall be what rises up in the world."

"Will she love me?" Lancelot, about 8-years-old at the time, asked me.

I puckered my face. "Who cares about such things?"

"I do," Lancelot insisted on knowing.

"I suppose so," I hedged.

"And what about you?" he asked.

"What about me?"

"Do you love me?" He looked up at me with his earnest blue eyes, and even as such a young boy, his hair was like a lion's crown of waves and curls atop his head.

"I suppose so," I answered, but there was an uncharacteristic softness in my voice and eyes that Lancelot noticed.

He smiled and threw his arms about me in an embrace. I couldn't help but chuckle. Love had always been the only thing that Lancelot wanted: to love and to be loved. He longed for affection, he was soft.

I taught him magic and swordplay. I forced him to work his body until he'd become a strong and fierce warrior. But beneath his body and armor of steel, I, the closest thing to a mother he had known, as the woman who raised him, could see that he had never changed. At heart, he would always be sensitive.

Even as a man, he was still an innocent. Nothing I did or said could take away that soft heart of his, that longed for romance above all else, and the kind of epic love that took him by storm. A storm that could be not be stopped or quenched, a storm that destroyed everything in its wake.

Lancelot's good looks, and agreeable, pleasing nature would take him far in life. Yet I also knew that those very things that got him promoted, would be his undoing.

I knew that Lancelot having an affair with Guinevere would bring about the fall of Camelot. It was just another way to thwart Merlin, and his precious plans and prophesies.

It was kind of a fun hobby of mine to ruin the plans of the "greatest wizard that had ever lived—" at least that's what he thought. But I knew that my careful planning, and plotting, with his casted off protégé, Morgana, would destroy his hopes and dreams.

That gave me something to look forward to. That, and turning Merlin into a tree. I was very much looking forward to that. I had my own axe to grand with the old kook.

Morgana and I were very aligned when it came to vengeance. She was my protégé now—the only female student I'd ever had. To my surprise, I found I preferred her to the men, who all fawned over me and fell all over themselves for me, to the point they could never learn much at all.

Even my son, Lancelot, to a certain extent, was in love with me. As part muse, it couldn't be helped. But I wanted my adopted son to fall in love and mate with the Queen. Yes, only the Queen herself would do for one so worthy as my darling.

~ ~ ~

Years later, beneath the ancient trees of Avalon, the boy stood beside Vivienne. He was perhaps fifteen now, growing lean and tall, with bright curious blue eyes. He was a sensitive boy, with the desire to hurt no maiden or lady. For his mother's influence, he didn't have it in him to hurt a woman. He had too much respect and concern for them. In his hands he held a small wooden staff.

"Focus," Vivienne instructed calmly.

Lancelot frowned in concentration. The wind rustled the leaves around them.

"Magic," she continued, "is not force. It is listening."

The boy closed his eyes. Slowly, the leaves around his feet began to stir. Then they lifted gently into the air, circling him in swirling rings.

Lancelot opened his eyes in amazement. Vivienne nodded with quiet satisfaction.

"Yes," she said. "The world already knows your name. You shall become a great knight. You have an important destiny, my son."

In silence, Lancelot continued practicing magic, and swordplay, preparing for the life that was to come. The magic became a part of him. A part of his heart, his intuition, ingrained in his mind, flowing with his essence, a much a part of him as the blood coursing through his veins.

And far across the sea, in lands of war and kingdoms yet to rise, destiny waited for the boy who would one day become the greatest knight of Camelot...

~ ~ ~

In a dream, Vivienne came to King Arthur, the night before he would be crowned King...

The lake was still when he came. A young king, not yet burdened by all he would become, stood at its edge. King Arthur did not yet fully understand the weight of the crown upon his head, but he knew enough to seek power—and guidance—beyond ordinary means.

Vivienne watched him from beneath the surface. "He doubts himself," she said softly.

"He should," came another voice, ancient and distant.

Arthur knelt at the shore. "I seek the sword," he called. "The one that shall prove I am worthy to rule."

Vivienne rose from the water like a reflection given form. In her hand was the blade—Excalibur, gleaming not with light, but with inevitability.

"You do not prove worthiness by holding a sword," she told him. "You reveal it by how you use it."

Arthur met her gaze, unflinching. "Then let me reveal it."

For a long moment, she said nothing. She studied him—not his posture, not his words, but the shape of his intent.

At last, she placed the sword in his hands. "Very well," she said. "But understand this, Arthur—what is given can also be taken away."

It was only a dream, but it was meant as a warning. The lake stilled again. And somewhere, far off, the future shifted.

~ ~ ~

Night lay softly over the forest of Brocéliande. The wind whispered through the high branches, and the moon cast pale silver across the moss-covered ground. In a quiet glade beside a still lake, Merlin stood waiting.

He had known this moment would come.

The water of the lake shimmered unnaturally, glowing with a faint purple light. From its surface rose the Lady of the Lake, her form emerging as though the water itself had shaped into a woman. Her light, almost pure white hair, clung to her shoulders and back like strands of starlight, and her eyes shone with ancient magic, silver blue.

Merlin watched her with a sad smile. "You came," he said gently.

The Lady stepped onto the shore to meet him. The water did not cling to her gown; it fell away like mist.

"I always come when you call, Merlin." Her voice was soft, but there was a tension in it tonight.

For a moment neither spoke. The forest itself seemed to listen for their next words.

"You know why I summoned you," Merlin said at last.

"I know," she replied. Merlin's eyes drifted toward the stars between the branches. For centuries he had read the turning of fate as others read words upon a page.

Merlin had seen kingdoms rise and fall. He had shaped destinies, whispered into the ears of Kings, bent the fabric of time itself. Magic was his language—and his domain.

"You taught me everything," she said, walking beside him through a quiet forest.

"Not everything," Merlin replied, amused. "Some things must be discovered for oneself."

"Yes," she agreed. "They must." There was a stillness in her tone that gave him pause. Too late.

The air tightened. The trees seemed to lean inward, their roots twisting beneath the earth. The world itself became a lattice of unseen threads—and Vivienne held them all.

"You see, Merlin," she said, her voice calm, almost gentle, "you taught me your magic... but not your limits."

Merlin's eyes seemed to glow a vibrant blue in the night as he looked at her. "I tried," he said simply.

"You fear what you cannot control," she continued. "And you cannot control me."

"The threads have been woven," he said quietly. "Arthur's reign must follow its course. And I... must step aside—for a time."

"You speak of fate as though you welcome it."

"I do not welcome it," Merlin replied sadly. "I merely understand it—and accept it."

The Lady moved closer to him. Her eyes searched his face. "You taught me how the roots of the world drink magic from the earth. You even taught me the binding of life to wood and stone."

Merlin nodded.

"And now I shall use that magic against you."

"Yes."

"You fear what you cannot control," she continued. "And you cannot control me."

He was silent. Her hands trembled. "You shall not fight me?"

Merlin smiled sadly. "There are some turns of fate even I cannot alter."

He stepped toward the center of the clearing where a patch of bare earth lay waiting. The soil was dark and rich, as though the forest itself had prepared the place.

"I have seen it many times," Merlin continued. "If I remain, I shall try to prevent what must happen. And if I prevent it, the world shall fall into a darkness far worse than the fall of Camelot."

The Lady's voice hardened. "So, the great Merlin shall be imprisoned... for a time."

"Not imprisoned," he said gently. "Transformed. And not forever." He knelt and placed his palm upon the earth. "The oak lives for centuries. I shall still see the sky. I shall still feel the wind. I shall simply become part of the forest I have loved."

The wind stirred around them, carrying the scent of leaves and water. Slowly, almost reluctantly, the Lady raised her hands.

The lake behind her began to glow brighter. Ripples of magic spread across the clearing like rings on water. "Once the spell begins, it cannot be undone for many years."

Merlin looked at her with warmth that held centuries of moments between them. The memories passed before his eyes as he looked at her. "I know."

Roots began to push up through the soil beneath his feet.

At first, they curled around his boots like living cords. Then they thickened, climbing his legs, wrapping his body.

Merlin did not resist.

His robes stiffened, darkening into bark. His fingers lengthened and split into twisting branches reaching toward the moon.

The Lady wept as she spoke the final words of power. "By earth and root, by time and stone...let life endure through magic alone."

The magic surged.

Merlin's voice came once more, already deep and distant, as though spoken through the heart of the forest. "I shall return—when the time is right."

His face slowly hardened into the rough grain of wood. With a final shimmer of light, the transformation was complete.

Where Merlin had stood now rose a mighty oak tree, its branches spreading wide beneath the stars. The Lady of the Lake stepped forward and placed her hand upon the trunk.

The bark was warm, alive. The wind passed through the leaves above, and the branches whispered softly in the night. She swore she feel Merlin's heartbeat through the bark of the tree.

She closed her eyes. "See you soon," she whispered, fighting the feeling her own heart, a feel of longing and love she pushed away.

The leaves rustled again, as though the tree itself had answered. With a final gesture, she sealed the spell—not cruelly, but completely. The great wizard was bound—not dead, not harmed, but removed from the world he had so long guided.

Vivienne watched him for a moment. Then she turned away.

~ *** ~

Chapter Nine
Bors and Lionel

The forest of Brocéliande did not welcome trespassers. Its paths shifted like thoughts half-remembered, its shadows clung too long, and the air carried the hush of old magic—watchful, patient. Even seasoned knights felt it pressing against their senses, urging them to turn back.

But Sir Bors did not turn. Nor did his brother, Sir Lionel.

They rode side-by-side beneath ancient boughs, their armor dulled by the green light filtering through the canopy. Neither spoke for a long while, as if words themselves might betray them to the forest.

At last, Lionel broke the silence. "She warned us," he said, his voice low. "We both heard her."

Bors did not look at him. "She warned us not to interfere."

"And we are not interfering?" Lionel pressed, a flicker of unease breaking through his usual boldness. "We ride to undo her work. That sounds very much like defiance."

Bors slowed his horse, eyes lifting to the towering oaks around them. "If what we were told is true... if she truly bound him there—trapped him between life and stillness—then this is not defiance."

"It isn't?" Lionel asked.

"It is mercy. It is time. We are destined to unbind Merlin from our foster mother's magic, and serve as Knights of the Round Table."

"Are you sure?" Lionel insisted.

"Yes," Bors told him simply.

They rode on.

It took hours—or perhaps days. Time had little meaning in that place. But eventually, they found it.

The oak tree where the great wizard Merlin was held captive.

It stood apart from the others, vast and silent, its trunk wide as a castle's hall, its roots clawing deep into the earth. Its bark was dark, almost black, and its branches reached skyward like frozen hands.

And there was something else. A presence.

Bors dismounted first, his expression tightening. "Do you feel it?"

Lionel slid from his saddle, frowning. "Aye. Like... a mind, half-asleep."

They approached cautiously. Bors placed a hand against the bark. At once, the world shifted.

Not in sight—but in sensation. A flood of awareness pressed into him—thoughts without words, longing without voice, time stretched into an endless, unmoving existence. Loneliness. Wisdom. Love. A magic greater than he had ever felt before.

Bors staggered back, breath catching. "It's him," he said hoarsely. "It's Merlin."

Lionel's jaw tightened. "Then we are wasting time—we must make haste before mother comes."

He drew his sword. The blade rang softly as it left its sheath—a human sound in a place that rejected such things.

"You think steel will break this enchantment?" Bors asked.

"No," Lionel said. "But it will start the work." Before Bors could answer, Lionel struck the tree. The blade bit into the bark—and at once, the forest reacted.

A wind rose from nowhere, violent and cold. The branches above them shuddered, leaves tearing free and spiraling like a storm of green blades. The ground trembled beneath their feet.

"Lionel—stop!" Bors shouted.

But Lionel struck again. And again. Each blow echoed not just in the air, but in something deeper—like a chain being strained to breaking.

Then—a voice. "Enough."

The wind died instantly. The leaves fell silent. And she stood there.

Vivienne did not emerge as mortals do. One moment the space was empty—the next, she simply was. Cloaked in flowing light and shadow, her eyes burned with a cold, fathomless fury.

Both knights froze.

"My sons," she said, and though the words were soft, they carried the weight of command. "What have you done?"

Bors lowered his sword—but did not kneel. "What was needed."

Lionel did kneel, bowing his head. "Lady... we mean no disrespect. But this—" he gestured to the oak "—this is not right. And we had a shared dream that this was the time to free the wizard."

Her gaze snapped to him. "Not right?" The air thickened, grew heavy with her rage.

"You presume to judge me?" Vivienne stepped forward, and the very ground seemed to recoil. "You, whom I raised? Whom I taught? Whom I loved as my own? You would stand in my forest and name my will unjust?"

Bors held his ground, though his voice remained respectful. "We would stand as knights. And as men who know suffering when we feel it."

For a moment, something flickered in her eyes—not doubt, not regret—but something more dangerous. Recognition.

"You touched it," she said quietly. "His mind." Bors nodded once.

"Then you know," she said, her voice sharpening, "why he was bound."

Lionel stepped forward now, his compassion clear. "We know only that he lives as neither man nor spirit—trapped, alone, enduring something no creature should."

"He chose it!" Vivienne's voice rose—not uncontrolled, but fierce. "He sought to bind me—to hold me as one holds a thing, a possession. He sought to control me! He would have stripped me of my will, my power—myself."

The forest seemed to lean closer, listening. "I gave him what he deserved," she continued. "A prison of stillness. A lesson in eternity."

"A punishment without end," Bors said quietly. Silence fell.

Vivienne's gaze hardened. "I want you leave. Now. And never touch this tree again."

Lionel lifted his sword slightly. "No, mother." The word struck like a spark in dry tinder.

In an instant, the air crackled with power. Light coiled around Vivienne's hands, the ground splitting faintly beneath her feet. "You would raise steel against me?" she asked, incredulous—and furious.

"I would stand against what is wrong," Lionel replied.

For a heartbeat, it seemed the forest itself might tear apart. Then—Bors stepped between them.

"Enough." His voice was not loud, but it carried. "We will not fight you," he said to Vivienne. "But neither will we abandon him."

He turned, placing both hands against the oak once more. "Forgive us," he murmured—not to her, but to the presence within.

Then he closed his eyes. Lionel followed, laying his hand beside his brother's. No swords. No spells. Only will. Pure will in a righteous cause.

For a moment, nothing happened. Then the tree... trembled.

A crack split the bark where Lionel's blade had struck. Light—faint, but real—seeped through it.

Vivienne's breath caught. "Stop," she said—not commanding this time, but warning.

They did not. The crack widened.

The presence within surged—not violently, but awakening. Like a man drawing breath after an age beneath water.

"STOP!" Vivienne's voice thundered now, power surging–

But it was too late.

With a sound like the breaking of the world, the oak split open. Light burst outward. And from within, falling to his knees upon the forest floor, came Merlin–no longer tree, no longer bound, but pale, trembling, and alive.

Silence followed. Heavy. Absolute. Vivienne stood motionless.

Her gaze moved from Merlin... to the shattered oak... to Bors and Lionel.

When she spoke again, her voice was very quiet. "You have undone me."

The words carried no immediate wrath–but something far deeper. Betrayal.

"You were mine," she said. "My students. My sons. My legacy."

Lionel bowed his head. "We are still yours."

Bors did not. "But not your tools."

The forest stirred uneasily. Vivienne's eyes lingered on them both–long, searching, as though weighing something unseen.

At last, she turned away. "Go," she said.

No fury. No spell. Just a single command.

"Take him," she added, not looking back. "And leave this place before I remember how easily I could end what I began."

Bors and Lionel did not hesitate. They lifted Merlin between them, supporting his unsteady form. As they turned to leave, Lionel glanced back once—but Vivienne was already gone.

Only the broken oak remained. And the echo of something long held captive, freed.

~ ~ ~

Chapter Ten
Merlin

Long before Camelot reached its glory, Merlin traveled through a mist-filled valley where no road appeared on any map. At its center lay a still, purple lake with mist rising from it like ghosts. The surface of the water was so calm it mirrored the stars.

Merlin approached the shore. "You summoned me," he said into the darkness.

The lake rippled.

From the water rose a woman clothed in silver mist. She was Lady of the Lake, guardian of ancient magic. Her eyes shone like moonlight on water. The wizard already knew her name, though this was their first meeting: Vivienne.

"So, this is the wizard who bends fate," she said. Merlin bowed slightly. "No, only listens to it."

Lady studied him carefully. "You walk between past and future. That power destroys most men."

Merlin smiled faintly. "Then I am fortunate to be only half a man."

For a long moment they stood in silence. Then she extended a hand from the water. In it was a blade glowing with quiet power.

"Someday," she said, "this sword shall belong to a King."

Merlin recognized it instantly. Excalibur. "The future of Britain rests on that blade," he whispered.

"And on the man worthy to wield it," the Lady replied. "You shall make sure he gets it?"

Merlin nodded. He looked at the woman he already knew he would grow to love, and who would ultimately be his undoing. He was not so different from the future King Arthur, in that respect.

~ ~ ~

Many centuries ago... The plains of Salisbury were silent beneath a pale moon. Before dawn, Merlin stood among massive stones brought from distant lands. But they did not yet form the monuments the world would remember as one of the great mysteries of the world.

This monument was Stonehenge.

Merlin raised his staff. "Spirits of earth and sky," he called. "Lend me your strength."

The ground trembled.

One-by-one, the enormous stones began to rise. The beings from other earths stood with him and helped him. Together, they lifted into the air like floating mountains. Villagers watching from afar fell to their knees in awe. Merlin moved his staff slowly, guiding the stones into their perfect circle. Each stone locked into place with a thunderous rumble.

When the final lintel settled upon its pillars, the monument shone briefly with the power of the universe. Merlin stepped back, breathing heavily. "These stones shall remember the stars, and my friends from other earths," he said. "And through them the future shall always speak to the past."

For centuries to come, people would stand in wonder before the mysterious circle. Few would ever know or believe the wizard and the creatures who had raised it.

~ ~ ~

Centuries later, the wind howled across the barren hills of ancient Britain as Merlin climbed the ridge alone. His gray cloak snapped in the gale like a torn banner. Before him stood a circle of ancient stones older than any kingdom.

He placed his hand upon the tallest monolith. The stone hummed. Not with sound–but with memory.

Merlin closed his eyes. Images rushed into his mind: giant beings raising the stones, stars shifting across forgotten ages, and a future where swords clashed beneath a crimson sky.

He whispered in the language of the old druids. The stones trembled. From the shadows of the circle emerged ghostly shapes–spirits of the land, ancient and patient.

One spoke in a voice like grinding rock. "Why do you wake us, child of demon and woman?"

Merlin opened his eyes, the wind whipping his long, silver hair. "Because the future of Britain hangs by a thread," he replied. "And only the old powers remember how to mend it."

The stones glowed faintly blue as the spirits considered his words. Then the earth itself began to answer him. A faint rumble began, growing louder, and vibrating beneath his feet.

He gripped his staff to ground himself until the mild earthquake passed. "Britain needs a new Kingdom," the beings in the stone told him. "One Kingdom under one King who is able to unite them all."

"I have foreseen that Uther Pendragon will father just such a King. A King to unite all kingdoms. His name shall be Arthur."

"Yes," the stone vibrated and glowed a vibrant blue. "King Arthur and his Knights of the Round Table."

"A Round Table?"

"Yes, a magical table of stone. Take one of us with you. Form a band of men to pledge allegiance to this King. The stone table shall aid this mission."

"Thank you," Merlin nodded. "And one last thing–what shall the Kingdom be called? I have not been able to see it."

The stones vibrated quietly, as if they were thinking. "This enchanted kingdom shall be called... Camelot. And it shall become a golden age of peace in Britain."

Merlin put his staff to a small stone that was destined to become a large round table, where the knights of the King would gather in the future. A future that Merlin envisioned.

~ ~ ~

Deep beneath Dinas Emrys, torches flickered against damp stone walls as soldiers dug into the hill. Their King, Uther Pendragon, had commanded a fortress built here–but every wall collapsed overnight.

Merlin stood beside the frightened workers. "Dig deeper," he said calmly.

They obeyed. Soon the ground cracked open. A terrible roar echoed through the cavern.

Two dragons burst from the earth–one red, one white, scales blazing like living fire. The soldiers fled in terror. But Merlin stood unmoving, not frightened in the least.

The dragons circled each other, roaring, claws tearing stone. Their battle shook the hill. The red dragon finally forced the white one into the depths, driving it back into darkness, wanting the men for itself.

Merlin turned to the trembling men. "The red dragon is Britain," Merlin said quietly. "The white dragon is the invading Saxons."

They stared at the wizard in awe. "You mean Britain will win?"

Merlin's eyes looked far beyond the cavern walls. "Eventually."

Merlin held out his staff and ice erupted from the end, some breaking apart and falling on the red dragon. The dragon roared in protest.

Then Merlin held out his staff and water began to flood and pour from the dragon. The great beast couldn't get out of the cave fast enough.

Then Merlin started a fire on the ground to dry the water that had flooded the small area, and to provide them with a little warmth in the cold caverns where they mined for gold and jewels for their King.

The men watched all this in silent wonder and amazement. "Now keep digging," Merlin instructed. And they did.

~ ~ ~

The road to what Merlin knew would one day be Camelot wound through green hills and misty valleys. One late autumn afternoon, when snow filled the sky and iced the ground, an old man in a weathered cloak sat beside the road carving runes into a piece of oak with a small knife. This man was Merlin, though few who passed him knew it.

Hoofbeats approached. A young boy rode past on a small horse, carrying a bundle of weapons nearly larger than he was. Behind him rode a tall knight in shining armor—his foster brother and master.

The knight shouted impatiently. "Hurry, Arthur! We are late for the tournament!"

The boy—King Arthur, though he did not yet know it yet—pulled his horse to a stop near the old man. "Sir," Arthur said kindly, "are you well? The road is cold this time of year."

Merlin slowly lifted his eyes. For a moment the world seemed to pause. In that instant Merlin saw everything.

He saw Arthur crowned King. He saw the glory of the Round Table. He saw war, betrayal, and the red fields of Battle of Camlann. All of it lived inside the boy's future.

Merlin smiled faintly. "Yes," he said softly. "I am quite well."

Arthur reached into his pouch and offered the old man an apple. It was his only food for the day. "Then take this, sir. No one should go hungry on the King's road."

Merlin accepted it. "You have a generous heart, sir," he said.

Arthur grinned awkwardly. "I'm no Lord. I'm just a squire."

Merlin chuckled quietly. "Yes," he replied. "For now."

As Arthur rode away, Merlin whispered to the wind: "The once and future King has begun his journey."

Snow dusted the courtyard of the London cathedral. Knights gathered in confusion around the great stone block. Embedded within it was a sword gleaming like starlight.

Above it were the words: WHOSO PULLETH OUT THIS SWORD SHALL BE KING OF ALL BRITAIN.

Merlin watched from the shadows. Great knights tried first–lords, warriors, princes. None could move the blade.

Then came a quiet boy looking frantic. Arthur. Merlin's eyes softened. He had waited and prepared a long time for this moment.

Arthur placed his hand on the hilt. With no effort at all... The sword slid free.

Kay and Arthur exchanged a few words. Then Kay kneeled before their new King.

Gasps echoed through the courtyard. The boy looked bewildered. Merlin stepped forward slowly, leaning on his staff.

"The land has chosen its King," he said. And in that moment, the fate of Britain changed forever.

~ ~ ~

Years later, Merlin sailed west beyond known waters. The sky turned strange there–purple at sunset, green at dawn. His small boat drifted through fog until an island appeared.

Avalon.

Apple trees heavy with silver fruit covered the hills. The air itself shimmered with magic. Waiting on the shore was the Lady of the Lake, her blonde almost white hair moving like water.

"You always return here, Merlin," she said. "Even when the world burns with war."

Merlin stepped onto the shore. "This island holds the memory of continents that have fallen into the sea," he replied. “And someday it will be the refuge of the greatest King Britain shall ever know.”

The Lady studied him. “You already know how Arthur’s story ends.”

Merlin looked toward the horizon where storm clouds gathered. “Yes.”

“But knowing the future,” he whispered, “does not mean I can stop it. Some things we must accept as fate. Like death... and love.”

Merlin pulled the lady of the lake into his arms. “Vivienne,” he whispered into her hair. “I’ve missed you.”

Vivienne’s usual crusty and cold exterior thawed a few degrees. For she had missed him too. “It’s been so long since you’ve come, I was afraid you were angry with me.”

Merlin shook his head.

“So, you forgive me for turning you into an oak tree and missing out on Arthur’s childhood?”

“I have forgiven you for far worse you shall do in the future.”

“Really?”

“Really,” Merlin assured her, then leaned down and kissed her perfect pink lips. “Now let’s make love beneath an oak tree so Avalon can hold the memory of our love forever.”

She would usually scoff at such sentimental words... but some magic in moonlight... or something in the sound of Merlin’s voice, or touch, seemed to have bewitched her too. She liked to think she never loved any of her conquests... but she and Merlin made love that night, and fell asleep afterwords beneath the branches of the very oak tree where had watched imprisoned him, and a sky full of stars.

In that moment, and in some part of her, she loved him. She hated him too. Wanted to best him, beat him, and compete with him. But she would miss him, and his last memory would be of her.

Of the two of them, it was Merlin who knew she would be the one to take his last breath. And he loved her enough to accept his fate, and live in this moment of love, holding it deep in his heart, forever.

~ ~ ~

Thunder rolled across the towers of Camelot as lightning split the sky. In the courtyard stood two figures facing one another. Merlin and Morgan le Fay.

Morgana's black cloak swirled like smoke as her eyes burned with fury. "You taught me magic," she hissed. "And now you dare oppose me?"

Merlin leaned on his staff calmly. "I taught you wisdom," he replied. "You chose power."

Morgana raised her hands. Dark lightning erupted from her fingertips, striking the stones with explosive force. Merlin slammed his staff into the ground.

A wall of golden light burst upward, deflecting the spell. The courtyard trembled with the power of the greatest wizard and sorceress Britain had ever known.

Morgana summoned a storm of shadow serpents that slithered across the stones, hissing and striking at him.

Merlin whispered ancient words older than the druids. The serpents burst into white fire.

Morgana's fury only grew. "Arthur will fall!" she cried. "His kingdom will burn!"

Merlin's eyes flashed with sorrow. "Yes," he acknowledged her words. "I have seen it."

Morgana froze for a moment. "You *know*... and you still protect him? *Why?*"

Merlin's voice became heavy with fate. "Because even doomed Kingdoms can change the world. Camelot is the greatest Kingdom this country shall ever know, and Arthur is the greatest king Britain shall ever see. He shall inspire the hearts of many for centuries to come. It is goodness that shall do so—his ability to put others before himself. He has more of your mother in him than you ever did, Morgana," he said sadly.

Morgana screamed and unleashed a final wave of magic that shattered stone and split the courtyard. Merlin lifted his staff one last time. Light and darkness collided like two storms crashing together. The explosion of magic shook the entire castle.

When the light faded, Morgana was gone—vanished into the night. Merlin stood alone among the shattered stones, knowing the war between them had only begun.

~ ~ ~

Deep within a cave beneath a sacred hill, Merlin knelt before a pool of perfectly still water. This was the Well of Ages, where time itself could be seen—past, present, and future.

Merlin lowered his hand into the water. The visions began.

First came the past. He saw the ancient giants building the great stones that would one day become Stonehenge. Then the water shifted.

He saw Arthur pulling the sword from the stone. Crowds cheering. Knights kneeling. The Kingdom of Camelot rising in glory.

Then the vision darkened. He saw Sir Lancelot and Guinevere together in secret. He saw betrayal spreading like cracks in glass until the glass finally shattered.

Then came war. The fields of the Battle of Camlann burned red with blood. Knights of the Round Table lay fallen.

Arthur struck down his enemy—his own son Mordred. But Mordred's blade struck Arthur as well. Merlin recoiled from the water. Yet the visions continued. The future stretched far beyond Camelot.

He saw castles crumble. He saw new Kingdoms rise. He saw iron ships crossing oceans and towers touching the sky. He saw himself lying beneath the Lady of the Lake, stiff and blue.

Finally, the water stilled, as the future ended with his. Merlin whispered to the empty cave: "I see all of time... but I can change so little."

The cave echoed with silence, filled with his sadness. Then a distant voice seemed to whisper from the water itself. "Even the smallest choice can reshape the future."

Merlin stared into the pool. And for the first time in centuries... the great wizard wondered if fate itself could still be rewritten. The cave was silent once more. The cave he returned to when there was danger and loss, or when he wished simply to look into the past, present or future, to see what he could to affect in any sort of positive way.

He knew that the Age of Camelot would one day come to an end. He had known since before it had ever begun. All good things must. Everyone must die, and every Kingdom must come to its end.

It is a fate that we must all accept. One could possibly delay it—but death inevitably takes us all in the end. And that night, Merlin allowed himself to grief the loss of Camelot, so that when the end came, he could face it, steady, stoic, and strong.

~ ~ ~

Night lay heavy over Camelot. Within the castle forge, the fire burned low and red as molten metal glowed like a captive star. No smith worked here tonight—only Merlin stood before the great circular slab of oak and iron that rested upon stone pillars. This would become the Round Table.

Merlin placed both hands upon the wood. Ancient runes carved along its rim shimmered faintly. "A Kingdom built on equality," he murmured. "Not pride."

He whispered words older than the druids. Magic stirred in the air like a rising wind. The symbols ignited with pale blue light. Visions appeared across the surface of the table: knights riding across distant lands, dragons slain, Kingdoms defended.

Then darker visions came. Broken promises. Broken swords burning castles. Knights fighting knights.

Merlin closed his eyes. "This is the cost of greatness," he said softly.

The magic faded, leaving the table silent once more. When the Knights of Camelot would sit at this table, none would sit above another. Merlin alone knew that this symbol of unity would one day witness the fall of everything it represented.

~ ~ ~

Mist rolled across the green valley as dawn broke over the hills. A young king stood beside an old wizard, both gazing across the empty land. The king was King Arthur, newly crowned and still uncertain of the weight of his destiny. Beside him stood Merlin, his staff planted firmly in the earth. Before them stretched a wide plain surrounded by gentle hills, sweeping mountains, lakes, and forests.

"There is nothing here," Arthur said.

Merlin smiled faintly. "Exactly."

Arthur frowned. "You brought me here to show me... nothing?"

The wizard tapped his staff on the ground. The sound echoed strangely, as if the earth itself were hollow.

"This," Merlin said, "is where your kingdom shall rise." Arthur looked around again. Wind swept through tall grasses, bending it like waves across the valley.

"It seems a strange place for a great city."

Merlin's eyes glittered. "Great things often begin in humble places."

He lifted his staff towards the sky. Clouds swirled above them. The ground trembled. Arthur stepped back as the earth itself began to shift.

Stones pushed upward from the soil. Foundations appeared as if carved by invisible hands. Towers rose slowly like mountains growing from the land.

Walls of white stone formed in great arcs. A castle appeared at the center, its towers reaching toward the morning sun.

Arthur stared in disbelief. "Is this...?"

"Yes," Merlin said.

"This is Camelot. This is the Kingdom that shall unite all Kingdoms of Great Britain."

The city gleamed in the rising sunlight as banners unfurled along the towers. The air filled with the sound of distant bells and unseen builders completing their work through magic and labor alike.

Arthur walked forward slowly. "This shall be the greatest Kingdom Britain shall ever know."

Merlin's expression grew thoughtful. "For a time."

Arthur turned toward him. "What do you mean?"

Merlin looked across the shining towers, already seeing their distant ruin. "Every kingdom rises," he said sadly. "And every kingdom falls. Just as every person who lives, shall one day die."

Arthur placed his hand upon the white stone wall. "Then we will make this one worthy of remembering."

Merlin nodded. "Yes, my King. And you shall be a King worth remembering."

~ ~ ~

The great halls of Camelot shined amber with torchlight. Hundreds gathered for the celebration: lords, warriors, ladies, and travelers from across Britain. Long tables overflowed with roasted boar, fresh breads, honey cakes, and goblets of wine.

At the center of the hall stood a massive circular table carved of stone from Stonehenge. It was the Round Table.

No throne stood at its head. For there was no head.

King King Arthur stepped forward, his crown gleaming in the firelight. Beside him stood Queen Guinevere, radiant in white and gold. Around the hall stood the greatest warriors in the land.

Among them were Sir Lancelot, noble and silent, Sir Gawain, fierce and golden, and many others who would become legends.

Arthur raised his hand. The hall fell silent. "Tonight," Arthur declared, "we create something the world has never seen."

He gestured to the table. "At this table, no knight shall sit above another. No pride of rank shall divide us. Not even the King shall rule it. Everyone who sits at this table is equal."

Murmurs spread throughout the great hall. No one had every heard of a humble King–a King who did not demand complete authority over everyone in their Kingdom.

Arthur continued. "We shall not fight for gold or glory alone. We shall fight for justice, for the weak, and for the peace and unity of this land–and all of Great Britain."

The knights looked at one another. Something powerful stirred within them. A respect that no other King before or after him had inspired. Merlin watched the lad with pride overflowing.

Arthur drew his sword and raised it. "Those who sit here shall be brothers. We shall vow blood loyalty and fidelity to one another. Brother-to-brother, knight and King, all peoples of all Kingdoms—brought together under one rule, with one group that fairly governs them, and fights for them, and seeks a justice for us all."

One-by-one, the knights approached the Round Stone Table. On their faces was a reverence, as if God and government had come together at last, for the good of all. They knelt before the King and swore their oaths: to defend the innocent, to honor truth, and to stand together until death. Until the end of the age of Camelot."

At the edge of the hall, Merlin watched silently. The firelight reflected in his ancient blue eyes. For a moment he saw the future again. He saw these same knights riding together in glory. He saw them in battles with the Saxons and feudal kingdoms. He saw them on quests and adventures. He saw some of them falling in love and marrying. He saw their children, and their children's children.

He also saw them falling in battle... and turning against one another. Yet in that moment the hall rang with laughter, music, and hope. In that moment, they were brothers. In that moment, they were of one mind, one purpose, and one heart.

The knights took their seats around the Round Table. And thus, was born the brotherhood that would become the greatest legend in all of Britain. And thus, the great Kingdom of Camelot and the Knights of the Round Table was begun.

~ ~ ~

Chapter Eleven
Kay

The winter wind swept through the training yard of Sir Ector's Manor, rattling wooden practice swords stacked against the fence. Young Arthur stood in the mud with a bruised lip and a split knuckle.

Across from him, his foster brother Sir Kay—bigger, older, red-faced with anger—held a wooden sword like a club. "Is that all you have in you, Wart?" Kay barked. "You swing like a girl milking a cow!"

Arthur raised his sword again, breathing hard. Kay charged without warning.

CRACK!

The blow knocked Arthur flat on his back.

Kay stood over him laughing. "You're meant to be my squire one day," Kay sneered. "You'll carry my shield, polish my armor, and hold my horse while I win tournaments. You need to be stronger and tougher than this!"

Arthur wiped mud from his face. "I'll do it gladly," he said quietly.

Kay frowned, confused by the lack of anger. "You're a fool, Wart." He tossed the practice sword aside. "A fool and a weakling."

Arthur only smiled faintly. "Maybe."

Kay's father, Ector, would often beat up his son. Then Kay would turn around and beat up Arthur. Yet beneath it all, love was there. Kay was never as rough on Arthur as his father was on him. And really, Arthur was the closest thing to a brother he had. Deep down, that's how he saw Arthur. Deep down, he cared about him. While he beat him up, he would never let Ector beat him, or any of the other boys from school.

When Ector went after him, he stood in between them and took his hard knocks. Same with the boys at school.

Arthur noticed that. He observed everything. He had learned to keep quiet and say little when emotions were high. But deep down, he loved Kay like a brother too. And Kay noticed his kindness, and wished he could be more like Arthur.

~ ~ ~

When Arthur was fourteen, and Kay was about twenty or so, crowds gathered in London around the sword set in the stone. The sword gleamed beneath the winter sun. A challenge had been proclaimed: whoever pulled it free would be the rightful King of Britain.

Knights tried. Princes tried. Nobles of all ranks tried. None succeeded.

That morning Kay had forgotten his sword before a tournament. "Wart!" he shouted. Arthur hurried to him. "Fetch my sword from the inn. Quickly!"

Ector, Kay, and Arthur were staying in an inn in London for the tournament, and for Kay to try his hand at pulling the sword in the stone.

Arthur ran as fast as he could through the empty streets. But the inn was locked. He began to panic.

Then he saw the sword in the stone. It stood there quietly, while all the rest of the men and crowds were at the tournament. It seemed... meant to be taken. Arthur grasped the hilt. It slid free as easily as drawing a knife from butter.

When Arthur found Kay at the tournament, he took the sword without looking. "It's about time!" he griped. Then he froze. His eyes widened. "Why Wart, this... this is the sword from the stone."

Arthur blinked. "Oh... is it?"

Kay stared at him in wonder. For a moment greed burned in his eyes. "I could say I drew it," Kay whispered. Arthur said nothing. Then Kay slowly handed the sword back. "No. That wouldn't be right."

Then without another word, he knelt. The crowd gasped.

Kay bowed his head before his younger foster brother. "All hail the King of Britain."

Arthur looked stunned. "Kay... you don't have to do this... please don't kneel to me."

Kay grinned crookedly. "Oh, I know. But it'll annoy the other knights if I don't." Merlin, the wizard, who they would soon get to know well, stood watching, looking as proud as a peacock.

~ ~ ~

Years later in Camelot, the Round Table was crowded with knights. Kay slammed his fist on the table. "I say we ride out now!"

A goblet toppled over. "Raiders burned three villages and we sit here discussing poetry!"

Across the table Sir Gawain sighed. "You break more cups than enemies, Kay."

Kay glared. "Come say that outside."

The room erupted in laughter. Arthur raised a hand. "Kay."

The single word and motion stopped him instantly. Kay leaned back in his chair, grumbling quietly to himself.

Arthur smiled. "You see why he sits closest to me?" The knights murmured complaints. Arthur continued, "Because if Kay weren't beside me, he would be starting fights with everyone else."

Kay snorted. "Not everyone." He glanced around the table. "...just most of them."

Yet when the war horns sounded, Kay was always the first to ride. And the last to retreat.

~ ~ ~

A few years after Arthur had become the King of Camelot, he and Kay rode together across a quiet hill.

Arthur spoke softly. "You used to bully me terribly."

Kay chuckled. "You deserved it."

Arthur raised an eyebrow. "Did I?"

Kay thought a moment. "...probably not."

They rode in silence. Then Kay admitted quietly, "I was jealous of you."

Arthur looked surprised.

"You were always better than me," Kay told him reluctantly.

Arthur chuckled. "Kay, I could barely hold a sword when we were boys, I was so skinny."

Kay shook his head. "You were kind. That's harder. I wish I could be more like you... but I know who I am and I know my place. We're the way we are a reason. You need a dunderhead like me to protect you when you're too kind. Kindness can get you killed in this world." He looked toward Camelot in the distance. "I'll fight anyone who threatens you."

Arthur smiled. "I know."

Kay rested his enchanted sword across his saddle. "Even fate itself."

Arthur nodded. "And that is why you sit beside me at the Round Table."

Kay smirked. "Also, because no one else will put up with me."

Arthur laughed. "Also, that."

And together they rode back to Camelot—the King and the once-bully, Kay, who had become his fiercest and most faithful companion.

~ ~ ~

One evening in the forest beyond Camelot, Kay found Merlin waiting for him beside a pool of moonlit water.

"You again!" Kay muttered. "Come to tell riddles?"

Merlin smiled. "I came to test you."

Kay rolled his eyes. "I hate tests."

"Good," Merlin said. "Then you will be honest." The wizard circled him slowly. "You are cruel."

Kay shrugged. "Sometimes. But life is cruel. Sometimes you gotta match fire with fire."

"You are hot-tempered and quick to anger."

"Usually."

"You are foolish."

Kay grinned. "Often."

"You love to fight—even when it's not necessary."

Kay threw him a devilish grin. "Hell yeah!"

Merlin stopped. "But you are loyal."

Kay's smile faded. An almost earnest expression crossed his face. "Yes."

Merlin tapped his staff against the earth. "Loyalty is the rarest magic in Britain—and the most valuable."

The ground shimmered. Ancient runes glowed around Kay's feet. Merlin raised his hand. "Britain has many knights," Merlin continued. "But only three who will wield magic as warriors."

Kay frowned. "You must be joking."

Merlin shook his head. "I need to choose two more, but you are my first choice to be one of the Three Enchanter Knights of Britain."

~ ~ ~

Not long after, night hung over Camelot like a dark cloak when Merlin summoned Arthur. Deep within a stone chamber beneath Camelot, three braziers burned with blue fire. Merlin stood before three knights.

Sir Kay leaned against a pillar, clearly bored. Beside him stood the calm and thoughtful Sir Gawain, whose golden hair gleamed in the torchlight. The third knight was the strange and enigmatic Sir Bedivere, a quiet warrior whose armor bore ancient runes.

Merlin raised his staff. "Britain has many warriors," he said. "But only three shall carry the magic of the old world."

Kay yawned loudly. "Yes, yes, you've given me this speech before."

Merlin shot him a look. "You are the most irritating knight in the Kingdom."

Kay grinned. "That's why Arthur keeps me around. I'm the only one around here with a sense of humor!"

Merlin just ignored him. He'd learned to do that a long time ago.

"You woke me up for this?" Kay continued to complain. "I was enjoying a wonderful dream about a delicious feast celebrating my prowess in battle."

Merlin went on as if Sir Kay had said nothing. "The old magic of Britain is returning. Darkness rises from the north, and swords alone shall not defeat it."

Arthur looked between the knights. "Three?"

Merlin nodded. "Three knights who shall wield magic as well as steel."

The second knight stepped forward. It was Sir Gawain, golden-haired and calm. Merlin spoke: "Sir Gawain, whose strength grows with the rising sun." Gawain's armor glowed faintly with a warm golden light.

Merlin continued, "Sir Gawain shall wield the magic of the sun. His strength shall grow with the rising day." Golden light flared around Gawain's hands.

The knight looked startled. "I feel...stronger."

Kay muttered loudly, "Show-off."

The third knight stepped forward slowly. A tall, quiet warrior whose eyes burned like coals. Sir Bedivere.

Merlin lifted his staff. "Bedivere, keeper of ancient runes and warder of enchanted blades...may the magic within you flow freely." Blue symbols shimmered along Bedivere's gauntlets.

Merlin turned. “Sir Bedivere shall also wield the magic of illusions and dreams.” Mist rose from the floor, swirling around the knight until three identical versions of him stood in the chamber.

Kay blinked. “Alright, that’s actually impressive.”

Finally, Merlin faced Kay. “And Sir Kay...” The wizard struck the stone with his staff. Fire erupted along the walls, “...shall wield the magic of flame and fury.”

Fire raced across Kay’s sword. The blade glowed like molten iron.

Kay stared. “Well.” He grinned wickedly. “That’s going to scare people.”

“Yes,” Merling continued. Sir Kay... whose temper burns hotter than dragon fire, shall wield the flames to the glory of Camelot.” A blaze of blue fire rushed through Kay’s body. He staggered. “What did you just do to me?”

Merlin smiled mischievously. “Something dangerous.”

Kay lifted his hand. Flames flickered across his fingers. He stared. “Well.” A grin spread across his face. “That’s going to make tavern brawls much more interesting.”

Arthur sighed. “God help Britain.”

Kay smirked. “God helps Britain by giving magic to me.”

~ ~ ~

The knights gathered around the great circular table. Wine flowed freely. Kay slammed his mug down, already drunk and the evening was early. “I say I could defeat ten Saxons alone!”

On the other side of King Arthur, Sir Lancelot smiled calmly. "Perhaps eleven, if they are all asleep."

The room erupted with laughter. Kay stood up. "You doubt me?!"

Arthur sighed. "Kay..."

But it was too late. Kay drew his sword dramatically. "Observe!"

The blade burst into flame. A jet of fire shot across the hall—and ignited a tapestry.

Knights leapt to their feet. "Fire!"

Gawain grabbed a pitcher and threw water at the wall. Merlin rubbed his temples. Lancelot calmly stood and smothered the flames with a cloak. The hall filled with smoke.

Arthur stared at Kay. Kay scratched his head. "...in hindsight that may have been unnecessary."

Arthur pointed to the burned tapestry. "That was from Byzantium."

Kay looked genuinely apologetic. "Do they have another one?"

Arthur buried his face in his hands. The tapestry with four hundred years old.

~ ~ ~

War came to Britain.

A Saxon warlord marched toward Camelot with an army twice the size of Arthur's. The battlefield roared with steel.

Arthur's army struggled. Then three riders charged down the hill. Gawain raised his sword to the sun. Golden light exploded across the field. His strength tripled as daylight blazed. He smashed through enemy ranks like a storm of light.

Beside him rode Bedivere. The Saxons suddenly saw an army of hundreds where only a few knights stood. Illusions surrounded them. Panic spread.

Then came Kay. Flames burst from his blade as he rode into battle. "OUT OF THE WAY!"

He swung once. A wall of fire blasted through enemy shields. Saxon soldiers fled screaming. Kay laughed like a madman. "This is fantastic!"

Even Arthur watched in amazement. Merlin murmured beside him, "Sometimes the loudest fool becomes the greatest weapon." Arthur laughed and nodded, as the battle waged on. It didn't take long for them to win. Suddenly Arthur was very glad that Merlin had given him Three Enchanter Knights to help them win against their endless enemies.

~ ~ ~

Years later, a traitor within Camelot struck.

During a moonless night an assassin slipped into Arthur's chambers. Arthur woke just as the dagger descended. Steel flashed. Arthur blocked it—but the assassin was faster. A second blade came towards his throat.

Suddenly—BOOM. The door exploded inward. Fire filled the room. Sir Kay stood in the doorway like a blazing demon. "NO ONE STABS MY KING."

The assassin lunged at him. Kay barely parried. The fight crashed through the chamber. The assassin was deadly, silent, relentless. But Kay was furious.

His sword erupted into roaring fire. He drove the assassin backward. With one final strike Kay blasted him across the chamber wall.

The assassin fell. Silence filled the room. Arthur slowly stood. "You... broke my door."

Kay shrugged. "You're welcome." Arthur laughed.

"Kay... you just saved my life." Kay wiped soot from his armor.

"Well." He smiled crookedly. "I did promise I'd fight fate itself if it came for you."

Arthur smiled. Kay pulled the mask off the assassin. It must have been a hired hit because it was no one they knew.

"It could have been sent by anyone," said Arthur. "Most likely from the Saxon camp."

"Could be," Kay mused. "But somehow this feels closer to home."

Arthur grimaced. "You're right. This feels personal."

"I will stand guard outside your chambers every night—indefinitely," Kay stated. Arthur tried to talk him out of it to no avail. When Kay's mind was made up, a fire-breathing dragon could not have budged him.

"Your safety is the most important thing in Camelot. And it's my job to keep you safe!"

"Thank you, Kay," King Arthur finally related, knowing it was more than the oath of the Knights that compelled Kay to protect him. It was brotherhood. It was love.

~ ~ ~

At dawn, Merlin watched Kay from a tower. The knight was below in the courtyard arguing loudly with three squires about breakfast.

Merlin smiled. Arthur approached. "You always knew, didn't you?"

Merlin nodded. "Kay is flawed."

Below, Kay accidentally set a training dummy on fire. Knights ran to put it out.

Arthur laughed. "That's one way to describe him."

Merlin continued, "But you know he would die for you, don't you?" he asked, suddenly serious.

Arthur was somber. "I know."

"Indeed, I believe he shall die for you someday, Arthur."

Arthur turned and looked at him sharply. "Is that a prophecy?"

Merlin said nothing, and that said it all.

~ ~ ~

A morning of gentle light glowed pleasantly in Camelot. The Round Table chamber was filled with knights. Everything was peaceful. Too peaceful.

Kay squinted suspiciously. "This is boring."

Across the table Sir Lancelot spoke calmly. "We are discussing diplomacy."

Kay waved a hand. Fire sparked from his fingertips. Suddenly Lancelot's goblet burst into blue flames.

Lancelot stared at it. The knights gasped. Arthur buried his face in his hands. "Kay..."

Kay grinned. "What? It's only a little magic."

Gawain leaned over. "You set Lancelot's wine on fire."

Kay shrugged. "It improves the flavor. Who doesn't like hot spiced wine on a Christmas Eve?"

Lancelot muttered, "This isn't spiced wine." Kay just laughed at him.

Bedivere muttered, "One day Merlin will regret giving you powers."

Kay raised his flaming goblet. "Nonsense."

Across the hall a banner accidentally caught fire. Knights leapt up. Arthur sighed. "I regret it already. How many things in this castle have you caught on fire now? I'm afraid I've lost count."

Kay grinned and roared in laughter. Merlin came over to Arthur and whispered in his ear, "And how many times has he saved you?"

Arthur's eyes narrowed. And he decided to laugh along with Kay. "They are only things," said King Arthur. "People matter more." Everyone who was there that night was impressed and grateful to have a King like Arthur, especially Sir Kay.

~ ~ ~

Winter winds howled as Arthur's army faced a sorcerer warlord in the north. The enemy wizard raised his staff. Lightning tore across the battlefield. Knights fell screaming.

Arthur shouted: "Enchanter Knights!"

Kay rode forward laughing like a madman. "Finally!"

He slammed his sword into the ground. A wall of roaring fire burst upward, devouring the enemy like lightning striking them all at once.

Gawain raised his blade to the rising sun. Golden light erupted across the battlefield, strengthening Arthur's soldiers.

Bedivere knelt in the snow. Ancient runes flared beneath the earth, inciting an earthquake.

The enemy sorcerer unleashed a storm of black shadows. Kay stepped forward. "Oh, I hate shadows."

He lifted both hands. A blazing inferno exploded from his palms, burning the darkness from the sky. The battlefield erupted with cheers. Arthur watched, half amazed and half horrified. "Remind me never to anger Kay again."

Merlin grinned. "I told you Kay would make a great Enchanter Knight."

~ ~ ~

Years later, during a brutal ambush in a dark forest, Arthur was thrown from his horse. Enemy knights surrounded him.

One raised a spear. Arthur struggled to stand. Too slow. The spear flew. Suddenly a wall of fire erupted between Arthur and the attackers. The spear melted in midair.

A familiar voice roared, "NOBODY KILLS MY BROTHER!"

Sir Kay crashed into the battlefield like a thunderstorm. His sword blazed with magic. Flames spiraled around him. Enemy knights scattered in terror.

Kay swung his blade once. A ring of fire burst outward, knocking the attackers to the ground.

Arthur stared up from the dirt. Kay helped him stand. "You alright?"

Arthur brushed ash from his cloak. "I was nearly killed."

Kay shrugged. "Nearly. But not quite."

Arthur smiled. "Thank you, Kay."

Kay looked embarrassed. "Don't mention it." Then he grinned. "But you owe me a new horse."

Unexpectedly, a lady emerged from the fire and flames. She had thick, bright red hair. She was big and buxom, wearing a corset that showed off her ample chest.

Sir Kay's mouth hung open. "Well, hello, stranger," she said flirting. "What you are you, a fire god?"

"What are you?" Kay stuttered. "I mean, who are you?"

"Lady Ray. Short for Rayvin."

"You're beautiful... I mean, a mean, that's a beautiful name!"

Lady Ray gave him a wicked smile, taking his hands, and leading him into the woods.

"Is it a trick?" Sir Bedivere worried.

"What kind of lady goes off the moment she meets a knight for a roll in the hay?" wondered Gawain.

Arthur just laughed. "The perfect woman for Kay."

Lady Ray led Kay to a babbling brook shaded by trees. "Take your clothes off," she ordered.

"All of them?" he gulped.

She laughed. "Yes, all of them. To do what I want to do, you can't really be clothed." He did he was instructed, lying down on a blanket of green grass and the hard ground.

Then he watched as she slowly removed her corset and skirt, her large, voluptuous body making him literally drool. She got on top of him and gave him the ride of his life!

Kay was madly in love, and without any unnecessary drama or fanfare, they married the next day in the chapel of Camelot. Merlin officiated the wedding, King Arthur was Kay's best man, and Sir Gawain and a suspicious Sir Bedivere were witnesses.

Kay had never been so happy in his life. When he wasn't in battle or protecting King Arthur, he was making love to his wife. And soon they had four red-haired and especially large kids to raise. When the children were born, Kay was happier than he ever thought possible. His heart, and his life were full.

~ ~ ~

At sunset the Three Enchanted Knights stood beside Arthur outside of Camelot. Gawain shone with the light of the dying sun. Bedivere studied glowing runes on his gauntlet. Kay roasted meat over a magical floating fire. Arthur watched them. "You three are dangerous."

Kay nodded happily. "Extremely."

Arthur sighed. "And yet you are my greatest champions."

Kay tossed Arthur a piece of roasted meat. "We're also some of your best friends."

Arthur laughed. Sir Gawain smiled. Sir Bedivere nodded quietly. And the three Enchanter Knights of Britain rode beside their King into legend...

~ *** ~

Chapter Twelve
Bertilak

Men whisper that I am a spirit of the forest, a giant born from moss and oak roots, or a demon sent to mock Kings. Others say I am a lord enchanted by ancient magic.

Let them wonder. I could hear the whispers about me, feel the fear. My tales and numerous and strange. But the tale I tell today is of the test.

What matters to this story, is the test.

For long had I watched the court of King Arthur—that shining company gathered around the Round Table. They spoke endlessly of honor. Of courage. Of truth.

But words are like the wind. Only trials reveal a man's heart. And so, one winter's day, I rode to Camelot...

Snow lay upon the fields when I entered the King's hall. The doors burst open before me as my horse's hooves rang upon the stone floor.

Every eye turned toward me. I wore green from head to heel—green armor, green cloak, even an axe hilts the color of deep forest leaves.

In one hand I carried a holly branch. In the other, my great battle axe. The knights stared in silence. Even the mighty Lancelot did not move.

I laughed. "Is this the court whose fame fills the world?"

My voice echoed across the hall. "Where are the warriors whose courage is sung across Britain?"

At last Arthur rose from his throne. "What game do you bring to Camelot, stranger?"

I planted the axe head into the floor. "A simple Christmas game."

I pointed to my neck. "Strike me once with this axe. A single blow." Murmurs spread through the hall. "And one year from today," I continued, "I shall return the same blow."

The hall fell silent. For who could strike such a blow knowing it must one day be repaid? Then one courageous knight stepped forward.

A golden knight bowed before Arthur. It was Sir Gawain, one of the Three Enchanter Knights.

"My lord," he said, "allow me to take this challenge."

Arthur agreed. Gawain took up my axe. The handsome knight did not hesitate. The blade flashed. My head fell to the floor.

Gasps filled the hall. Yet as my body stood there, unmoving, my hand reached down... and lifted my severed head back onto my shoulders. I screwed my head back into my body.

My eyes looked directly into Gawain's. "In one year," I said calmly, "come to the Green Chapel and receive your blow." Then I rode away from Camelot, my battle axe swinging like a silent threat of what was to come.

~ ~ ~

For twelve long months I waited. Winter turned into spring. Spring gave way to warm summer heat. Few men would have kept such an appointment.

But I believed Gawain might. He had courage.

Yet courage alone is not enough. A knight must also possess honesty, humility, and honor. And so, I prepared the deeper test.

~ ~ ~

When Gawain journeyed toward the Green Chapel, a week or so before the appointed time, he arrived at a castle hidden within the forest. That castle was mine. Though he did not know it.

Disguised as its lord, I welcomed him warmly. During the days we hunted together. But each morning while I rode out, my lady visited Gawain in his chamber.

She tested his honor. Flattered him. Tempted him. The young knight resisted her considerable charms bravely.

Yet on the final day she gave him a green silk girdle—a charm she claimed could protect its wearer from death. And Gawain accepted it.

Not from lust. But from fear. For he knew the axe awaited him.

He kept the girdle secret from me. That secret was the crack in his armor.

~ ~ ~

On Christmas Eve, exactly one year since we had first met, Sir Gawain found me waiting at the Green Chapel. He knelt before me bravely.

Few men would have done the same. I raised my axe. After the first swing I stopped short. The second swing I also held back. But the third blow I allowed to fall.

The blade only nicked his neck. A small wound. Gawain leapt back in anger. "Enough!" he cried. "You have struck me!"

I laughed and revealed the truth. The first two feints matched the first two days he had been honest with me. But the third cut was payment for the secret he kept—the green girdle hidden beneath his armor.

Yet his fault was small. He had faced death with courage. Few men would have done better. I told him the truth of my identity.

I was the Bertilak de Hautdesert, the Green Knight sent to test the honor of Camelot; my enchantment placed upon me by the sorceress Morgana. Gawain bowed his head in shame for his small failure. But I told him this: "You are the most honorable knight I have ever tested."

Gawain returned to Camelot wearing the green girdle as a reminder of his imperfection. But the knights of the Round Table chose instead to wear green sashes in his honor. For a man who admits his fault is greater than one who pretends perfection.

And as for me—I returned to the deep forests where green things grow and ancient magic lingers.

Still watching.

Still waiting.

For another knight brave enough to accept the game. Waiting for new games to play.

~ *** ~

Chapter Thirteen
Gawain

Among the knights of Camelot, none were more beloved than Sir Gawain. But few knew the full truth of the magic within him.

It was Merlin who first revealed it. One morning at dawn, Merlin summoned Gawain to the high cliffs overlooking the sea.

"The sun rises," Merlin said. "Do you feel it?"

Gawain closed his eyes. Warmth filled his body like fire in a forge.

Merlin nodded. "Your strength is tied to the sun itself."

As the first golden ray crossed the horizon, Gawain felt power surging through him. His muscles tightened. His senses sharpened. The wind seemed to whisper secrets.

"You shall grow stronger with the rising sun," Merlin said. "And be strongest at midday."

Gawain opened his eyes. Light shimmered along the blade of his sword.

Merlin smiled. "Britain shall soon have a knight whose power rises with the heavens. You are the second Enchanter Knight I choose."

~ ~ ~

Years after Merlin dubbed Kay, Bedivere, and Gawain the Three Enchanter Knights, giving them their powers, which had always lied dormant within them, Arthur's army faced a monstrous giant in the Red Vale.

The creature towered above the knights like a living mountain. One swing of its club easily crushed three men. Arthur's army faltered.

Then Gawain rode forward. The sun was rising. Golden light poured across the valley. As the sunlight touched Gawain's armor, it blazed like polished gold.

The giant roared and charged.

Gawain leapt from his horse. At sunrise his strength doubled. By midmorning it tripled. The giant swung its club downward.

Gawain caught it with both hands. The earth cracked beneath his feet. The giant stared in disbelief. Then Gawain lifted the enormous weapon... and snapped it in half.

By noon the giant lay defeated. The knights began to whisper a new name for him: *the Sun Knight of Camelot.*

~ ~ ~

The wind howled through the jagged peaks of the Snowdonia, carrying with it the smell of ash and burned earth. Below the cliffs, an entire village lay in ruins.

Blackened stone. Charred fields. Melted church bells. All signs a dragon had come. And King Arthur had answered the call of his people.

Arthur stood beside the smoking ruins with three of his greatest champions. First stood Sir Gawain, his armor gleaming faintly in the morning light. The rising sun was climbing over the mountains, and with it his strength grew.

Beside him was Sir Bedivere, quiet and watchful, ancient runes glowing faintly along his enchanted gauntlet. And leaning casually against a rock with a flaming dagger spinning in his fingers was Sir Kay.

Kay squinted toward the mountains. "So... we're hunting a dragon," he said with an excited gleam in his eyes.

Arthur nodded. Kay grinned. "Finally—something interesting."

"Let's go," said Sir Gawain.

The knights climbed higher into the mountains until the path narrowed along a sheer cliff. Then the earth trembled. A thunderous roar shattered the air. The dragon rose from a cavern below them.

Its wings were as vast as a ships' sails. Its scales burned red like molten iron. Smoke poured from its jaws. Even Arthur's horse reared in terror.

Kay whistled. "That's... bigger than I expected." The dragon lunged. Flames erupted down the mountainside.

But the sun had risen high. Golden light poured across the valley. Sir Gawain stepped forward.

His armor blazed like a second sunrise. The dragon swung its massive claw. Gawain caught the blow with his shield, sliding back across the stone but holding firm. At this hour his strength was at its peak.

With a roar he leapt upward, slashing across the dragon's chest. Golden sparks burst across its scales. The beast recoiled in shock.

Kay laughed. "Look at him go!"

The dragon spread its wings. It lifted into the air. From above them, it rained fire upon the knights. But Sir

Bedivere knelt and struck the earth with his glowing gauntlet.

Ancient runes ignited across the mountainside. The ground rumbled. Massive stone pillars erupted from the earth like the teeth of giants. The dragon crashed into them, unable to gain height.

Bedivere whispered in the old language of Britain. "Sleep, ancient mountain. Rise for your king." The cliffs themselves seemed to obey.

"Now that's faith that can move the mountains!" joked Kay.

"Stop with the jokes, and help them!" Arthur ordered.

Then Sir Kay stepped forward, obeying his King. He stretched his fingers. Flames danced across his hands.

"Oh, you want fire little dragon?" Kay taunted. "I'll show you fire!"

He thrust both hands forward. A blazing torrent erupted from his palms like a living inferno. The dragon roared as Kay's magical flames met its own breath.

Fire against fire.

Heat against heat.

For a moment the entire mountainside glowed like a furnace. Arthur shielded his eyes. "Kay is enjoying this far too much," he said to no one in particular.

Blinded by flame and trapped by stone, the dragon thrashed wildly. That was the moment Gawain needed. With the power of the noon sun blazing through him, he ran straight up the rocky slope.

Leaping from a fallen boulder, he launched himself onto the dragon's neck. With a single mighty strike, his enchanted blade plunged deep beneath its scales.

The dragon gave one final thunderous roar. Then the great beast collapsed against the mountainside. Silence fell over the valley.

Smoke drifted through the peaks. Arthur walked toward the fallen dragon. "You three nearly burned down Wales."

Kay shrugged. "Dragon problem solved."

Bedivere wiped soot from his gauntlet. "The mountain will recover."

Gawain rested his sword against his shoulder. "The village will rebuild."

Arthur looked at them all and smiled. "My Three Enchanter Knights."

Kay poked the dragon's enormous claw with his boot. "Can we keep the head?"

Arthur sighed. "Why?"

Kay grinned. "It'll look great in the hall at Camelot. And it will replace that tapestry I burned."

Arthur shook his head. But he was laughing. And far below in the valley of Wales, the people would tell stories for generations of the day three enchanted knights slew a dragon in their mountains.

~ ~ ~

The wind whispered through the ancient trees as King Arthur rode alone, separated from his knights in the deep forest. A sudden thunder of hooves broke the stillness. From the shadows emerged a grim French knight clad in dark armor—Sir Gromer Somer Joure.

"Arthur," he growled, "you trespass upon lands that are not your own."

Arthur's hand moved toward Excalibur, but the knight raised a gauntleted hand.

"No blade today. Instead, I give you a choice. Answer me a question within one year—or die."

Arthur straightened in his saddle. "Speak it."

The knight's voice lowered, heavy with menace: "What do women most desire?"

Arthur frowned. "Is that all?"

"You shall find the answer is not so simple," Gromer said coldly. "Fail to answer correctly—and your life is forfeit."

With that, he vanished into the trees.

For months, Arthur searched across Britain. He asked queens and maidens, wives and widows: "Riches," said one. "Beauty," said another. "Lust," whispered some. "Flattery," claimed others. But none agreed.

At last, weary and desperate, Arthur wandered once more into the forest—where fate awaited him. From beside a gnarled oak came a voice—harsh, grating, unnatural.

She was hideous beyond measure—her face twisted, her skin blotched, her teeth like broken stones. Yet her eyes gleamed with terrible intelligence. "I know your riddle," she said.

Arthur leaned forward. "Then tell me—and you shall be richly rewarded."

She laughed, a dreadful sound. "I want no gold."

"Then what?"

She pointed toward Camelot. "I will give you the answer... if Sir Gawain agrees to marry me."

Arthur recoiled. "Gawain? One of the enchanter knights?"

"Yes," she nodded. "Now agree—or die."

Back in Camelot, Arthur spoke in anguish. "I would not condemn you to such a fate," he told Gawain.

But Gawain—ever loyal, brave and true—smiled calmly. "My King," he said, "your life is worth far more than my comfort."

He was handsome, with golden skin and hair, like a sun god from the south. All the maidens wanted him. He could take his pick of them. It was not fair to condemn him to such a marriage.

Arthur shook his head. "You do not know what you agree to."

"I know enough," Gawain replied. "If this marriage saves you, then I accept it freely. And if I may say so, my dear King—and my dear friend, it is my choice to accept." King Arthur reluctantly agreed.

~ ~ ~

Arthur returned to the French knight, Gromer Somer Joure. "I have my answer," he declared.

The dark knight folded his arms. "Speak it."

Arthur lifted his chin.

"What women most desire... is sovereignty—the power to choose their own lives." The forest fell silent.

Gromer's face darkened with fury—but he could not deny it. "You have been told," he spat. "But the answer is true." And Arthur lived.

~ ~ ~

The wedding feast was uneasy. Knights averted their eyes. Ladies whispered behind their sleeves.

Ragnelle entered in all her grotesqueness—yet she walked proudly, as though she were the fairest lady alive. Only Gawain greeted her warmly, ever the gentleman. "My lady," he said, bowing deeply, "I am honored to take your hand in holy matrimony."

She studied him carefully. "You do not mock me?"

"Never," he said simply. And so, they were wed. But the wedding "feast" felt more like a funeral in the Kingdom of Camelot, as golden as Sir Gawain himself.

That night, in their chamber, Gawain turned to his bride—and gasped. Before him stood not the loathly woman—but a lady of breathtaking beauty.

Her skin shone like ivory, her hair like gold in firelight, her eyes soft and luminous. "You see me as I truly am," Ragnelle said gently.

Gawain stared in wonder. "What sorcery is this?"

"A curse," she replied. "But I may yet be freed."

She stepped closer. "You must choose. I can be beautiful by day and foul by night... or foul by day and beautiful by night."

Gawain fell silent.

At last, he spoke. "My lady... the choice should not be mine. It would selfish for me to choose for you."

She looked at him, startled. He continued softly: "You are the one who must live with it. Choose as you will—and I shall be content."

For a heartbeat, there was only silence. Then her face lit with joy. "You have given me what I desired most." A soft glow filled the chamber. "The curse is broken."

They both grinned and laughed. "May I kiss you, my lady?" Gawain asked his wife with the utmost respect.

"Oh, come here," Ragnelle said, coming at him with fierce passion.

They made love by the gentle light of dozens of candles. They made love all night. When the morning came, Sir Gawain became fierce with the passion of the sun, and they made love all day, falling asleep in each other's arms, by the light of a full moon...

From that night onward, Dame Ragnelle remained forever beautiful—not just in form, but in spirit. Their marriage became one of rare happiness in Camelot.

Where others saw only a strange union, those close to them saw something deeper: Gawain's unwavering kindness, Ragnelle's fierce intelligence and wit, and a love built not on appearance—but on mutual respect.

They smiled and laughed often. They walked the gardens together. They spoke as equals. They loved each other with the passion of a thousand suns.

~ ~ ~

In time, they had a son: Gingalain, known as *the Fair Unknown*. The child inherited his father's nobility and his mother's quiet strength. Ragnelle held him once and whispered: "You shall grow free, my son. No curse shall bind you." For the last thing she wanted was for her son to endure a curse as she had.

But happiness in Camelot is rarely eternal. After five short years, Ragnelle fell ill. Gawain stayed by her side day and night.

"Do not leave me," he whispered, gripping her hand. "You are my perfect match."

She smiled faintly. "I was given more years than I was meant to have," she said. "Because of you."

Tears filled his eyes. "You gave me everything," he said.

She shook her head gently. "Yes... but you gave me myself. If it hadn't been for you... I would have had nothing to give."

Her hand tightened around his for a moment more—then fell limp onto the sheets.

When she was gone, something in Sir Gawain broke. The court still saw the smiling knight—but those closest to him knew the truth.

He never loved again as he had loved Ragnelle. For she had not only been his wife—she had been his equal. And so, the tale endured: of a king saved by a riddle, of a knight who chose sacrifice over pride, of a woman who demanded sovereignty—and received it. And above all—a story proving that true love is not found in beauty, but in the freedom to choose, and to be chosen in return.

~ ~ ~

In legends told by the fires of old Britain, people spoke of three knights with magical powers: Sir Kay, whose fire and fury burned like a dragon. Sir Gawain, whose strength rose with the sun. Sir Bedivere, master of runes and ancient magic.

Together they stood beside King Arthur. The Three Enchanter Knights of Britain. The guardians and champions of Camelot. And heroes whose stories would echo long after the fall of Camelot.

~ *** ~

Chapter Fourteen
Owain

Owain, the son of Morgana and King Urien, was raised among the lords and warriors of Britain during the golden age of King Arthur. His father had ruled the northern kingdom of Rheged, and his mother—sister to Arthur—was known for her cunning mind and mysterious knowledge of magic.

After Morgana killed Owain's father, she had abandoned him to the courts of Camelot. From childhood, Owain showed both courage and compassion, two qualities that would define his destiny. Beneath the banners of the dragon and the white horse, he was welcomed into the fellowship of the Round Table.

Among knights such as Lionel, Bors, and Percival, Owain quickly earned respect. Though still young, he possessed a quiet confidence and a fierce loyalty to justice. But the deed that would make him legendary had not yet come.

One summer, while riding alone through a deep and ancient forest, Owain heard a terrible struggle ahead. The air was filled with the snarling of beasts and the hiss of something monstrous.

He pushed through the trees and came upon a dreadful sight. A great black lion was locked in combat with a massive serpent. The serpent had coiled itself around the lion's body, squeezing with terrible strength, while its venomous fangs struck again and again.

Owain paused.

The lion was fierce but noble in appearance. The serpent, however, moved with cold cruelty. Owain knew that nature itself was locked in battle before him. Yet his heart told him which creature deserved aid. Without hesitation, he spurred his horse forward.

Owain leapt from his horse and drew his sword. The serpent turned its terrible eyes towards him and lunged. Its body lashed like a whip, but Owain stepped aside and struck. His blade bit deep into the creature's scaled flesh.

The serpent recoiled and hissed with fury, attacking again. Owain fought with the skill he'd learned on the grounds of Camelot. The forest echoed with the clash of steel against, scale and the roar of the lion struggling in the coils.

At last, as the serpent reared to strike once more, Owain drove his sword straight through its neck. The creature collapsed, writhing once before lying still.

The forest fell silent.

Owain wiped the serpent's blood from his blade and turned to the lion. The great beast slowly rose. For a moment, man and lion regarded one another.

Owain expected the creature to flee back into the forest. Instead, the lion bowed its head. Then it walked to Owain and gently placed one massive paw against his shield, as if pledging itself to him.

From that moment forward, the lion refused to leave Owain's side. Wherever the knight rode, the lion followed–through forests, across plains, and into battle itself.

~ ~ ~

Word soon spread across Britain of the knight who traveled with a black lion at his side. Enemies fled when they saw the pair approach: a fearless warrior and a loyal beast whose roar shook the battlefield. Thus, Owain earned the name by which he would forever be remembered: *Owain, the Knight of the Lion.*

Together, the knight and the lion experienced countless adventures—defending the weak, defeating tyrants, and bringing honor to the court of King Arthur. And though Owain was born the son of kings and sorceresses, it was not his birth that made him great. It was the moment he chose compassion over indifference—and saved a creature that would become his greatest companion.

~ ~ ~

Not long after earning fame as Owain, the Knight of the Lion, he heard a tale at the court of King Arthur that stirred his heart with the desire for adventure.

The Knights of the Round Table were gathered in the great hall of Camelot, when seasoned knight spoke of a strange and enchanted place hidden deep within the forest of Brocéliande.

He claimed there stood a mysterious fountain beneath a great tree. Beside it hung a silver basin. The knight told them that if anyone poured water from the basin onto the stone beside the fountain, a terrible storm would rise from nowhere—thunder would shake the forest, lightning would split the sky, and the guardian knight of the fountain would come riding forth to challenge the intruder.

That guardian knight was called Esclados the Red. Many had tried the challenge. Few had survived.

Owain listened closely, his eyes bright with curiosity. Before dawn the next morning, he and his lion quietly left Camelot to seek the fountain himself.

After days of travel through thick forest and winding paths, Owain at last found the place described in the tale. A great ancient tree spread its branches like a crown above a clear stone fountain. Beside it hung the silver basin exactly as the knight had described.

Owain dismounted. The forest was silent. He filled the basin and poured the water upon the stone. At once the world changed.

The sky darkened as if night had fallen in a single heartbeat. Winds roared through the trees. Thunder crashed overhead, and lightning struck the earth with blinding flashes. The storm raged like the fury of the gods.

Then, through the rain and thunder, a knight came galloping from the forest. His armor gleamed red like fire.

And he knew... It was Esclados the Red, guardian of the fountain...

~ ~ ~

The two knights lowered their lances and charged. Their horses thundered across the clearing. The lances struck with a crash that echoed through the storm. Both shattered, and the knights were nearly thrown from their saddles.

They drew their swords and fought on foot, steel clashing again and again beneath the roaring sky. Esclados fought fiercely, for he was defending both his land and his honor. But Owain's skill—honed at Camelot—matched him blow for blow.

At last, Owain struck a powerful blow that broke through his enemy's guard. Esclados staggered back, mortally wounded, and fled toward his castle. Owain pursued him to the gate, where the guardian knight collapsed and died. But as Owain stepped through the gates after him, a portcullis crashed down behind him, trapping him inside the castle of the fallen knight.

~ ~ ~

Within the castle lived the widow of the slain knight: Laudine, the Lady of the Fountain. She was renowned for her beauty and wisdom, and the entire land depended on the guardian knight to defend the enchanted fountain and its surrounding forests.

Now that guardian was dead.

At first, Laudine burned with grief and anger towards the knight who had slain her husband. But fate intervened through her clever servant, Lunete.

Lunete secretly helped Owain hide within the castle and later spoke to her lady with careful reasoning. She told Laudine that the enchanted fountain still needed a protector.

Enemies would soon come if the land had no champion. And who better to guard it than the knight strong enough to defeat its former defender?

Laudine slowly realized the wisdom of these words. When she finally met Owain face-to-face, she saw not a cruel conqueror—but a noble knight of honor and courage. And as for Owain, the moment he looked upon her, his heart was imprisoned in love for her forever.

~ ~ ~

Before long, grief turned to understanding, and understanding to admiration. Owain, and his black lion, pledged to defend the fountain, the forest, and all of Laudine's lands, with their very lives.

In time, the two were married. Thus, the warrior who had come seeking glory found something greater instead—love and responsibility.

Owain became both the Knight of the Lion and the Lord of the Fountain, guarding the enchanted spring beside his lady. And though many more trials awaited him—trials that would test his honor, loyalty, and courage—this moment would forever mark the beginning of a legendary romance.

For a time, Owain, son of Morgana and King Urien, lived happily beside his wife, the beautiful Laudine, as lord and protector of the enchanted fountain. The forests were peaceful, the lands prosperous, and the people loved their new knight. But the call of adventure soon returned.

One day, Sir Bors arrived at the castle while traveling through the region. When he learned that Owain had settled into a quiet life, he laughed good-naturedly and spoke bluntly.

"Have you become a house knight now?" Bors teased. "The greatest warriors of the Round Table ride across Britain seeking glory, while you sit beside a fountain."

Owain protested, but the words stung him. Bors urged him to return to the tournaments and quests of knighthood. Reluctantly, Owain brought the matter to Laudine.

She loved him deeply, but she knew the nature of knights and honor. At last, she agreed to let him leave—but only under one condition. "You may ride out and seek glory," she said. "But you must return to me within one year and one day. If you fail to come back by then, you will have broken your word, and my love will be lost to you forever."

Owain swore the oath. Then he rode away.

~ ~ ~

At first, Owain fought bravely in tournaments and adventures across Britain. His skill was unmatched, and his reputation grew even greater. He rode beside knights like Gawain and Lancelot, defeating champions and rescuing the helpless.

But glory has a dangerous power.

Days turned into months. Months turned into a year.

Owain became so caught up in the thrill of victory that he forgot to count the passing of time. The appointed day came and went, and Owain did not return.

~ ~ ~

One afternoon, as Owain rested after a tournament, a maiden rode into the field carrying a message. She wore the colors of Lady Laudine. Owain's heart froze as she approached.

Without speaking kindly or softly, she removed a ring from her hand–the very ring Laudine had given Owain as a symbol of her love. "You were given a year and a day," the maiden said coldly. "You swore by your honor to return."

Owain tried to speak, but the words would not come.

You have broken your oath," she continued. "My lady sends this ring back to you. She declares that she will never love you again."

The maiden threw the ring at his feet and rode away. Owain stared at the ground. The truth struck him like a sword. He had lost everything that mattered...

Overwhelmed by grief and shame, Owain fled into the wilderness. His mind shattered under the weight of his failure.

He tore off his armor and wandered deep into the forest like a wild man. His once noble appearance faded; his hair grew tangled, his clothes tattered. The great knight of the Round Table lived like a beast among the trees. He hunted animals for food, slept beneath the open sky, and forgot the world he had once belonged to.

The black lion attempted to remain by his side, but Owain looked at the beast as an enemy, no longer remembering or recognizing it as a friend and companion. At last, even the black lion left him.

Some travelers glimpsed a wild man of the forest, fierce and unpredictable. They never guessed he had once been one of the greatest knights of King Arthur.

~ ~ ~

Then at last, mercy found him. A noble lady traveling through the forest encountered the broken knight. Her servant recognized something in his bearing–something noble buried beneath the madness.

The lady possessed a magical ointment bequeathed to her long ago by the wise enchanter: *Merlin.* When the ointment was placed upon Owain's skin, the spell of madness slowly lifted.

His mind returned. And with it came the crushing memory of his broken oath.

Owain wept. The lady who healed him did not mock him. She was kind.

She told him, "A knight who recognizes his failure may yet regain his honor."

Owain rose to his feet once more. He swore that he would spend the rest of his life performing deeds of courage and mercy, hoping someday to prove himself worthy again. And it would be during these new adventures that the greatest companion of his life would return to him–the loyal lion he had once saved from the serpent.

He no longer sought glory for its own sake. Instead, he vowed to perform deeds of courage and mercy that might someday restore the honor and love he had lost when he broke his oath to Laudine.

Not long into his wandering, fate reunited him with the companion who had once chosen him in the forest–the great black lion he had saved from the serpent. The lion appeared from the trees as if summoned by destiny itself.

It approached Owain calmly and bowed its mighty head. From that moment forward, the beast again walked beside the knight, never leaving him again. Thus, the two companions rode together: Owain and his lion.

One afternoon, as they traveled along a lonely road near the edge of a forest, Owain heard desperate cries carried on the wind. He followed the sound until he came upon a terrible sight.

A young lady of nobility was being dragged toward a rocky hill by a monstrous giant, a creature twice the height of a man with arms like tree trunks and skin hardened like stone.

The lady struggled and screamed as the giant laughed cruelly. Owain's hand went immediately to his sword.

"Release her," he called. The giant turned slowly, glaring down at the knight with contempt.

"And who are you," the monster growled, "to command me?"

Owain stepped forward. "A knight who shall not allow injustice in the lands of King Arthur." The lion beside him gave a thunderous roar.

The giant hurled the lady aside and seized a massive iron club. With a roar he charged.

Owain dodged the first terrible swing of the club, which smashed the ground and sent stones flying in every direction. The lion leapt forward, claws flashing, and sank its teeth into the giant's leg. The monster bellowed with pain and tried to kick the beast away.

Owain seized the moment and struck with his sword, slicing deep into the giant's side. But the creature was enormously strong.

It swung its club again, striking Owain's shield with such force that the knight was knocked to the ground. The giant raised the club for a killing blow.

Before the club could fall, the lion sprang upward with fearless fury. It landed upon the giant's back, clawing and biting with savage strength.

The monster staggered, roaring in rage and pain as it tried to shake the beast loose. Owain rolled to his feet and rushed forward.

With one final strike, he drove his sword deep into the giant's heart. The monster froze. Then it collapsed to the earth with a thunderous crash that shook the hillside.

Silence followed.

The rescued lady ran to Owain, her eyes filled with relief and wonder.

"You have saved my life," she said, bowing deeply. "I feared no knight would dare face such a monster."

Owain helped her to her feet. "A knight's duty," he said simply, "is to defend those who cannot defend themselves."

The lady also knelt before the lion, who sat calmly beside Owain like a silent guardian. "Then I owe my life to two heroes," she said.

Word of the deed spread quickly throughout the nearby lands. People spoke with awe of the knight who traveled with a lion and defeated giants and tyrants.

Each brave deed slowly restored Owain's reputation across the kingdoms ruled by King Arthur. The name Owain, the Knight of the Lion was once again spoken with admiration.

Yet one honor still remained beyond his reach. The forgiveness of Lady Laudine. And destiny would soon lead him back to the enchanted fountain where he would face the final test that might win back her love.

~ ~ ~

After many adventures restoring his honor, Owain, son of Morgana and King Urien, at last felt the pull of destiny guiding him back to the place where his greatest joy—and his greatest failure—had begun. The enchanted fountain.

For years he had ridden across the lands of Britain performing noble deeds beside his faithful lion. Tales of the Knight of the Lion spread across the realm. Yet none of these victories could erase the sorrow in his heart.

He had broken his oath to Laudine, the Lady of the Fountain. Only her forgiveness could truly restore him. At last, Owain returned to the deep forest where the ancient tree spread its branches above the magical spring. The lion padded quietly beside him as he approached the stone basin.

For a long moment, Owain simply stood there. Memories flooded his mind—the storm he had summoned, the duel he had fought, and the love he had once been given. Then he lifted the basin and poured water onto the stone.

~ ~ ~

Immediately the sky darkened. Thunder rolled across the forest just as it had years before. Rain poured down in sudden torrents, and lightning cracked through the clouds. But this time the challenge was different.

Word had spread across the land that the Knight of the Lion had come to the fountain. Many knights, eager to prove themselves, began arriving to challenge him.

One after another they rode into the storm. And one after another, Owain defeated them—always sparing their lives and showing mercy.

His lion stood beside him like a living banner of courage. The defeated knights returned to their homes with tales of a warrior both powerful and merciful. Eventually the stories reached the castle of the Lady of the Fountain herself.

Within the castle, the clever lady Lunete—who had once helped Owain win Laudine's love—recognized the truth before anyone else did. She suspected that the mysterious Knight of the Lion was none other than Owain himself.

But Laudine still carried the wound of betrayal. So Lunete devised a careful plan. She went before her lady and spoke of the knight defending the fountain.

"My lady," she said, "this warrior protects your lands better than any champion before him. Should he ask a reward for his service? Would it not be just to grant it?" Laudine agreed.

"A knight who serves so faithfully deserves a fair reward," she said. Only then did Lunete bring the Knight of the Lion before her.

Owain entered the hall quietly. His armor was scarred from countless battles, and beside him walked the great black lion, whose courage had also become legendary. Laudine studied the knight carefully.

There was something familiar in his bearing. Something that stirred old memories. Then Owain removed his helmet. For a moment the hall fell completely silent.

Laudine's eyes widened. "Owain..."

The name escaped her lips like breath she had held in for years. Owain knelt before her. "My lady," he said softly, "I broke my oath and deserved your anger. But since that day I have lived only to regain the honor I lost—and to prove myself worthy of you again."

He bowed his head. "If forgiveness is impossible, I would ask for it... but I will accept your judgment." The lion sat beside him, calm and watchful.

Laudine stood motionless for a long moment. The memory of her anger warred with the sight before her: the knight who had returned after years of courage and humility.

Finally, she spoke. "You did wrong, Owain," she said. "But the knight who stands before me now is not the careless man who once forgot his promise."

She stepped forward. "You have defended my lands and proven your honor."

Then, slowly, she offered him her hand. "I forgive you."

Owain looked up, astonished. The great hall erupted with joy as the two embraced. Thus, Owain, the Knight of the Lion, regained not only his honor but also the love he had once lost.

And together, Owain, Laudine, and the faithful lion ruled once more beside the enchanted fountain, where the storm still rose for any knight brave enough to challenge it.

~ *** ~

Chapter Fifteen
Galahad

The night that set destiny in motion was woven of deception, longing, and fate's quiet inevitability. Elaine of Corbenic had heard the stories long before she ever saw him—the unmatched prowess, the impossible beauty, the tragic devotion of Sir Lancelot.

To her, he was not merely a knight, but something closer to a vision: the man chosen by heaven, though bound to a love that could never be sanctified. And in her father's halls, whispers grew into intent.

King Pelles, keeper of ancient mysteries and guardian of relics tied to the divine, knew of prophecy that was tied to the Holy Grail. The sacred vessel of Christ's last supper would one day be fully revealed not to kings, nor to warriors of renown, but to a knight of perfect purity. This knight, it was foretold, would be born of Lancelot.

But Lancelot's heart was already given, and it was given in a way that could never yield such a child. So, the king devised a plan.

On a night thick with enchantment, Elaine was brought to Lancelot's chamber, cloaked in illusion. Through magic, she was made to appear as Queen Guinevere—the one woman Lancelot loved beyond reason, beyond honor, beyond salvation itself.

When Lancelot beheld her, his guarded heart broke open without question. There was no hesitation, no suspicion—only love, desperate and consuming.

And thus, he lay with Elaine, believing her to be Guinevere. By morning, the illusion shattered.

When Lancelot realized what had been done, grief and fury tore through him. He felt betrayed not only by Elaine and her father, but by himself—for being so easily led, for betraying the very woman he worshipped. In anguish, he fled, leaving behind a woman who had gained what she sought, yet lost what she truly desired.

Elaine bore his son in quiet reverence. The child was named Galahad.

From the beginning, there was something different about him. He did not cry as other infants did; his gaze seemed steady, almost knowing. He grew swiftly in body and spirit, raised in a place where faith was not doctrine, but living presence. While other boys played at war, Galahad listened to silence. While others sought glory, he sought understanding.

He became a great knight. He took a vow of chastity, and meant it. His destiny was tied to his celibacy. He never lay with a woman, or married.

When he came of age, he was sent to Camelot. There, among the greatest knights in the world, Galahad's arrival felt less like a beginning and more like a return. Even before he spoke, there were whispers. Some said he resembled Lancelot; others said he surpassed him.

It was at the Siege Perilous—the empty seat at the Round Table, reserved for the one knight destined to achieve the Grail—that Galahad's fate revealed itself. For years, the seat had stood untouched, for any unworthy man who dared sit there met swift death.

Without fear, without arrogance, Galahad approached. And he sat. As if it had always been his sit.

Nothing happened—no thunder, no divine wrath. Only a quiet certainty settled over the hall. The seat, at last, was filled.

Lancelot watched from across the table, a storm of emotions rising within him. Pride, confusion, awe—and beneath it all, a deep, aching awareness. He knew, though none had yet spoken it aloud.

That Galahad was his son.

Not long after, the quest for the Holy Grail began. Knights of the Round Table set out across the land—Sir Percival, steadfast and devout; Sir Bors, loyal and enduring; and Lancelot himself, driven by a desperate hope that he might yet be worthy.

But the Grail was not a prize to be taken by strength or cunning. It was a revelation, granted only to those whose souls were aligned with divine grace.

Lancelot came closest. Closer than any before him, perhaps. In a sacred place, he glimpsed the Grail from afar—radiant, untouchable. But as he reached for it, an invisible barrier held him back. His sins, his divided heart, his love for Guinevere—beautiful though it was—bound him to the world in ways the Grail would not allow.

He fell to his knees, weeping, not in anger, but in understanding. He was not meant to have it. It was not meant for him.

Elsewhere, Galahad's journey unfolded not with struggle, but with clarity. Where others faltered, he remained steady. Where others doubted, he believed without question. Percival and Bors traveled alongside him, bearing witness to a purity they could not fully comprehend, yet deeply respected. They too were knights of purity, who had taken vows of chastity.

The air grew thinner the higher they climbed. Not with cold alone, but with something unseen—something that pressed gently against the soul. Sir Galahad walked ahead, unarmored save for a simple white surcoat, his steps unhurried, as though he followed a path only he could perceive. They were taking a dangerous path, a hidden path, which no one else had ever wandered.

Behind him came Percival, breath steady but eyes searching, and Bors, whose hand never strayed far from the hilt of his sword. Lancelot had stayed back at Camelot this time, believing they might fare better without him.

They had ridden through secret forests that whispered, crossed rivers that ran backward, and passed ruins where no birds dared sing. Each trial had stripped something from them—fear, doubt, pride—until only the truest parts remained.

At last, they reached the summit. Before them stood no castle, no chapel, no throne of gold—but a vast, open expanse of white stone, smooth as still water. At its center rose a low altar, ancient beyond reckoning, and above it... light.

Not sunlight. Not fire. Something alive.

The three knights stopped as one. "This is the place," Percival murmured, his voice barely more than breath. "I feel it... as though my heart has been waiting for it all my life."

Bors said nothing. He had seen battlefields soaked in blood, had heard the cries of dying men—but here, his strength felt small, almost irrelevant. His sword seemed a crude thing in a sacred space.

Only Galahad stepped forward.

At last, they had reached the place where heaven touched the earth. There, the Holy Grail revealed itself fully—not as an object alone, but as a presence, a living embodiment of divine grace.

Galahad beheld it. And in that moment, he was fulfilled. Not triumphant, not exalted—simply complete. For him, the quest was never about seeking. It was about being.

The Grail did not test him, nor deny him. It received him, as one might welcome something long awaited. And when his purpose was fulfilled, Galahad did not return.

As his foot touched the white stone, the light above the altar brightened—not violently, but in welcome. The air seemed to resonate, like a chord struck in the fabric of the world itself.

Then, slowly, it appeared. The Holy Grail.

It was not large, nor adorned as kings might decorate a treasure. It was simple—perfect in its simplicity. A crude wooden cup, radiant with a light that did not blind, but revealed. Within it, something shimmered like liquid gold, yet deeper, as though it held not substance, but presence.

Percival fell to his knees at once. “I am not worthy,” he whispered, tears already streaming down his face.

Bors followed, though more slowly. “No man is,” he said quietly. “And yet... we were brought here.”

Galahad alone remained standing. Not in pride—but in stillness.

He approached the altar, and with each step, the world seemed to fall away. The weight of armor, of history, of name—everything that had ever defined him as a man—slipped from him like shadows at dawn.

When he reached the Grail, he did not reach for it. Instead, he bowed his head. And the light responded.

It descended—not as flame, but as something softer, deeper. It surrounded him, passed through him, and for a moment, Percival and Bors could no longer see him as flesh and bone. He was something else—something luminous, something divine.

Perhaps it was his essence, his very soul that stood before them. Pure light, gentle and stronger than any sword.

Then came the voice.

Not heard with ears, but known.

A presence that filled the space, vast and immeasurable, yet intimate as a breath.

Percival trembled. “Do you hear it?” he asked, though he knew the answer.

Bors nodded, unable to speak.

Galahad lifted his gaze.

And for the first time, he reached out.

His hands did not grasp the Grail—they received it. And as his fingers touched its surface, the light surged, filling the sky, the stone, the very air they breathed.

As he sipped from the sacred cup, visions unfolded before them. Not dreams, but eternal truths.

They saw kingdoms rise and fall, saw the suffering of men and the quiet acts of grace that redeemed them. They saw Camelot—not as it was, but as it had been meant to be. They saw Lancelot, kneeling in sorrow, and in that sorrow, was something sacred.

Percival wept openly now. Bors pressed his forehead to the ground. And Galahad... smiled. Not with triumph, but with peace. The light began to draw upward, and with it, Galahad himself.

"Will you leave us?" Bors finally cried, lifting his head. Galahad looked back at them—not distant, not fading, but clearer than he had ever been.

"I do not leave," he said softly. "I become."

The Grail rose higher, and Galahad with it, until the light consumed him completely. Then—silence.

The altar stood empty. The summit remained, vast and still, but forever changed.

Percival and Bors stayed there for a long while, neither speaking. At last, Percival rose, his face transformed, steadied by something holy and deep. "He was what we were meant to seek," Percival said.

"And what we could not be," Bors replied.

Below them, the world waited—unchanged, imperfect, human. But they would return to it carrying something no sword could win; no King could command. They had seen the Holy Grail. And it had seen them.

When Lancelot heard that they had finally discovered the Holy Grail, and that Sir Galahad, his son, had been taken up into heaven, he did not speak for a long time. At last, he bowed his head–not in shame, but in acceptance.

His son had become what he could not. And in that truth, there was both sorrow and a strange, fragile peace.

~ *** ~

Chapter Sixteen
Tristan and Isolde

Among the most tragic romances connected to the legends of King Arthur is the story of Tristan and Isolde—a love born from magic, loyalty, and fate, destined from the beginning to end in sorrow.

Tristan was the nephew and greatest knight of King Mark, ruler of Cornwall. Brave, noble, and unmatched with the sword, Tristan defended his uncle's kingdom from many enemies.

The name of Tristan traveled ahead of him like a rumor—half admiration, half warning. Knight, exile, lover, warrior. His life did not follow the clean lines of chivalry that men at court preferred to recite. It surged and broke like the sea that had first carried him toward his fate.

Friend of Sir Lancelot, and one of the greatest Knights of the Round Table, we share here the end of his great tale. For Tristan was known best not for his adventures, but for his love, Isolde.

~ ~ ~

One day Ireland demanded tribute from Cornwall, enforced by their champion, the giant warrior Morholt. Tristan challenged the giant to single combat. The battle was brutal.

After a long struggle, Tristan killed Morholt—but not before the giant's poisoned blade wounded him deeply. The poison slowly began to kill him.

Desperate, Tristan sailed across the sea disguised as a wandering minstrel, hoping to find a healer in Ireland. There he was cared for by a young woman of great beauty and wisdom: Isolde.

She did not yet know that the wounded knight she was healing had slain her uncle Morholt. With herbs and skill, she cured him. Tristan returned to Cornwall, carrying with him the memory of her kindness.

Years later, Tristan traveled again to Ireland—but this time with a mission. King Mark wished to marry the Irish princess, Isolde, to strengthen peace between their kingdoms.

Tristan agreed to escort her across the sea to become his uncle's queen. Though neither Tristan nor Isolde spoke of it openly, both felt a strange pull toward one another during the journey. Yet they remained honorable.

Before Isolde left Ireland, her mother had prepared a magical love potion. The potion was meant to ensure that Isolde and King Mark would love one another forever. Isolde's maid kept the potion safe during the voyage. But during the long journey across the sea, Tristan and Isolde—thirsty and unaware of its power—drank the potion by mistake.

On the voyage, beneath an open sky and a quiet sun, after they drank the potion, nothing happened at first. There was no thunder. No sudden blaze of magic.

Just a moment. A glance. And then—everything.

"You..." Isolde whispered, as though seeing him for the first time. It was if the whole of the universe was exchanged between them in that moment.

Tristan did not answer. He could not. The world had narrowed to the space between them, to a truth neither had chosen and neither could escape.

What followed was not joy. It was inevitability. They came together in a love that was bound in magic.

Love surged through them like fire. A love so powerful that neither honor nor reason could defeat it.

They tried to resist. They remembered King Mark. But the magic bound their hearts forever.

When they reached Cornwall, Isolde married King Mark as planned.

Yet Tristan and Isolde's love continued in secret. They met in hidden gardens, forest clearings, and quiet halls where no eyes could see them. But secrets rarely remain hidden for long.

King Mark began to hear whispers. Jealous courtiers watched the lovers carefully, hoping to expose them. Though Mark loved Tristan like a son, suspicion slowly poisoned his heart.

At times the lovers were discovered and forced apart. At times Tristan was exiled from Cornwall. Yet no matter how far he traveled, he could not escape his love for Isolde.

~ ~ ~

Finally, King Mark exiled the two star-crossed lovers. Exile is quieter than war. Driven from court by King Mark when he learned of their love, hunted by rumor and suspicion, Tristan and Isolde fled into the wilderness. There, in the Forest of Morois, they carved out a fragile existence between longing and fear.

No courtly splendor. No golden halls. Only trees, shadows, and each other.

"This was not how it was meant to be," Isolde said one night, watching the fire burn low.

"No," Tristan agreed. "But it is how it is."

He did not speak of honor. Of loyalty. Of the King he had betrayed. Some truths were too sharp to hold.

They lived as outcasts, sustained by something neither could name without breaking it. Love, yes—but also guilt. And the knowledge that the world beyond the forest still waited.

Eventually, it found them...

Forgiveness is rarely clean. Through cunning, through time, through the strange mercy of circumstance, Tristan found his way back into the court of King Mark.

So too did Isolde.

Nothing was spoken plainly. It never could be. Mark watched them both with eyes that saw too much and understood too little. Or perhaps understood everything—and chose silence.

Tristan resumed his place as a knight. Isolde, her place as Mark's Queen. And between them—an invisible line, drawn by duty and crossed by desire, again and again.

~ ~ ~

sTristan and Isolde could not stop finding a way to each other. Tristan, fearful of getting them both exiled again, fled back to Camelot. Yet he was haunted by the woman he loved.

Years passed. Tristan fought many battles and traveled far from Cornwall. During one such battle he was struck by a poisoned weapon–much like the wound that had nearly killed him long before.

His strength faded like a tide pulling away from shore. There was only one person who could heal him. Isolde.

"Bring her," he said to his closest friend, Sir Lancelot. "Bring Isolde. For I cannot live without her love."

A ship was sent by his friend, who understood all too well the endless, cursed love of a Queen not his own. "If she comes," he told Lancelot, "Raise white sails. If not... black."

The wounded knight waited anxiously by the sea. Days passed. At last, a ship appeared on the horizon.

Tristan, too weak to rise, asked his friend what color they were. The shadows cast the sails in darkness.

The answer came–quiet, final. "Black."

Something in him broke–not loudly, not dramatically, but completely. He turned his face away. And died.

Moments later, the truth arrived. The sails had been white, obscured and blinded by the sun to appear dark. And Isolde–Isolde–came too late, her grief echoing across a story that had never allowed them peace.

When she saw Tristan lying lifeless before her, she collapsed beside him. Overcome with grief, she died there with him.

The tragic tale of Tristan and Isolde was messy. It was not a story of perfect knighthood, nor of triumph unmarred. It was a story of contradictions—of both loyalty and betrayal, of love that defied reason and destroyed what it touched.

And yet, it endured. Because in all its tragedy, it spoke to something unyielding: that even in a world of oaths and crowns, the human heart remains the most dangerous force of all.

The lovers were buried on opposite sides of a churchyard. But according to legend, a thorny vine grew from Tristan's grave and crossed the wall to entwine itself with the vine growing from Isolde's.

No matter how often it was cut, it grew back again. Even in death, the two lovers could not be separated.

And so, the tragic love of Tristan and Isolde became one of the most famous romances of the age of Camelot—forever remembered beside the legends of King Arthur.

~ *** ~

Chapter Seventeen
King Arthur

A storm wind swept across the tidal flats surrounding Mont Saint-Michel, driving gray clouds over the jagged island like fleeing armies. The sea had pulled back with the tide, leaving vast stretches of wet sand and black rock exposed beneath the towering abbey. But the land did not feel empty.

Fear hung in the air.

Behind King Arthur, a group of villagers huddled together near the edge of the marsh. Their faces were pale, their voices trembling as they pointed toward the cliffs above.

"It lives there," one old fisherman whispered. "In the caves beneath the rock."

Arthur rested his hand on the pommel of Excalibur, studying the steep slope that rose toward the abbey. Beside him stood Sir Bedivere, gripping his spear.

"You do not have to face it alone, my king," Bedivere said.

Arthur shook his head. "The creature asked for a champion," he replied quietly. "It will have one."

He turned to his knights. "Wait for me below. If I do not return..."

Bedivere interrupted firmly. "You will."

Arthur gave a faint smile and began the climb.

The wind howled around the rocks as Arthur reached the higher slopes of the island. Jagged stone towers rose above him, and the dark mouth of a cavern gaped open like a wound in the cliff. Bones littered the ground outside. Human bones.

Arthur stepped forward, drawing Excalibur. "Come out!" he called.

For a moment there was only the wind. Then the ground trembled.

From the cave emerged the giant. He was monstrous—twice the height of any man, his shoulders broad as a warhorse's body. Matted hair hung around his face, and in his massive hand he carried a club carved from a whole tree trunk.

His eyes burned with savage hunger. "So," the giant growled, his voice echoing off the rock. "Another knight comes to die."

Arthur held his ground. "I am Arthur, King of All Britain."

The giant laughed, a terrible sound. "I have eaten kings before—princes too!"

With a mighty roar he charged. His club swung downward, towards Arthur, with crushing force.

Arthur leapt aside just as the weapon smashed into the stone, shattering rock and sending fragments flying across the slope. Arthur darted forward, slashing Excalibur.

The enchanted blade cut deep into the giant's thigh. The monster bellowed in rage and kicked at Arthur with enormous strength. The blow struck Arthur's shield and hurled him across the ground.

Arthur rolled to his feet; breath knocked from his lungs. The giant came again, raising the club high overhead. Arthur rushed beneath the swing, striking again and again—Excalibur flashing like lightning against the creature's flesh.

The giant staggered back, wounded but still deadly. "You are small," the monster snarled.

Arthur wiped blood from his brow. "Small," he replied, "but fast."

The giant lunged forward, grabbing for him with a massive hand. Arthur ducked under the grasp and climbed the rocky slope beside the creature, scrambling up the jagged ledge.

The giant turned to follow—and Arthur leapt.

With a shout he drove Excalibur downward with all his strength. The blade plunged into the giant's throat. The monster staggered backward, clutching the wound as dark blood poured down his chest.

For a moment the giant swayed on the edge of the cliff. Then he collapsed with a thunderous crash, the ground shaking as his body struck the rocks below.

Silence returned to the island.

Arthur stood breathing heavily, Excalibur still in his hand. Far below, Bedivere and the waiting knights saw the giant fall. A roar of triumph rose from the shore.

Arthur looked out across the vast tidal flats as the sea slowly began to return. Another terror had fallen. Another legend had begun.

~ ~ ~

The wind howled across the high ridge of Battle of Badon Hill, carrying the bitter smell of smoke and iron. Below the hill stretched the Saxon host—thousands of warriors gathered beneath grim banners of wolves and ravens. Their shield wall spread across the valley like a dark tide, their axes glinting beneath the pale morning sun.

For years they had ravaged the lands of Britain. But here, at Badon, they would go no farther.

At the crest of the hill stood King Arthur, mounted upon a white warhorse. His armor gleamed beneath his crimson cloak, and in his hand, he carried the sword Excalibur, its blade catching the light like fire.

Behind him waited the warriors of Britain—knights and spearmen from many kingdoms, gathered under one banner for the final stand. Among them stood Sir Kay, gripping his spear, and Sir Lancelot, his shield raised.

They had fought eleven great battles against the Saxons already.

This would be the twelfth.

Sir Bedivere rode forward slightly. "The Saxons are forming their shield wall," he said.

Arthur watched the enemy ranks tighten below the hill. Thousands of shields locked together. Thousands of spears raised.

"They believe we will wait," Arthur said quietly.

Kay frowned. "They outnumber us three to one."

Arthur lifted Excalibur. "Then we shall not give them time to use it."

He turned to the gathered warriors. "Men of Britain!" he shouted, his voice carrying across the ridge.

The army fell silent. "For years these invaders have burned our homes... slain our people... and claimed our land."

He pointed his sword toward the valley. "Today we end it."

A roar answered him. Arthur lowered his visor. "When the charge begins," he said, "do not break your line. Follow me."

He raised Excalibur high. "FOR BRITAIN!"

The trumpet sounded. Arthur drove his heels into the horse's flanks. The charge began.

Down the slope thundered the knights of Britain—hundreds of armored riders descending the hill like a storm of iron. Hooves tore through the grass, shields lifted, lances lowered. Arthur rode at their head.

The Saxons saw them coming and roared in defiance, bracing their shield wall. Spears angled forward. Axes raised.

The two forces collided with earth-shaking force. Arthur struck the line first. Excalibur flashed in a deadly arc, cleaving through the first Saxon shield and the man behind it. Without slowing, Arthur drove deeper into the formation, his horse smashing aside warriors as the King's blade rose and fell again and again.

A Saxon lunged at him with a spear. Arthur caught the shaft with his shield and cut the man down in the same motion. Another swung an axe. Arthur parried and struck back instantly, his enchanted sword slicing through helmet and bone.

Around him the knights of Britain crashed into the Saxon ranks, breaking the shield wall apart. But Arthur did not slow.

He rode like a force of nature through the enemy host, Excalibur blazing in the sunlight as warrior after warrior fell before him. The Saxons began to falter.

Where Arthur passed, their line shattered. Where he struck, men fell. The charge carried him straight through the heart of the Saxon army, leaving a trail of broken shields and fallen warriors behind him. By the time Arthur reached the far side of the battlefield, the Saxon line had collapsed entirely.

Their banners fell. Their warriors broke into desperate flight. Arthur wheeled his horse and raised Excalibur once more. "Drive them from Britain!" he shouted.

The Britons surged forward with a thunderous roar. By sunset the field belonged to Arthur. The Saxon army had been destroyed.

On the hilltop, as the red light of evening spread across the battlefield, Merlin approached King Arthur. "They are fleeing to the coast," he said. "The war is finished at last."

Arthur looked out across the valley of Badon Hill. Broken shields lay scattered across the grass, and the wind carried the distant cries of the defeated enemy. For a long moment he said nothing.

Then he slid Excalibur back into its scabbard. "Britain is ours again," he said quietly.

And for a generation, peace would follow the victory at Badon Hill—the greatest triumph of the King who would become legend.

~ ~ ~

After the final battle to unite the kingdoms of Britain under one high king, Merlin came to Arthur and told him it was time. Time for him to take a wife. Arthur was ready.

And of course, the old wizard knew just who he should marry. Spring sunlight poured over the courtyards of Camelot, warming the pale stone towers and filling the air with the scent of apple blossoms. Knights and nobles gathered along the castle walls, watching the road that wound up the green hill toward the gates.

King Arthur stood beside the great entrance arch, his crimson cloak stirring lightly in the breeze. Though he had faced battlefields and giants without fear, today there was a quiet tension in his posture.

Beside him stood Merlin, leaning on his staff. "You look as though you are waiting for war," the old wizard murmured.

Arthur gave a faint smile. "I would rather face a hundred Saxons than an uncertain marriage."

Merlin chuckled softly. "Sometimes destiny arrives more gently than a battlefield."

At that moment the riders appeared on the distant road. At their center rode Guinevere, daughter of King Leodegrance, escorted by her father's knights.

As the procession approached the gates, Arthur's gaze settled on the young woman. And for a moment the world seemed to grow very still.

Guinevere dismounted as the guards opened the gates. Her gown flowed like white silk across the stones, and sunlight caught in her dark hair. She lifted her eyes—and saw Arthur watching her.

Neither spoke.

Yet in that quiet moment something passed between them—an understanding as swift and certain as lightning. Merlin noticed the King's sudden stillness.

"Well?" the wizard asked quietly. "Did I do well for you?"

Arthur did not take his eyes from her. "I think," he said softly, "I have already lost my heart."

Guinevere stepped forward, and Arthur descended the steps to meet her. "My lady," he said.

"My king," she replied. Their hands touched briefly in greeting. Both felt the spark.

~ ~ ~

The next day, they were wed. After the vows were spoken and the halls of Camelot rang with celebration, the castle slowly grew quiet. Moonlight silvered the towers and gardens.

Inside the royal chambers, Arthur removed his crown and placed it gently upon the table. Guinevere stood near the window, looking out across the sleeping kingdom.

Arthur approached slowly. "Do you regret it?" he asked.

She turned toward him, surprised. "Regret marrying you?"

"You did not know me before yesterday."

Guinevere smiled softly. "Strangely," she said, "I feel as though I have known you for a very long time."

Arthur stepped closer. The candlelight danced across the walls as their shadows met.

"When I first saw you at the gate," Arthur said quietly, "I forgot every speech I had prepared." Guinevere laughed gently. "I noticed."

"And yet you seemed very calm."

"That," she admitted, "was only because I was trying not to stare."

Arthur reached for her hand. "Why?"

Her eyes met his. "Because the moment I saw you...I understood something."

"And what was that?"

"That my life had just changed forever."

Arthur brushed his fingers lightly against her cheek. "Then we share the same fate."

The room fell quiet except for the soft crackle of the fire. Arthur drew her gently into his arms, and Guinevere rested her head against his shoulder. The burdens of crowns and kingdoms seemed far away in that moment. Only two newly married hearts remained.

Arthur lifted her chin and kissed her softly. Guinevere returned the kiss with warmth and tenderness, her hands resting against his chest. It was hard to explain or define, but they loved each other from the start.

Outside, the moon shone over Camelot, and the banners stirred lightly in the night wind. Inside the chamber, the King and his Queen held one another close, beginning a love that—like the legend of Camelot itself—would shape the fate of a Kingdom.

As we lay there together, entwined in each other's arms, my mind drifted back to the events of the day. Merlin had chosen her to be my bride. Yet I recalled his warning to me right before we took our vows. "Guinevere is your fate—but she shall also be your undoing."

I was shocked that he would say such a thing right before we were married. So shocked, I never responded. Now as I held Guinevere in my arms, a restless, unsettled feeling plagued me.

Time would reveal how right Merlin's warning had been...

~ *** ~

Many happy years of marital bliss followed. The torches in Camelot burned low, their golden light trembling against the stone as night settled like a hush over the kingdom. Within the royal chamber, King Arthur lay awake, though the world believed him at rest.

Beside him, Guinevere slept. Or seemed to. Arthur watched her in the quiet, his breath slow, careful—as though even the air might disturb her. Moonlight spilled through the high window, silvering her hair where it lay across his arm, soft as silk, warm despite the chill of the night.

He had faced warlords without fear. He had drawn the sword from the stone. He had stood against Kings and carved a Kingdom from chaos. And yet... nothing unmade him quite like this.

His gaze traced her face as if committing it again to memory: the curve of her lips, the softness at the corner of her eyes, the way her brow smoothed in sleep, free from the weight of the crown and court and expectation.

Here, she was not Queen–she was simply Guinevere. His Guinevere.

Arthur shifted slightly, brushing his thumb along her hand. Even that small touch felt like a vow renewed.

How is it, he thought, *that I can command armies, yet feel conquered by a single glance from her?*

Every day he carried the burden of being King–justice, war, duty, the fragile unity of Camelot. But in the stillness of night, all of it fell away. What remained was startling in its simplicity.

He loved her.

Not as a King loves a Queen for alliance or legacy–but as a man loves the one soul that feels like home.

He remembered the first time he saw her. How the world had narrowed, how everything else had blurred. That feeling had never left him. If anything, it had deepened–rooted itself so completely that the thought of life without her felt like standing at the edge of an abyss.

Arthur leaned closer, pressing the faintest kiss to her temple. "I would give all my victories for one more moment like this," he murmured, so softly even the night could barely hear it.

Guinevere stirred, her hand tightening faintly around his. "I know," she whispered, eyes still closed, voice laced with sleep and something deeper. "And I would not let you."

Arthur smiled, though there was an ache behind it. Because morning was coming.

Without the need for words, they came together. There was a strong, almost feverish urgency in their movements. A need to become One, to connect, to find in one another, the missing piece of themselves.

There were passion and depth and desire and need between them. But as King, there was also a whole kingdom, a whole country full of needs and demands between them too. His heart remained with Guinevere, but the demands of running his Kingdom, took him away from her, more than either of them would have liked.

Too many days went by without them seeing each other. Too many nights his Queen dined and slept alone. And Arthur worried.

Dawn came too quickly. They'd made love through the night. The pale gold light of morning spilled across the chamber, chasing away the intimacy of the darkness.

His armor stood ready, lying on a nearby chair. The sword waited. The King must return to his endless duties. Arthur fastened his cloak in silence, though he could feel her watching him. He could already feel the wedge of separation had come down like a sword between them.

"You are leaving again," Guinevere said—not a question.

He turned.

She had risen, standing by the window now, wrapped in a simple gown, her hair loose over her shoulders. In the daylight, she was every inch the Queen—but her eyes betrayed something rawer.

"I must," Arthur replied gently. "There are lands beyond our borders that need aid. Knights have gone missing. Merlin believes—"

"I know what Merlin believes," she interrupted, not harshly, but with quiet weariness. "There is always something. A battle. A giant. A dragon. A rebellion. A quest. A cause greater than ourselves."

Arthur stepped toward her. "Camelot depends on me."

"And I depend on you." The words landed heavier than any blow he had taken in battle.

Guinevere looked away, her voice softening. "When we wed, I knew I would share you with a Kingdom. I did not know I would lose you to it piece by piece. Nor did I know how much I would love you, and how much it would hurt every time we say goodbye."

Arthur reached for her, gently turning her back to him. "You have not lost me."

"Haven't I?" she asked, searching his face. "First it was battles. Now it is quests—endless, distant, dangerous quests. Each time you leave, I wonder..." Her voice faltered. "Will this be the one you do not return from?"

Arthur's jaw tightened. That fear lived in him too—unspoken, ever-present. He cupped her face, his touch steady despite the storm within. "Every road I take leads back to you. That is what brings me home."

"But it does not stop you from leaving."

"No," he admitted quietly. Because he was King. Because the world demanded it. Because he could not turn away from his people and their needs—he could rest for the alleviation of their suffering. Yet he suffered too, missing his Guinevere.

She leaned her beautiful face into his hand, closing her eyes for just a moment. "I do not wish to begrudge Camelot," she said softly. "I just wish... for once... that it did not take you from me."

Arthur pulled her into his arms then, holding her tightly, as if he could somehow make the moment last longer forever.

"If I could choose," he murmured into her hair, "I would never leave this room."

"But you will."

"Yes."

They stood like that, suspended between love and duty, neither strong enough to overcome the other.

At last, Arthur drew back. He pressed a lingering kiss to her lips–gentle, reverent, filled with everything he could not say.

"For you," he said. "For Camelot. For all that we are building... together."

Guinevere nodded, though her eyes shone with unshed tears. "Then come back to me, as quickly as you can."

"I always do."

Arthur turned, forcing himself not to look back as he left the chamber. But even as he walked away–towards the Knights of the Round Table, towards danger, towards destiny–his thoughts remained behind him.

His mind, his heart, his soul, his destiny... was with her. Always. Until the bitter end.

~ *** ~

Chapter Eighteen
Morgana le Fay

The ivy twisted around the gigantic oak outside my window. The birds were singing, the crickets chirping. The sun was shining over the deep emerald grass in Camelot. It was a bright and happy day. And I was anything but.

After my father had been killed by mother's second husband when I was but six, I knew exactly what I wanted.

Power. Control. Status.

I planned to marry up. I wanted the security and creature comforts that wealth would provide.

Love wasn't real. It was only an illusion–an enchantment concocted by clever sorcery. "It's just as easy to love a Prince, as a Pauper, after all." That's what my mother had always told me. And it was true. Love was byproduct of marrying a man who took care of you.

The romantics believe that everyone thinks and feels like them. Their idealistic view of the world is foolish and naïve. Those who married for love, were often disappointed by the result.

I would create the life I wanted by taking control my fate. Love would have nothing to do with it. Marriage was about prestige, comfort, security, titles, your rank and standing in the world. It was a business arrangement.

And it would be temporary. What I really wanted was to be free. I want to be the Priestess of Avalon. And I knew that day would come.

But first, my mother and foster father, Uther Pendragon, devised a strategic plan to capture the heart of King Urien.

I was meant to be more than lady. I would become the Queen of Rhegard. That title would be mine long after Urien lay six-feet-under.

Getting what you want is not about looks, or even intelligence. It's all about manipulation, and I was good at that. I knew how to play people for a fool.

King Urien was no different from my many other conquests. In fact, he was an easier target because his ego was the size of his country. Ego makes a man weak.

I wanted more for my life than my mother and sisters had. I wanted everything.

And I got it. First, I lived a wonderful life in the Land of Maidens. Then I married King Urien, becoming a warrior Queen. Then I killed him.

I took my son, Owain, and we entered the land of Camelot, where the brother who I had vowed to exact revenge on, rule. He was young, he had only just become King a few years hence. He was in his twenties by then, and I was in my mid-twenties.

The war with the Saxons had only just begun.

I hated my brother, Arthur, but I wanted him too. Wanted his seed deep inside my body and soul, mixed with the blood we shared.

I want to bear his son, and I wanted that son to be his undoing. I had planned it all my life.

I told the truth when I came to Camelot. For it is always smart to mix lies with truth, to be more believable.

I told him how I was his half-sister. I told him about the truth of his origins, which he did not know. He had never been told.

Night had settled over Camelot. Torches burned low along the stone corridors, and most of the castle slept after the long feast. In the high chamber overlooking the courtyard, Arthur sat alone beside the fire, weary from council and war. This was before his marriage to Guinevere. Before the twelfth battle that won them the war with the Saxons.

His door opened softly. Arthur looked up, "Morgana?" She stepped inside, cloaked in green velvet, her long black hair falling over her shoulders and down her back like a curtain. Her expression was gentle–too gentle.

"You looked troubled tonight, my King," his erotic sister with long black hair said to him, seeming to be genuinely concerned with his welfare. He could not help but notice her beauty.

Arthur sighed and rubbed his brow. "The Saxons gather again in the east. Every victory only buys us time before the next battle."

Morgana moved to the table where a goblet of wine waited. She opened the bottle with a smooth and practiced finesse, pouring the wine into a goblet. Before handed it to him, she poured a concoction of herbs into his glass.

"Then tonight," she said softly, "forget the burden of the crown. Let yourself relax and unwind and enjoy life a little, before the next fight."

Arthur studied her for a moment before accepting the cup. "You are kinder to me than most tonight."

A faint smile crossed her lips. "Drink, your highnance. Please. Rest. Make merry."

"And make merry with you, aye?" he laughed.

"Of course," Morgana laughed with him, flipping her hair to one side seductively, with the sleek subtleness of a snake.

"Let us toast to you, my beautiful sister," Arthur smiled, and raised the goblet, drinking deeply. Even before he drank, Morgana could feel the electricity and attraction between them. In those days, many a King married his sister or cousin to keep the royal blood in the family. And for a moment, she wanted him, really wanted him, body and soul–bound to her, and she to him.

As they continued to drink the wine from their goblets, outside, the wind stirred the banners of Camelot. For a moment they spoke quietly. Arthur's voice gradually slowed, his thoughts growing heavy.

"Morgana..." he murmured, setting the cup down. The room seemed to sway. "What was in that wine?"

Her expression changed. The warmth vanished from her eyes. "Only a little magic," she replied calmly.

Arthur tried to rise, but his strength failed him. The chamber blurred around him. "But why?" he stuttered.

She stepped closer, looking down at him with a cold, calculating gaze. "Because you took everything from me without ever knowing it," she said. "My father. Our mother. My childhood. My destiny."

Arthur struggled to remain conscious. "I thought you didn't blame me... that you forgave me?"

"No" she answered him, her voice low and quiet. "That was always a ruse. And through you, a King shall be born."

He would remember none of this in the morning, why hide the truth from him now? Her voice carried the weight of prophecy. "Your son shall one day bring down everything you have built."

Arthur's vision darkened. The last thing he saw was Morgana standing above him, the firelight reflecting in her eyes like twin flames.

Outside, thunder rolled across the sky. And somewhere in the shadows of fate, the future of Camelot had just been sealed with the seed planted deep in Morgana's womb.

~ ~ ~

After she knew for certain that she was pregnant, she left Camelot for the life she really wanted...as priestess of the Isle of Apples. She left her son Owain behind in Camelot, as once her mother had left her behind, for he destined to become a Knight of the Round Table.

Soon after her night with King Arthur, soon after she conceived her half-brother's son, Mordred, before the knights of Camelot rode across Britain in endless adventures and quests, there was a night when Morgana crossed a threshold from which she would never return. That was the night she became Morgana le Fay.

Morgana had always possessed strange Gifts. As a child she could feel the breath of the wind before storms came.

She could hear whispers in ancient stones. Animals sometimes bowed their heads when she passed.

Yet the court called these things *unnatural*. They feared her. They whispered about her. Even the great wizard Merlin watched her with caution.

"You are powerful," Merlin once warned her. "But power must be balanced with wisdom and humility–or it will destroy everything in its wake–including itself." Morgana did not like limits. She did not like being told what to do–especially by men

This magical night, about a year after Morgana had left Camelot, she rode alone into the ancient forests beyond Avalon the Land of Maidens. The moon shone like silver through the trees. And she was restless.

After hours of wandering, she reached a place older than the Kingdoms of men. She entered a hidden a grove where a ring of black stones stood tall. They were carved with symbols that twisted and moved like living serpents.

This was the place Merlin had once forbidden her to go. It was the place where the ancient magic of the fae still lingered.

Morgana stepped inside the circle of dark stones. The air changed instantly. The wind stopped. The forest fell silent. Then the stones began to glow.

Whispers rose from the stones. Soft. Tempting. Ancient. "Daughter of power..."

"Child of the old blood..."

"Take what is yours."

Morgana felt the magic surge through her veins. Not the careful, disciplined magic Merlin taught her.

This was older. Wilder. Darker. Free. Without limits. Without boundaries. Without rules. This was what Morgana had always sought.

A cold wind spiraled around her as shadows formed shapes in the air—faces of ancient spirits. "The world fears you," they whispered.

"But we do not."

Morgana lifted her hands.

Lightning flickered from her fingertips, out into the sky full of stars.

She laughed softly. "What must I give?"

The shadows answered in one voice. "Everything."

Morgana knelt in the center of the stones. The ground cracked open. Black fire erupted from the earth and wrapped around her body.

Her hair whipped about her face in a storm of magic. Her eyes burned green with power. The ancient spirits poured their strength into her.

She saw visions of hidden realms. Of enchanted islands. Of forgotten gods. Of the mystical land called Avalon, where magic ruled the world.

Her voice echoed across the forest. "I claim this power as my OWN!"

The stones blazed with blinding light.

When the storm ended, Morgana rose slowly to her feet. The forest itself seemed to bend around her.

She was no longer merely a sorceress. She had become something more. Something feared. Something legendary.

She had become Morgan le Fay, the priestess of Avalon.

~ ~ ~

At dawn, she returned to the outskirts of Camelot to see the wizard. Knowing he would know. Knowing he was waiting for her. The old wizard stared at her with quiet dread. “You went to the stones.”

Morgana smiled faintly. “Yes.”

Merlin felt the magic radiating from her like heat from a forge. “You have bound yourself to the ancient powers of the fae.”

Morgana stepped closer. “They have given me a new name.” Her voice carried a strange echo now, as if other spirits spoke through her. “Morgana...le Fay.”

The wizard closed his eyes briefly. For he knew what the name meant.

She was not simply a sorceress now. But a woman of the fae. A mistress of the Otherworld. A being whose power no longer belonged to the mortal world alone.

Merlin spoke softly, “This path shall lead to destruction and war.”

Morgana looked toward the towers of Camelot. Toward the kingdom of her brother. Her smile was cold and mysterious. “Then let the war begin. For I am ready.”

And from that night forward, the sorceress of Britain was no longer merely Morgana. She had become Morgana le Fay–the most powerful sorcerous Britain would ever know.

~ *** ~

Chapter Nineteen
Bedivere

Sir Bedivere was the quietest of the Three Enchanter Knights. He was the most magical of them too. The magic had lied dormant in his blood more than the others.

Thus, Merlin took special care with him, showing him the way of magic, and using runes for your own ends. The wizard knew the day would come when magic fought against magic, and they would need Bedivere's quiet strength to win the day. Because Sir Bedivere didn't say much, when he did, people listened.

His reputation proceeded him. Everyone respected him.

While Gawain drew power from the sun, Sir Bedivere drew power from older magic. Older even than Camelot. One night deep in the forests of Britain, Merlin led Bedivere to a circle of ancient standing stones. It was the same stone circle he had warned Morgana not to go to. But Bedivere's spirit was good. Merlin knew he would not use the only magic for his own gain.

"These were carved long before the Kingdoms of men," Merlin told him.

Strange glowing symbols appeared along the stones. Runes. Merlin placed a gauntlet in Bedivere's hand. "Wear this."

The metal was as cold as moonlight. The runes carved into the gauntlet began to glow when Bedivere touched them.

"You are not merely a knight," Merlin told him. "You are a keeper of ancient magic."

Bedivere lifted his hand. The runes flared. The earth trembled. Roots burst from the ground like serpents.

Merlin smiled. "You shall learn to command the magic beneath the soil of Britain herself."

Bedivere seem to take everything in stride. After Merlin ignited the fire of magic within his soul as an Enchanter Knight, Bedivere seemed to learn the way of magic quickly.

Soon Bedivere became known for enchanting weapons before battle. On the eve of a great war, Arthur approached him. "Can you strengthen the blades of our knights?"

Bedivere nodded. He knelt before a line of swords. One-by-one he touched them all with his glowing gauntlet. Ancient runes flowed into the steel like liquid fire. The blades hummed softly. "Strike true," Bedivere whispered.

The next day those enchanted weapons shattered enemy shields like glass. Arthur later said that Bedivere's magic saved half the army in that battle.

~ ~ ~

Storm clouds gathered over the fields outside Camelot. But the thunder above the Kingdom was not natural. The sky itself twisted with unnatural shadows. Shadows cast by magic, not the sun.

From the dark hills came the army of Morgan le Fay—witches, warlocks, and sorcerers wrapped in black robes, carrying staffs carved with cursed runes. At their head rode Morgana herself.

Her voice echoed across the valley. "Camelot shall fall tonight, brother!"

Within the castle walls, King Arthur stood beside his champions. Knights filled the courtyard. But Arthur's gaze rested on three men. The Enchanter Knights of Britain.

Sir Gawain was glowing dimly, for Morgana had come in the dead of night, when Sir Gawain's power would be at its weakest. Sir Bedivere's runes burned along his enchanted gauntlet. And leaning casually against a pillar with flames dancing along his fingers—Sir Kay.

Kay cracked his knuckles. "So... evil sorcerer army." Arthur nodded. Kay grinned. "Finally, a fair fight."

The battle began in silence. Then Morgana raised her staff. She was the silent but deadly type. Like Bedivere, she didn't say much. When she spoke, it mattered.

Black lightning split the sky. The earth tore open beneath Arthur's army. Knights were thrown from their horses as shadow creatures crawled from the cracks in the ground.

Arthur drew Excalibur. "Hold the line!" he ordered. But the sorcerers chanted together. His sister knew his fighting style. She had prepared for it.

A massive wall of darkness began rolling toward Camelot like a living storm. And these shadow entities had a form, had a strength, and they pushed Arthur's army back, imprisoning them in the darkness of their own shadow selves.

The men screamed in torture as their worst thoughts and deeds overtook their minds. They were lost to the darkness... at least for now.

It turned out that the shadows were only their chains. Their dungeon bars were on the way... from the Lady of the Lake came a wall of ice, growing strength and scope as it headed towards Camelot, until it last, it surrounded all of Arthur's knights with a wall of ice.

All but three knights. The Three Enchanter Knights. But Gawain had far less power in the dead of night, for his power source was the sun. And the strength of the cold and ice made from the magical waters of Avalon, made it so only sparks came from Kay's fingertips. This time, it was up to Bedivere.

It was Bedivere against Morgana. She had planned the attack well. Merlin had been missing for days. So Bedivere was the only one with magic. The powerful and excellent sword fighting of King Arthur would be rendered useless against Morgana and her army of magical maidens.

Sir Bedivere did some quick thinking. He knelt on the battlefield. He pressed his glowing gauntlet into the soil. Ancient runes exploded outward in a circle.

The ground beneath Morgana's army began to tremble. Stone pillars burst from the earth. Massive roots wrapped around the legs of the enemy soldiers. The very land of Britain rose to defend its king.

Bedivere whispered the old words, "By the ancient stones... Britain stands." The sorcerers found themselves trapped in a living maze of stone and earth.

Enraged, Morgan le Fay rode forward. Her eyes burned green with magic sorcery. She lifted her staff and unleashed a storm of black lightning at the three knights.

The sky shattered with magic. Gawain raised his golden blade, deflecting the lightning. Bedivere carved glowing runes into the air, forming a shield of ancient symbols to protect them.

The Three Enchanted Knights stood together before their King. Morgana hissed, "You cannot defeat me!"

Kay grinned. "Maybe not."

Gawain raised his sword. "But we can delay you."

Bedivere's runes ignited across the battlefield. The earth surged upward, knocking Morgana from her horse. From the first rays of the sun, Kay and Gawain gained strength.

Kay looked out across the battlefield. Hundreds of dark sorcerers stood chanting spells. Kay cracked his neck. "Well... this seems like my kind of problem."

Flames burst across his hands. He raised them to the sky. A roaring storm of fire erupted from his palms. Not ordinary flame. Dragon-fire.

A blazing inferno swept across the battlefield, colliding with Morgana's ice wall surrounding Arthur's army. The air itself screamed and sizzled with heat as fire devoured the ice and darkness.

Kay laughed like a madman. "Oh, this is FUN."

Arthur shook his head. "Someone really should have told Merlin not to give him magic. I told him giving Sir Lancelot magic would have been safer." Kay glared at him.

As gentle morning sun rose higher in the sky, Sir Gawain stepped forward, ready to fight. As sunlight touched his armor, it blazed like molten gold.

His strength surged. His sword shone like a beacon. With a shout he charged the shadow creatures. Each swing of his blade scattered them like mist.

The dark sorcerers recoiled. One screamed: "The Sun Knight!" The golden light of dawn pushed the darkness back across the field.

Arthur rode forward, Excalibur blazing. His knights were behind him. The Three Enchanter Knights stood before him, in brave protection.

Morgana vanished into shadow before the blade could strike. Her army scattered in panic. The battle was over.

The battlefield was quiet again. Smoke drifted across the fields. Arthur stood beside his three champions. "You saved Camelot today."

Kay brushed soot from his armor. "Of course we did."
Gawain sheathed his blade. "We would have lost without Bedivere. He saved us all.

"The light defeated the darkness," responded Sir Bedivere, infinitely humble, always deflecting praise.

Bedivere looked out over the valley. "The land of Britain stood with us."

Arthur smiled. "The Enchanter Knights of Britain."

Kay looked toward the retreating sorcerers. "Think Morgana will try that again?"

Arthur sighed. "Definitely."

Kay grinned. "Good."

Flames flickered across his fingers. "Because I'm just getting warmed up."

~ ~ ~

A strange silence had fallen over Camelot. For a week now, Merlin had been missing. Since before the battle with Morgana.

The court whispered nervously. Without Merlin, the magic that protected Arthur's kingdom felt... weaker somehow.

King Arthur summoned the three knights who had once been given magical power by the wizard himself. Arthur spoke grimly. "Merlin has been taken."

Bedivere nodded, "I suspected as much.

Gawain frowned. "Taken where?"

Arthur pointed toward the distant sea. "To Avalon."

Kay groaned. "Oh great. The magical island full of weird things that want to eat us."

Arthur nodded. "Yes."

Kay sighed. "Well...let's go rescue the old wizard."

They all agreed to leave after dinner. By sunset the three knights reached the lonely shore where the veil between worlds grew thin.

A heavy fog rolled across the water. Bedivere studied ancient runes carved into standing stones along the coast. "This is the gate," he told them.

Gawain looked uneasy. "The land of Avalon is not bound by the laws of our world."

Kay cracked his knuckles. "Neither am I."

Bedivere put a comforting hand on Gawain's shoulder, "And neither are we." Bedivere touched the stones with his glowing gauntlet.

The runes ignited. The sea split open like a doorway of mist. A ghostly island appeared beyond it... Avalon.

Kay stepped forward. "If something eats me, I'm haunting both of you." Then the three knights crossed the veil... into a world where Time stands still.

~ ~ ~

The moment they entered Avalon, the world changed. The sky shimmered like liquid glass. The trees whispered. Strangest of all... time was absent here. There was no past or future... only the present moment.

Yet time could also be manipulated here. As they were enemies of Avalon, in a mere instant, the knights turned from young men... into old men. The next instant, their armor rusted and their hair turned gray.

Then suddenly they were young again. Gawain gripped his sword. "A time illusion," he whispered, looking about him as if the trees themselves might hear.

Bedivere nodded. "The forest feeds on the memories of past travelers."

From the shadows stepped strange creatures—half-deer, half-shadow. Ancient spirits of Avalon. They lunged at them.

Kay rolled his eyes. "Of course, the trees have monsters in them." Flames erupted from his hands. Fire lit the forest.

The creatures shrieked and fled from the burning light. But the illusion of time grew stronger.

Kay suddenly saw himself as an old man. Gawain saw Camelot in ruins. Bedivere saw Arthur dying.

The visions tried to break their minds. But Bedivere slammed his rune-gauntlet into the ground. Ancient symbols flared.

"Truth over illusion!" he demanded. They had never heard him raise his voice.

The magic shattered. The forest returned to normal. Kay wiped sweat from his face. "I hate magic forests."

"They evidently hate us too," said Sir Gawain.

Kay looked him wide-eyed. "Was that a joke, Sir Gawain?"

Gawain smiled, and they continued on. The Three Enchanter Knights were all very different in skill and personality, but they had become the best of friends as the years went by.

At the heart of the island stood a lake of silver water. Floating above it in chains of light was Merlin. And guarding him—were three enormous beings... ancient gods of Avalon.

Their forms shifted like living stone and storm clouds. One spoke in a voice like thunder. "No mortal may take the wizard."

Gawain stepped forward. "We are not ordinary mortals."

The sun broke through the clouds above Avalon. Golden light filled Gawain's armor. His strength exploded. The battle began.

One of the gods hurled lightning across the lake. Kay blasted it apart with a wall of roaring fire. Another god raised the water itself into towering waves. Bedivere carved glowing runes through the air. The runes hardened into shimmering shields. Gawain charged the third god directly. His blade burned like the sun itself.

The creature roared as Gawain's strike cracked its stone armor. Kay laughed wildly as he hurled firestorms across the lake. Bedivere's runes bound the giants in chains of glowing symbols.

Together the three knights forced the ancient guardians back. The gods sank slowly into the lake once more. The way to Merlin was open.

Bedivere stepped forward and studied the chains holding Merlin. "Time magic."

Kay crossed his arms. "So... complicated."

Gawain raised his glowing sword. "With light, truth, and fire combined."

The three knights struck the chains at once. Gawain's sunlight. Bedivere's runes. Kay's fire.

The magical prison shattered. Merlin dropped gently to the ground. The old wizard looked at them and smiled. "Well. It looks like I chose the Three Enchanter Knights well."

Kay folded his arms. "You're welcome."

Merlin chuckled. "I see my Enchanter Knights have grown powerful."

Bedivere cracked a smile. None of them could remember him ever smiling before. "We had a good teacher," he said.

~ ~ ~

When the four returned through the gate of mist,. Arthur rushed to meet them. "You found him."

Merlin bowed slightly. "I had complete confidence in them."

Kay whispered to Gawain: "He absolutely did not." Gawain smiled.

Arthur looked at the three knights proudly. "You faced the magic of Avalon itself–and won."

Bedivere nodded quietly. "We serve the King."

Gawain raised his sword to the sun. "For Camelot."

Kay stretched his hands, sparks dancing across his fingers. "And if Avalon ever kidnaps Merlin again..." He grinned. "We're charging them a rescue fee."

Merlin laughed. And the legend of the Three Enchanter Knights of Britain grew even greater across the lands of Arthur.

~ *** ~

Chapter Twenty
Guinevere

Just as Arthur had arranged to marry me from the Saxon Kingdom, in order to foster peace in our realms, he'd sent for Sir Lancelot to come and join his Knighthood from France, in order to foster peace in his neighboring country.

Arthur became best friends with Lancelot, and he became the head of the Knights of the Round Table. Arthur dubbed him, "Lancelot the Valiant."

I loved Arthur. Yet we were always saying goodbye. As the years passed, the separation from his constant leaving caused a chasm between our hearts. We continued to love each other. We continued to make love when he returned home. But we could never quite become One flesh, for the Kingdom of Camelot itself lay between us, like a dam or a river without a bridge—we could not bridge the gap.

Night had fallen over the Castle of Camelot. Torches flickered along the walls of the great fortress of King Arthur. The castle had grown quiet after the evening feast. Music and laughter had faded into the corridors as nobles and knights retired to their chambers.

In the Queen's private garden courtyard, moonlight poured across the stone fountain. Guinevere walked slowly along the path. Her cloak was wrapped tightly around her shoulders. She often came here when the castle slept; the quiet helped her escape the constant noise of court.

Arthur was away again. The time had come that she no long asked him where he went, or when he would return. For he always came home later than he expected.

A breeze stirred the ivy on the walls. Then came the faint scrape of metal. Guinevere turned.

A shadow moved near the archway leading into the garden. A man stepped forward into the moonlight. It was Maleagant. His dark armor reflected the torchlight behind him, and his expression held an unsettling intensity.

"My Queen," he said softly.

Guinevere stiffened. "Sir Maleagant. You should not be here at this hour."

"I have waited too long already."

She moved a step back. "You were dismissed from court for your conduct. The King forbade you from returning."

Maleagant's jaw tightened. "King Arthur does not understand what I feel... and besides, he is not here. He is never here."

"What you feel," Guinevere said firmly, "is not welcome."

He moved closer. "You rule beside him," Maleagant said, his voice growing sharper. "Yet he barely sees you. I do. I see your strength. Your beauty. Your loneliness."

Guinevere's eyes flashed. "You mistake courtesy for loneliness. Leave this place before I call the guards."

Maleagant shook his head slowly. "I cannot–I must have you, even it is against your will."

Two cloaked figures stepped from the shadows behind him. Guinevere's breath caught. "You planned this."

"I planned to save you," Maleagant insisted. "Camelot is a cage. With me you could rule lands far greater than Arthur's Kingdom."

"I would never choose you."

His expression hardened. "I will give you time to reconsider. Then I will have you—like it or not!"

He seized her wrist. Guinevere struggled immediately, "Release me!" she demanded. But what were her protests against Maleagant and his men?

Maleagant's men moved quickly, wrapping a cloak around her to muffle her cries as they dragged her toward the archway. A distant guard called from the battlements. Maleagant hurried them forward.

In the outer courtyard, horses waited in the darkness beyond the gate. Guinevere fought fiercely as they lifted her onto the saddle before Maleagant.

"You will regret this," she said through clenched teeth. "Arthur will hunt you to the ends of the earth." Maleagant swung up behind her. "Let him try."

The gate creaked open. Beyond Camelot's walls the road vanished into the dark forests. As the horses thundered away from the castle, Guinevere looked back once at the distant towers glowing under the moon.

Somewhere within those walls were the Knights of the Round Table. One knight in particular whose loyalty to her had never wavered. Though she did not yet know it, the moment her absence was discovered, this knight would not wait for an army.

Lancelot would come for her the moment he heard she'd be taken.

By morning storm clouds rolled across the sky above the fortress of the traitor knight Maleagant. Lightning flickered along the stone towers where torches burned in the wind. Inside the highest chamber of that darkness, a single window looked out across the black countryside. Iron bars sealed it like a cage.

Days passed in what seemed to be an endless storm, as if the gods themselves were angry. Within the chamber stood Guinevere, Queen of Camelot, her hands resting against the cold stone sill.

Behind her, the door opened with a groan.

Maleagant stepped inside. "You should not stand so near the window," he warned. "The wind has been harsh for days."

Guinevere did not turn. "The wind does not trouble me nearly so much as your presence."

His expression darkened, though his voice remained measured and polite. "I have treated you with every courtesy," he insisted. "You could rule beside me here. Camelot would forget you soon enough."

Now she faced him, her eyes bright with anger. "I would sooner remain a prisoner forever than give you what you ask."

Maleagant stepped closer. "You will change your mind."

A thunderclap shook the tower. Then came another sound. The sound of metal clanking and straining echoed in the cell.

Maleagant froze. The iron bars over the narrow prison door shuddered violently. For a moment nothing moved—then with a terrible groan the bars bent outward. Another wrenching sound followed. And suddenly the iron tore free.

A figure stepped through the shattered barrier. Rain and lightning framed him in the doorway.

Sir Lancelot.

His hands were bleeding where the metal had cut them, but his eyes burned with determination. "Release the Queen," he demanded, with baited breath. His blue eyes held a glint of violent rage and nearing madness.

Maleagant's hand moved towards his sword. "You dare break into my fortress?"

"I would break the gates of hell itself if she were held within," he growled.

Maleagant drew his blade—but Guinevere barely saw the clash that followed. Steel flashed in the storm light. The chamber rang with the sound of swords.

Maleagant fought fiercely, but rage clouded his strikes. Lancelot fought with purpose.

At last, Maleagant stumbled back, disarmed, his blade clattering across the stone. "Go," Lancelot said coldly. "Leave us now—or you will die."

The defeated knight fled the chamber, leaving the storm and silence behind him. For a moment neither Lancelot nor Guinevere spoke.

Then he turned to her. "My Queen... are you harmed?"

Guinevere crossed the room before he could say another word. Her hands reached for his injured ones. "You broke through iron with your bare hands," she said softly.

"I would have broken the world to get to you."

Their eyes met. Years of unspoken feeling lived in that single moment. Without a thought, they came together, kissing passionately with all the pent-up emotion and desire that had been building inside them for so many years, ever since the first moment their eyes had met.

Later, after they had returned to Camelot under the cover of night, the castle slept quietly around them. In the chambers given to Lancelot within the great fortress of King Arthur, a fire burned low in the hearth. Guinevere stood near the window, the moonlight soft against her face.

"I should not be here," she said quietly. Lancelot closed the door behind her.

"We crossed that line the moment I entered that tower."

She turned slowly toward him. For years they had lived side-by-side in Camelot—duty holding them apart, silence guarding what neither dared confess. But tonight, the walls between them had finally fallen. And all that was left, was the love.

"You came for me," she said.

"There was never a question."

He stepped closer. Guinevere reached up, touching his face, his arms, covered in bruises and scrapes. "You could have died."

"Then I would have died knowing I tried to save the woman I–" He stopped himself. But she already knew the word he had not spoken. Her hand rose to his lips.

"You have never needed to hide that truth from me," she whispered.

The distance between them vanished. Their kiss began gently, years of longing finally allowed to breathe. What had once been carefully restrained now unfolded with quiet intensity, each touch carrying the weight of everything they had denied for so long.

The firelight flickered across the room as they held each other, not with hurried passion but with the deep tenderness of two hearts that had loved in silence for years. Outside, Camelot slept unaware.

Inside Lancelot's chambers, the knight and the Queen finally surrendered to the love that had long lived between them–no longer hidden, no longer denied, but shared in a moment that felt as timeless as the legends that would one day be told of them.

~ ~ ~

Moonlight lay softly over the gardens of Camelot, turning the marble paths silver and the roses pale as ghosts. The court had long since gone quiet, and only the distant murmur of the fountain broke the stillness.

Guinevere stood beneath an arbor heavy with climbing roses, her fingers brushing the petals as though she were trying to steady her thoughts. The night air was cool, but her heart was restless.

Footsteps approached along the path. She knew them before she turned. Lancelot stepped into the moonlight, his armor gone, dressed simply in white cloth. Without his armor and banners of the day, he seemed almost vulnerable.

"Your Majesty," he said softly, though his voice carried warmth rather than formality.

Guinevere slightly grimaced. "You have called me that all day. Must you do so even here?"

Lancelot hesitated, then shook his head slightly. "Guinevere." Her name lingered between them like the soft caresses of a cool wind in a summer heat.

For a moment neither spoke. The scent of roses filled the air, and somewhere a nightingale sang, soaring through the skies.

"You should not be here," she said at last, though there was no true command in her voice.

"Nor should you."

Their eyes met, and the truth they both tried so carefully to bury stood plainly between them. They had vowed that their first night together would be their only night together. But their hearts had called out for one another, their bodies aching and yearning to make love again.

Guinevere looked away first. "Camelot sleeps, Sir Lancelot. Tomorrow you shall ride beside the King again, and I shall sit beside him on the throne. We both know what the world expects of us."

"And yet," he said quietly, stepping closer, "here we are."

The moon caught the gold in his hair as she turned back to him. "Why do you make this harder than it must be?"

"I do not know how to make it easier," he admitted.

There was no armor now between them–no court, no one to bare witnesses. Only the fragrant garden and the truth neither could deny. This was not just a need of the flesh. This was love.

He reached for her hand slowly, giving her time to pull away.

She did not.

Her fingers were warm in his, and for a moment the world seemed to narrow to the space between them.

"I would cross a thousand battlefields without fear," Lancelot said, his voice barely more than a whisper. "But standing here with you feels more dangerous than any war."

Guinevere laughed softly, though her eyes shone with something deeper. "Perhaps because this is the one battle neither of us can win."

He lifted her hand to his lips, pressing a gentle kiss to her knuckles.

"Then let us not fight tonight," he said. "Let us come together... as we did before."

She stepped closer, the moonlight outlining them both in silver. For a heartbeat she studied his face–the knight beloved by the kingdom, the man she should never have loved. Then she rested her hand against his cheek.

"One more time," she murmured.

Their kiss was soft at first, hesitant, as though both feared the moment might vanish if they moved too quickly. But the quiet of the garden held them, and the years of unspoken feeling finally found their voice in that single, fragile embrace.

Above them the roses stirred in the night breeze, scattering petals across the path. And for a little while, hidden from the world, Camelot's greatest knight and its Queen forgot everything but each other.

One more night turned into weeks, months, and years of constant craving. His body became her home. They couldn't seem to stop. Their passion was never spent.

The more they got of each other, the more they wanted of each other.

Both had always had a restless spirit. As much as being with Lancelot excited and enthralled her, at the same time it also calmed her. His face...

~ *** ~

Something in the way he looked at me. As if he needed me. As if he truly knew me, understood me, loved me above all else.

Not like Arthur... Arthur had his Knights of the Round Table, his quests, his magic with Merlin, his precious Kingdom and all the people therein. And for so long I had only had him. When I been dead last on his set of priorities.

Now with Lancelot, I felt as if I was his whole world, and even though I fought it—no, the more I fought it, he became mine. And I became him.

One day, we were so overcome by passion, we needed to be inside each other more than we needed air to breath. And then we pulling and yanking and unbuttoning and untying each other's clothes and skirts and corsets, until at last we were naked, making love to each other as if our lives depended upon.

We could not get enough.

We were in love.

Madly, wildly, passionately, recklessly in love. It was bliss. And it was torture.

Because I loved Arthur too. I wanted my husband too. I wanted them both.

~ ~ ~

We were both overcome by guilt—terrified that Arthur would find out. We didn't want to hurt him. We both felt death would better than that.

Yet we also talked about running away together. Or faking our own deaths. We fantasized about doing something so that we could be together.

"But do you love me so much more than Arthur, that you would be okay to live forever without him?" he asked me once.

"And what about you? What about your friendship with him? Does that mean so little?" I countered.

He looked at me, deep into my eyes, and my stomach was suddenly overtaken by butterflies. He took my hand, and ran his fingers gently up my arm. Then he slowly kissed me all over my body, and all our thoughts were lost again in the emotion, the passion, the love...

Later that night, I had dinner with my husband Arthur. And in bed with my husband, we made love. And it was also magical and beautiful, in such a different way.

I felt horrible about myself for what I was doing. But I truly loved them both. Did I love Lancelot more than Arthur? Could I be happy with only one of them? Could this happiness—and torture—last forever, or were we heading into a disaster?

I stared at myself in the mirror. My cheeks were a bit flushed. And I felt something shift within me.

I was truly divided, split in the middle, and torn in two. Truth be told, I loved them both. And the worst part, was that they both truly loved me, and also each other, as friends.

A few more weeks passed... then we were discovered. And in the end, because I could not choose one or the other of them... I lost them both.

~ *** ~

Chapter Twenty-One
Lancelot

Among the knights of Camelot, none shone brighter than Sir Lancelot. He was the greatest swordsman of the Round Table, a warrior whose courage seemed almost supernatural. It was said no knight could defeat him in battle unless fate itself intervened.

One spring morning he rode out from Camelot beneath a sky of pale gold. Villagers had come to the castle gates with desperate news.

A cruel lord had imprisoned travelers in a fortress deep within the forest. Lancelot did not hesitate.

He rode through the dark woods until the iron towers of the fortress appeared above the trees. Guards mocked the lone knight at their gates.

But their laughter did not last long. Lancelot shattered the gate with a charging strike of his shield. Steel rang across the courtyard as soldiers rushed at him from every direction.

Yet none could stand before him. One-by-one they fell until the tyrant himself emerged in black armor. Their duel lasted only moments. Lancelot's blade flashed like lightning.

When it ended, the captives were freed and the cruel lord lay defeated. The people called Lancelot a hero. But the greatest battle he would ever fight was not with a sword.

~ ~ ~

The moment that changed his life forever came when he first saw Queen Guinevere. She stood beside King Arthur in the great hall of Camelot, her dark hair shining beneath a golden crown.

Lancelot had faced giants, dragons, and armies without fear. But when Guinevere smiled at him for the first time, his heart trembled.

From that moment on, he loved her. It was a love he knew he must never reveal. For she was the Queen. And Arthur was not only his King—but his best friend.

~ ~ ~

During battles that led to the golden age of Camelot, the roads of Britain were filled with danger—bandits, monsters, rogue lords, and strange magic from forgotten ages. To protect the land, King Arthur often rode out himself with the warriors of the legendary Round Table. These journeys became the great adventures that bards would sing about for centuries.

One summer morning, a desperate messenger arrived at Camelot. A cyclops had come down from the northern mountains, destroying farms and carrying away livestock and people alike.

Arthur gathered several knights to hunt the creature: Sir Lancelot, Sir Gawain, and Sir Kay. They rode north through dark forests until the hills rose like black teeth against the sky.

There they found the cyclops. It was enormous—twice the height of a man. Sir Kay charged first but was thrown aside by the giant's massive swing. Sir Gawain attacked next, striking the creature's leg with a powerful blow. But the giant barely noticed.

Then Lancelot rode forward. He leapt from his horse and faced the creature alone. The giant roared and swung its club. Lancelot rolled beneath the blow and struck upward with his sword, cutting deep into the monster's arm.

The giant stumbled. Arthur seized the moment and charged him with his spear, driving it into the creature's chest. With a thunderous crash the giant fell, shaking the ground.

The people of the nearby villages cheered for their King and his knights. But many said it was Lancelot's courage and quick thinking and acting that had saved them all.

~ ~ ~

On another adventure, Arthur and several of his knights rode into a forest rumored to be cursed. Travelers who entered it often vanished without a trace.

With Arthur rode Sir Lancelot, Sir Tristan, and Sir Lionel. The deeper they rode, the stranger the forest became.

Mist curled between twisted trees. Shadows seemed to move on their own.

Soon the knights realized they had become separated from one another. Lancelot rode alone through the fog until he reached a clearing where a strange knight in black armor waited silently.

Without a word, the dark knight attacked.

Their swords rang like bells in the quiet forest. The stranger fought with unnatural strength. But Lancelot's skill was unmatched.

After a long duel he finally knocked the black knight's sword aside and struck him from his horse. As the helmet fell away, the body beneath vanished into smoke.

The forest magic broke instantly.

The mist lifted.

The other knights rode into the clearing, suddenly able to find one another again.

"Another spell broken," Arthur said. "And another victory for Lancelot."

~ ~ ~

Perhaps Lancelot's greatest adventure came when several knights of the Round Table were captured by a cruel warlord who ruled a fortress deep in the mountains. Among the prisoners were Sir Gawain and Sir Percival.

When the news reached Camelot, Arthur immediately prepared to lead an army. But Lancelot rode ahead alone. As he often did.

After days of travel, he reached the fortress. Its walls were high and guarded by dozens of soldiers. Still, Lancelot refused to wait.

Under cover of night, he climbed the outer wall and slipped into the fortress courtyard. One-by-one he defeated the guards silently. Then he fought his way into the dungeon tower.

Chains rattled as the imprisoned knight stared in disbelief. "Lancelot?" Sir Gawain exclaimed. "I thought we were doomed."

Lancelot cut their chains. "Not while I still draw breath."

Soon the prisoners were armed once more. Together they stormed the fortress gates just as Arthur's army arrived at dawn.

The warlord surrendered before the combined might of Camelot's knights could destroy his entire fortress. Arthur clasped Lancelot's arm proudly. "You have saved your brothers," the King thanked him.

Lancelot only smiled. "A Knight of the Round Table never abandons his own."

These adventures were only a few among hundreds. The knights of Camelot traveled across Britain and beyond—slaying monsters, defeating tyrants, and defending the innocent. And always among them rode Sir Lancelot, the greatest knight in the world.

To the people, he was a living legend.

To his fellow knights, he was a brother.

And to King Arthur, he was the most trusted champion of Camelot.

Yet even during these glorious adventures, fate was quietly weaving the threads of tragedy that would one day bring their golden age to an end.

But for now, the banners of Camelot still flew proudly across the land—and the knights of the Round Table rode on toward their next adventure.

~ ~ ~

As the years passed, the secret love within Lancelot for Guinevere grew stronger. He rode on countless quests, defeating enemies and protecting the weak. Yet every victory felt empty unless Guinevere was there to witness it.

Sometimes he would stand silently in Camelot's garden, watching the light in her chamber window long after the castle had gone to sleep. He began to waste away with longing.

One day the burden became too great.

Overcome by grief and love he could not fulfill; Lancelot wandered alone into the wilderness. There, far from Camelot, he lost himself in madness.

Madness is a quiet thing at first. Lancelot wandered the forest, stripped of armor, of name, of purpose. Love had undone him. Guilt had hollowed him.

He wandered through forests like a wild man, sleeping among the trees and speaking only in broken whispers. Knights searching for him passed by without recognizing the greatest warrior of the age.

For many months he lived this way, driven mad by love for Guinevere.

Even the forest had forgotten his name. Branches tore at him as he moved, or perhaps he tore at them—it no longer mattered. Leaves clung to his hair, his beard had grown wild, and his once-bright armor lay rusting somewhere far behind him. What remained of Lancelot was not a knight, but a shadow—thin, restless, and unmoored.

He laughed at nothing. He wept at less.

"Guinevere..." he whispered, again and again, as though the name itself were a spell that might summon her. But the forest gave no answer—only echoes, broken and distorted.

Days blurred into nights. Hunger came and went. Time loosened its grip.

He drank from streams, slept in mud, fought things that were not there. Once, he raised a branch like a sword and challenged the wind itself, shouting oaths to a court that existed only in memory.

"Stand, sir knight!" he cried hoarsely. "Stand and answer—!"

But there was no one there.

Only the slow unraveling of a man who had once been the greatest among them.

~ ~ ~

The lake did not belong to the forest. It appeared where and when it wished. And on this day, it lay waiting—still as glass, untouched by the madness that circled it.

Lancelot stumbled toward it without knowing why. He fell to his knees at the shore, staring into the water. For a moment, his reflection stared back—gaunt, hollow-eyed, unrecognizable.

He struck the surface with his fist. The image shattered. "Gone," he muttered. "All gone. The King... the court... her..."

"Not gone." The voice was calm. Certain.

Lancelot froze. From the center of the lake, she rose—not as something sudden or violent, but as something inevitable. Water parted around her, forming no ripple, no resistance.

Vivienne regarded him with quiet interest. “So, this is what love has made of you,” she said.

He recoiled, scrambling backward like a wounded animal.

“No,” he said sharply. “No spirits. No tricks. Leave me—”

“Leave you?” she repeated. “You have already been left. By yourself.”

He did not recognize the woman who approached him. But Vivienne recognized him.

“Still breathing,” she said. “That is something.”

He did not answer.

She circled him slowly, studying what remained. Not the knight—no, that was buried—but the core beneath it.

“You were meant to be the greatest of them,” she told him. “And instead...” Her words trailed off.

His breathing grew ragged. His hands clawed at the ground. “Guinevere...” he murmured again, desperate now. “I must go to her—I must—she needs—”

“She does not need this,” Vivienne said, her voice cutting cleanly through the frenzy. “And neither do you.” Something in her tone—unyielding, absolute—broke through the noise in his mind.

For the first time in months, he hesitated. “I... I cannot stop,” he said, the words coming like a confession dragged from him. “She is—everything—”

“Yes,” Vivienne said. “And that is the problem.”

She stepped onto the shore, the water releasing her without a sound.

"Love," she continued, "is not meant to consume the self. What you feel is not love anymore—it is obsession."

Lancelot shook his head violently. "No—no, you do not understand—"

"I understand perfectly."

She moved closer. He tried to rise, to flee—but his strength failed him. He collapsed again, trembling, caught between instinct and exhaustion.

Vivienne knelt before him. "Look at me," she ordered.

He did not want to, but he did.

Her eyes held no anger. No pity. Only clarity. "You are Sir Lancelot," she told him. "Knight of the Round Table. The man who stood unbroken against armies. The man who chose honor when it cost him dearly."

"That man is dead," he rasped.

"No," she said. "He is buried."

She reached out and placed her hand against his brow. At once, the world fractured. Not outward—but inward.

Memories surged—not the fevered fragments that had haunted him, but whole, unbroken moments. The first time he had ridden into King Arthur's court. The weight of his oath. The laughter of the Knights at the Round Table. The quiet, terrible beauty of Guinevere—not as obsession, but as truth, as pure love as a mother for her child.

Then the pain came. Not dulled. Nor softened. Seen. Felt. "You cannot erase it," Vivienne said, her voice now distant and everywhere at once. "You must carry it."

"I... cannot..." he gasped.

"You can. You are stronger than you think you are."

The madness resisted–it clawed, it twisted, it begged for the easy oblivion of chaos. But Vivienne's magic did not destroy it. It ordered it. Piece-by-piece, she drew the storm into form–grief, guilt, love–each given its place, its boundary.

The noise in his mind quieted. Not gone. But no longer in control.

Lancelot collapsed forward, breathing hard, his body shaking as though he had been pulled from deep water. Silence settled. Real silence. He lifted his head slowly.

The forest was still the forest. The lake, still the lake. But the world no longer spun.

"Guinevere..." he said again–but this time, it was different. Not a cry. Not a plea.

A name. He closed his eyes. "I love her," he said.

"I know," Vivienne replied.

"I betrayed him," he continued.

"I know."

He swallowed hard. "And I must return."

Vivienne studied him for a long moment. "Yes," she said. "You must."

She rose, stepping back toward the water. For the first time, there was no madness in him–only resolve.

"You will find your way back," she told him. "Or you will not. That choice is yours."

For a moment, clarity flickered in his eyes. "Lady, Mother..." he whispered. But as he looked up again, she was already fading, her form dissolving into the still surface of the lake.

Her voice came one last time, soft as the water itself. "Be worthy of the man you have remembered. Be worthy of the son I raised."

Then she, and her lake, were gone.

Lancelot rose unsteadily to his feet. The forest did not seem smaller—but he did not feel lost within it anymore.

Step-by-step, he began the journey home. To Camelot. Toward the unspoken love that burned inside him for the Queen, for this was before they finally came together.

Toward whatever remained of honor in a life that had nearly been consumed by love. This time, he did not run. He walked.

~ ~ ~

Back in Camelot, Guinevere heard of Lancelot's disappearance. The news struck her heart like a blade. For though she had hidden it well, she too loved him.

In the quiet of her chamber, she wept. "I never wished to harm him," she whispered.

Yet she knew the truth. Their love was dangerous. And someday it might destroy everything Arthur had built.

When Lancelot finally returned to Camelot, thin and weary from his wandering, Guinevere was the first to see him.

Late one evening in the castle gardens she found him standing beside the fountain. Moonlight reflected in the water.

"Lancelot," she said softly.

He turned. For a moment neither spoke. Then he knelt before her. "My Queen," he said, his voice trembling.

Guinevere gently lifted him to his feet. “You must not kneel to me tonight,” she whispered.

The air between them seemed to glow with unspoken emotion. They walked together beneath the roses climbing the garden walls.

Their hands brushed once. Then again. Finally, Lancelot took her hand in his.

Neither pulled away.

In that quiet garden, far from the eyes of the court, they walked hand-in-hand, finding comfort and healing in that simple connection. These were the moments Lancelot lived for. These were the moments that made him crazy, and long for death too.

~ ~ ~

Soon after this, the exiled knight kidnapped Guinevere and Lancelot rescued her. Then their affair was begun, continuing on for years.

Their love gave Lancelot a reason for living, as they shared a happiness he had never known before.

On another evening when Arthur was away, rain fell softly against the castle windows. Guinevere sat beside the fire in a hidden chamber where only a few trusted servants knew the door.

When Lancelot entered, the storm seemed to fade into silence. “You should not be here,” she said gently.

“I know,” he replied. “But I could not stay away.”

She stood and stepped closer. “You are among Arthur’s most loyal knights.”

“And you are his queen.”

Lancelot nodded, sorrow in his eyes. "That is why this love is both my greatest joy...and my greatest curse."

Guinevere placed her hand upon his cheek. For a moment they simply stood together, sharing the warmth of the fire and the closeness they could never show before the world.

Outside, thunder rolled across the hills. Inside the chamber, their forbidden love grew stronger with every passing day. Though they fought it, they always seemed to find a way back into each other's arms...and beds.

For years the secret remained hidden. But in the shadows of Camelot, enemies watched and whispered. And though the Golden Age of Camelot still shone brightly, the love between Sir Lancelot and Queen Guinevere had planted the first seed of the tragedy that would one day destroy the enchanted Kingdom.

Even Merlin, long before his disappearance, had foreseen it. For sometimes the greatest heroes in the world cannot escape the power of love.

~ *** ~

The night was cold and still in Camelot when Mordred moved quietly through the shadowed halls of the castle. His expression was calm, but his mind burned with calculation.

For years he had watched the court of King Arthur—its loyalties, its weaknesses, its secrets. And he had discovered the greatest secret of them all: the forbidden love between Guinevere and Sir Lancelot. Tonight, he would make sure others saw it too.

Mordred knocked heavily on a chamber door. Inside, Sir Kay opened it with an annoyed expression. "What do you want, Mordred? It's the middle of the night. I need my beauty sleep, ya know?"

Mordred lowered his voice dramatically. "I have discovered treason."

Kay frowned. "Treason?"

Behind him stood Sir Gawain, still half dressed in his tunic. "What kind of treason?" For Mordred had waken up Sir Gawain first.

Mordred looked between them carefully. "The kind that will destroy Camelot if it remains hidden."

Kay crossed his arms. "Then speak it plainly."

Mordred leaned closer. "It concerns the Queen."

Gawain's face hardened immediately. "Mind your words."

Mordred raised his hands calmly. "I wish they were lies."

He lowered his voice further. "If you doubt me, come see for yourselves."

Kay glanced at Gawain. Both knights were fiercely loyal to Arthur. Any rumor about the Queen could not be ignored.

Kay sighed heavily. "Fine. But if this is some ridiculous trick–"

Mordred smiled darkly. "It is no trick."

The three men walked quietly through the corridors of Camelot. The torches flickered as they passed. Mordred led them deeper into the royal wing of the castle.

Kay frowned. "This leads to the Queen's chambers."

Mordred nodded, “Yes, I know.”

Gawain’s voice was tense. “You had better be certain.”

Mordred stopped before a closed door. Light flickered faintly beneath it. He looked back at the two knights. “See for yourselves.”

Kay pushed the door open. The room fell silent.

There, within the Queen’s chamber, were Guinevere and Lancelot, naked, together in a moment that left no doubt about the truth Mordred had hinted at.

The greatest knight of Camelot. And the Queen of Britain. Both froze as the door burst open.

Kay stared in disbelief. “You...?”

Gawain’s face went pale with shock. “Lancelot...”

For a long moment no one moved. No one even dared to breathe. Then Mordred stepped forward slowly, his voice quiet but triumphant.

“The greatest betrayal in Camelot.”

Guinevere looked toward them in horror. “Please–”

But the damage had already been done. Kay turned away angrily, with no hint of his usual humor. “This will destroy Arthur.”

Gawain closed his eyes briefly, “The King must know,” he sighed. Behind them, Mordred watched the scene unfold with cold satisfaction. The seed of Camelot’s downfall had just been planted. And soon... the kingdom would tear itself apart.

~ *** ~

I am the orphan prince of King Ban, of the lost kingdom of Benoic in France. I was raised by the Lady of the Lake, Vivienne. Like Arthur, I was raised with magic. It was a strange upbringing.

My mother lived in the waters of Lake Avalon. I lived in a small castle on the shores of France. Even though I was a Prince, I was a Prince who had lost his kingdom. In strange parallels, I was like Arthur. We had so much in common, and our lives had been so different, that we bonded over those things.

For what happened at the end of my life and this story, I am remembered. Yet there is more to me than my greatest mistake. And even though I regret with all my heart, hurting Arthur, who I will always consider to be the greatest friend of my life, I cannot regret loving Guinevere, who I cannot help but believe, was the greatest love of my life.

I am writing my story at the end of my life. As an old man I am looking back and reflecting on all I have lost. As a boy, I lost my father's kingdom. As a man, I cost the world the Kingdom of Camelot, by my own actions.

I take full responsibility for what I cost the people I love the most. And worst, what I cost the world. Because the age of Camelot was an enchanted place and time. King Arthur was a great man, who had a special way of bringing peoples and Kingdoms together.

He was such a great leader, we knights were honored to follow him. I followed him into many battles, and gladly would have died to protect him and his grand vision of not just his Kingdom, but the uniting of all countries on the earth.

It is so darkly ironic, that my actions cost him both his Kingdom and his life. Of course, I deeply regret that.

Yet if the world could look into my heart, they would see that even now, I am in love with Guinevere. And I truly loved her, for who she was, and for who we were together, the man she made me.

I came to Camelot with all the courage and valor of a knight, of a prince who'd lost his Kingdom, and found my truest home in Camelot. I fell in love with the land, with the people, with the idea, with the vision of Arthur's that I gladly followed.

At the same time, I had love at first sight with the Queen. We did not immediately jump into bed. We spent a handful of tortured years denying the passion we both felt for each other immediately.

It was a matching of hearts and souls, our love was. And I'd been trained in magic, by the Lady of the Lake, who I considered my mother. And yet, the greatest part of me was born when I fell in love with Guinevere.

When we at last consummated our love, it was as if I had finally found myself. I found myself in her arms. It was as if two puzzle pieces had finally fit into place.

No, sadly enough, it was worse than that. It was as if Arthur, Guinevere, and myself were all soul mates, as if somehow, we completed one another. That's why Guinevere could not choose between us. That's why she felt compelled to be with both of us. And that's why as much as we loved Arthur, we simply had to be together too.

It is hard to explain the magnetic pull of love to anyone who has not felt it. I will never say that cheating is right. And yet it felt right to be with her.

I was never more alive, more myself, or freer, than in the moments we shared. It was more romantic infatuation. I loved Guinevere for who she really was. I knew her, from the heart.

And she knew my heart too. It was not mere lust that brought us together. Our love was real, and true, as was our love for our King...

That's what made it all so impossible. We knew we headed for disaster, of course, and yet we could stop our seemingly fated descent and ascent into actions that destroyed that whimsical age of Camelot.

So as sorry as I am for what transpired, I also cannot in all honesty and truth tell you that I would change a thing. Please do not judge me too harshly.

I know that anyone who has tasted even a moment of love like this, will not judge me. They will understand that painful pull of love, that can only be comforted by being the arms of the object of your affections.

Guinevere was the only woman I ever loved. I was alone before. I've been alone ever since.

The memory of our times together, the bliss that we shared, has filled my mind for as long as I've lived. I've pined away for her. I've lived a quiet life, isolated and alone, away from the madding crowds, missing her, missing the best friend I'd ever known–Arthur, missing the Knights of the Round table, missing the best part of my life...the Age of Camelot.

~ *** ~

Chapter Twenty-Two
Mordred

Night wrapped Avalon in deep blue shadows. Far from the great Kingdome where knights feasted and laughed, a smaller castle in the forests of the Isle of Apples burned with quiet candlelight. The room smelled faintly of herbs and parchment; the tools of study and magic scattered across a heavy oak table.

Beside the window stood Morgana. Her dark hair fell across her shoulders like a cloak of shadow as she watched the stars above the sleeping kingdom.

Behind her, a young boy sat on the floor with a wooden practice sword in his hands. He was perhaps eight-years-old.

His name was Mordred.

The boy swung the wooden blade clumsily through the air. "Like this?" he asked.

Morgana turned from the window. "Again," she said calmly.

Mordred rose and swung harder this time, striking an imaginary enemy with fierce determination. Morgana stepped forward and gently adjusted his grip.

"Strength is not only in the arm," she told him. "It is in patience... in knowing when to strike."

Mordred nodded seriously, trying the movement again. He swung.

This time the motion was smoother. Morgana allowed herself a small smile. "You learn quickly."

Mordred lowered the wooden sword. "Will I be a knight someday?"

Morgana studied him for a long moment before answering. "Yes," she said. "But you will be more than that."

The boy's eyes brightened. "More?"

She knelt before him so they were face-to-face. "The world believes your father is the greatest King who ever lived," she said quietly.

Mordred frowned slightly. "My father?" He had asked about him before, but Morgana had never answered fully.

"Yes," she said softly.

"Who is he?"

Morgana reached out and brushed a strand of hair from the boy's face.

"His name is King Arthur."

The name carried power even in the quiet room. Mordred blinked in surprise. "My father is the King?"

"Yes."

Mordred's thoughts raced. "Then...am I prince?"

Morgana's expression remained calm, though something colder flickered behind her eyes.

"Not the kind Camelot would ever accept."

"Why?"

"Because your father fears what you are."

Mordred looked down at the wooden sword in his hands. "I don't understand."

Morgana rose slowly and returned to the window, looking out over the moonlit towers of Camelot.

"Arthur built his kingdom on ideals," she explained to her son. "Honor. Loyalty. Justice."

She turned back toward the boy. "But even kings can lie to themselves."

Mordred waited quietly. "You were born from a secret he wishes to bury," Morgana continued. "If he knew where you were... he would see you as a threat."

Mordred's small hands tightened around the practice sword. "So, he doesn't want me?"

Morgana walked back to him and placed a hand on his shoulder. "No," she said firmly. "That is not the truth."

"Then what is?"

She knelt again, her voice dropping to a quiet whisper. "The truth is that the world belongs to those strong enough to shape it."

Mordred looked deeply into his mother's emerald eyes.

"And you will be strong," she told him.

He nodded slowly.

"But what does that have to do with my father?"

Morgana's gaze hardened.

"Because one day you will face him."

The room seemed suddenly colder. "Why?" his question sounded small and innocent next to the scope of her vision for his future.

She placed both hands on the boy's shoulders. "Because your destiny is tied to his."

Mordred swallowed. "What will happen?"

Morgana held his gaze without blinking. "One day," she said softly, "you will stand before Arthur as a man." The candle flames flickered in the quiet chamber. "And when that day comes... the fate of Britain will rest in your hands."

Mordred's voice was barely above a whisper. "What must I do, mother?"

Morgana's answer came slowly and deliberately. "You must end him."

The boy stared at her, shocked. "Kill him?"

"Yes."

She stood, her shadow stretching long across the stone floor. "Arthur's age must end before a new one can begin."

Mordred looked down at the wooden sword in his grip. It suddenly felt heavier.

Morgana walked back to the window, staring once more at the distant towers of Camelot glowing in the moonlight which they could view from their highest tower.

"Train," she instructed him quietly. "Learn. Grow strong."

Mordred lifted the practice sword again, though uncertainty still lingered in his young eyes.

Behind him, Morgana whispered almost to herself, "The greatest Kings fall not by armies... but by the blood of their descendants."

Outside, the wind moved across the towers of Camelot. And far in the future, the seeds of Battle of Camlann had just begun to grow.

~ ~ ~

The great hall of Camelot glowed with torchlight as the knights of the Round Table gathered beneath banners of the dragon and the cross. At the center of the hall sat King Arthur, ruler of Britain, the sword Excalibur resting beside his throne. Around him stood the greatest warriors in the realm—among them Lancelot, Gawain, and many others whose names were sung across the land.

To Arthur, Camelot represented the highest dream of knighthood. Honor. Justice. Brotherhood. But within that shining dream, a shadow had already taken root.

Among the gathered knights sat a young warrior whose face was calm and watchful. His name was Mordred. And though Arthur did not know it, the young knight was his own son.

Years earlier, through deception and dark magic, Arthur had unknowingly fathered a child with his half-sister, the sorceress Morgana. That child had been Mordred.

Raised far from Camelot, Mordred grew up hearing stories of the great King—stories of honor and glory that filled the land. But in his heart, those stories bred resentment.

Arthur had built a kingdom of light. Mordred would prove it was built upon lies.

So, when he came of age, Mordred rode to Camelot and presented himself as a knight seeking service. Arthur saw only a capable young warrior. He welcomed him gladly. So, the son took a seat among his father's greatest champions: a hidden enemy in plain sight.

Mordred proved himself skilled in battle and clever in speech. Slowly he gained influence within the court. Yet he watched everything.

He studied the friendships and rivalries of the knights. He listened to whispers in the halls. He observed the quiet glances between the Queen and the greatest knight of the realm—Guinevere and Lancelot.

Mordred alone understood the power of such knowledge. Camelot was built on ideals of honor. Expose a single betrayal—and the entire kingdom might fracture. The ideal vision might unravel. So, Mordred waited patiently, for when the time was right. His mother had taught him well.

~ ~ ~

When Mordred, Kay and Gawain found Guinevere and Sir Lancelot in bed together, the moment froze like a blade poised above the kingdom itself.

Lancelot fought his way free, escaping through the chaos, but the truth could no longer be hidden.

By dawn, the entire court knew.

When Mordred brought the accusation before Arthur, the King sat in terrible silence. For Lancelot had been his greatest friend. Guinevere was his Queen. Yet Arthur's law was clear. No one—not even those he loved—stood above it...

~ ~ ~

The Knights of the Round Table split apart. Most remained loyal to Arthur. Others sided with Lancelot, refusing to see the greatest knight in the world condemned.

War soon followed.

Castles burned. Brothers in arms faced one another across battlefields.

The dream of Camelot began to crumble. And behind it all stood Mordred.

He watched the chaos unfold with quiet satisfaction. The Kingdom Arthur had built with honor was tearing itself apart from within. The poison Mordred had planted had taken root.

Soon father and son would face one another on the battlefield, though Arthur still did not fully understand the truth of the blood between them. And the final chapter of Camelot—the tragic battle of Battle of Camlann—was imminent.

~ ~ ~

A gray mist lay over the valley of Camlann, drifting slowly across the trampled grass and the silent ranks of two armies waiting in uneasy stillness.

On one side stood the warriors of Camelot, battered but loyal—knights who had followed King Arthur through decades of war and victory.

Across the narrow field stood the army of Mordred, armored men who had joined the rebel lord after he seized the throne during Arthur's absence. His uncle Cador had sent him thousands of men.

"May not one knight from the Round Table stand," he had told his nephew the last time he visited his mother and his nephew in Avalon. "May my money and power fuel your army until Camelot has fallen. And may King Arthur die, as once his father killed our father."

Between the two hosts stretched a strip of empty ground. A truce meeting had been called.

Arthur rode slowly forward with a small company of knights, among them were the Three Enchanter Knights. Across the field, Mordred approached as well, preparing himself to tell his father the truth.

They stopped within speaking distance. For a long moment there was silence.

Finally, Arthur's voice broke the silence. "You were raised in my court," he said. "You sat at my table and called me King."

Mordred's expression was hard beneath his helmet. "And you left Britain undefended," he replied coldly. "Someone had to rule."

"You did more than rule," Arthur said. "You crowned yourself. At my worst point–when betrayal had struck down with the madness of losing the two people closest to me."

A bitter smile crossed Mordred's face. "The throne was always mine to take."

Arthur paused. There was something in his words... "What do you mean, Mordred?"

"Twenty-five years ago, you spent a night with a woman."

Arthur looked at him blankly. "What? Who?

"You slept with my mother–your sister–Morgan le Fay. And she bore me for such a time as this. As such, I have more right to the throne than any here."

Arthur looked faint, and ready to collapse with the truth. Kay put a hand on his shoulder. His touch seemed to make him come back to his senses.

"I had no idea, Mordred. Can't we discuss this and work something out?"

The two armies watched in absolute silence. Arthur lowered his voice. "End this, Mordred. Lay down your claim. Britain has bled enough. Please. Become the son you always should have been... if I had only known... I would have welcomed you in, embraced you... as my son."

For a moment Mordred said nothing. Then he laughed softly. He was no longer the little boy who longed for his father's love. "You still believe this kingdom belongs to you."

Arthur's hand tightened around the reins. "It does."

"No," Mordred said quietly. "It belongs to the man strong enough to take it."

The wind stirred the grass between them. Arthur glanced at the two armies waiting behind their leaders.

"So, we make peace here," he said. "Or we destroy each other."

"Peace?" Mordred scoffed.

Then—a sudden hiss came from the grass.

A snake slithered between the soldiers gathered for the meeting. One nervous knight cried out and drew his sword, striking the serpent in a flash of steel.

For a heartbeat the world froze. Then horns blared. Both armies saw the blade drawn. Both believed the truce had been broken.

The battlefield erupted.

Warriors surged forward with shouts of fury. Steel clashed. Shields shattered. The Battle of Camlann had begun...

On one side stood the banner of Camelot. On the other... rebel host of Mordred, Morgana le Fay's son and both King Arthur's nephew and son.

The battle was brother against brother. Knight against knight. At the center of Arthur's army stood the King himself, fighting for his life and all that he had built.

King Arthur wore battle armor darkened by years of war, but in his hand burned the blade of kings—Excalibur.

Merlin was gone, never to be seen again. Arthur suspected the great wizard had finally been murdered.

Beside him stood his final magical champions. The Three Enchanter Knights of Britain. Sir Kay, whose temper burned like a forge. Sir Gawain, radiant with the strength of the sun. Sir Bedivere, whose ancient runes protected the kingdom itself.

Arthur looked across the battlefield. "This will be our last battle."

Kay cracked his knuckles. "Good. I'm tired of rebellions."

Gawain gazed at the rising sun on the horizon. "My strength is with us today. I am ready to fight for the last time," he answered bravely.

Bedivere touched the earth quietly. "The land of Britain stands with the King."

Arthur nodded. "Then let us end it. Let us die with the dream of Camelot, and the vision of the Knights of the Round Table."

A lightning bolt of grief pierced through all their hearts. The horns of war screamed. Two great armies charged. Steel clashed steel.

The last dawn of Camelot rose red over the field of Battle of Camlann. Mist clung to the valley like the breath of ghosts. Ravens circled above the hills, as if they already sensed the feast to come.

On one side of the field stood the army of King Arthur, the once-great fellowship of the Round Table gathered for what they all knew might be their final battle.

Armor gleamed beneath the rising sun. Among Arthur's host stood the greatest knights ever known: Gawain, Percival, Bors, Kay, Bedivere, even Owain, the Knight of the Lion who chose the vision of King Arthur over the fidelity of his mother and half-brother.

Beside Arthur's banner snapped the red dragon of Britain. Across the valley waited the rebel host. At its head rode Mordred.

The knights and lords who had joined his rebellion filled the opposite hills with dark steel and bitter hatred. Mordred lifted his sword toward Camelot's army.

The son prepared to destroy the father.

A horn sounded across the valley. Then another. Arthur raised Excalibur high. "FOR CAMELOT!"

The armies surged forward.

The ground shook beneath thousands of charging horses. Lances lowered, banners whipping in the wind. The two forces collided with a thunderous crash. Lances shattered like dry branches. Horses whinnied in protest. Steel rang against steel as knights hurled themselves into battle.

The field of Camlann became a storm of violence and a river of blood. Sir Gawain, one of the Enchanter

Knights, rode like a blazing comet through the enemy ranks.

Three rebels fell before him. Five more. But a spear struck his side, opening the old wound he had carried since the wars with Lancelot. Gawain slew his attacker before collapsing in the saddle.

Farther across the field, Sir Lionel battled a circle of rebel knights. His blade moved like lightning, cutting one down after another before a crossbow bolt pierced his chest.

Sir Percival fought with quiet fury, defending Arthur's banner against overwhelming numbers.

Even the wise and gentle Enchanter Knight, Bedivere, was forced into brutal combat as the rebel tide surged forward.

Everywhere across the field, the fellowship of the Round Table fought and fell. The brotherhood that had once represented the highest ideals of knighthood was being shattered forever.

Amid the chaos rode Owain, the Knight of the Lion. Beside him bounded the great black lion that had followed him through so many adventures. The beast roared as it leapt upon a rebel horseman, tearing him from the saddle.

Owain's sword flashed again and again, cutting through Mordred's soldiers like a storm through wheat. They were brothers who shared the same mother. But Owain finally saw his mother for what she was and what she did: she used her magic for evil, and for herself.

He fought for Arthur, his uncle, against his brother, and his mother, who he'd always been loyal too, even after she'd killed his father. But even the bravest knight could not stop the tide of death spreading across the field.

At last, the two armies collapsed into exhaustion and slaughter. The battlefield lay covered with the fallen. Then a second wave of Mordred's forces surged forward like a dark tide. Behind them marched sorcerers loyal to Morgana. Black magic erupted across the battlefield. Armies from the Duke of Cornwall, Cador, covered the land on sides.

Lightning struck Arthur's knights. Shadows swallowed entire companies. Arthur raised Excalibur. "Enchanter Knights!"

Sir Kay stepped into the storm of magic. Sorcerers hurled curses toward him. Kay answered them with fire. Flames erupted from his hands in a roaring inferno. Entire waves of shadow creatures vanished in blazing light.

Kay laughed wildly as he hurled fire across the battlefield. "You want magic?" He raised both his arms in a mad fury. "I'll give you MAGIC!" A massive firestorm erupted, scattering Mordred's sorcerers.

Even Arthur's knights stared in shock.

Then a seven-foot piece of ice struck Kay on his head. He was the first of them to fall. With the last of his life, he used his magic to cast fire and flames from his fingertips. The castle of Camelot took flame.

Morgana herself stood over Sir Kay, staring right into his dying eyes. With quick, powerful motions, she wielded her sword to cut off the head of Sir Kay.

"Nooooo!" King Arthur cried, rushing towards her. But she seemed to merge into the shadows themselves, disappearing swiftly.

Sir Kay died in the raging fire he had created. The fire seemed to devour him whole, until all that was left of him was ashes, and the love of his brother, King Arthur.

Meanwhile Sir Gawain fought at the center of the battlefield, like the sun itself. The sun climbed higher. With every passing hour his strength grew. He struck down enemy knights with unstoppable power. But Mordred had prepared for him.

A group of dark sorcerers surrounded Gawain. They cast a terrible curse.

A spear of shadow pierced through Gawain's armor. The Sun Knight staggered. Still, he fought on, glowing like a dying star. Arthur saw him fall to one knee.

"Gawain!"

But even wounded, Gawain raised his sword. "For Camelot!"

With one final surge of sunlight, he shattered the sorcerers surrounding him. Then the Sun Knight collapsed. The sky above battlefield darkened.

The darkness seemed to gain power and strength, with the fall of the Enchanter Knight of the sun. But the darkness in the heart of Camelot was far worse.

Seeing Gawain fall, Sir Bedivere unleashed the full power of his runes. He struck the earth with his gauntlet.

Ancient symbols blazed across the battlefield. Stone walls erupted from the ground, protecting Arthur's knights. The earth itself rose against Mordred's army.

Bedivere whispered ancient words into the wind. "Camelot shall not fall today," he vowed bravely.

But the battle was turning. The armies were exhausted. Bodies and blood flooded the field. And through the smoke rode Mordred himself.

The traitor prince rode directly toward the King. "Father!" he called out.

Arthur raised Excalibur. "You chose this path—you could have had a place by my side—as my son!"

Mordred only glared, lowering his spear. "Camelot must end. It is a mere dream. You fight for a fantasy. I fight for the right to govern Britain alone!"

They charged. The clash shook the battlefield. Steel struck steel. Arthur's blade cut deep into Mordred's armor. But Mordred's spear drove forward.

The weapon pierced Arthur's side. Both men staggered.

Arthur summoned the last of his strength. With a final blow from Excalibur, he struck Mordred down. The rebel King collapsed.

But Arthur fell with him. The battle slowly faded into silence. The armies were shattered. The Kingdom was broken.

Only a few knights remained standing. Among them... Sir Bedivere.

He rushed to Arthur's side. The king lay dying beside the forests that led to Avalon. Excalibur rested beside him. Arthur spoke weakly. "Bedivere...take my sword... return it to the Lady of the Lake."

Bedivere nodded sadly, quick to obey his King. He carried the sword to the water's edge and cast it into the lake.

A mysterious hand rose from the depths and caught the blade. Then it vanished. Bedivere feared his King would be dead upon his return. But the King was waiting.

"It is done?" Arthur asked his friend.

Sir Bedivere nodded. "It is done."

Arthur closed his eyes peacefully. In the distance, the mists rolled across the lake.

A mysterious barge approached. Morgana rose from the waters. Bedivere's eyes narrowed at its approach.

"My son is dead?" she asked, for confirmation.

Sir Bedivere nodded.

"My brother is dead?"

The knight nodded.

"Guinevere and Lancelot have fled?"

Bedivere nodded.

"And Camelot has fallen?"

"Yes, m'lady," Sir Bedivere told her, ever the gentlemen, even to the end. "You have won. Everything you wished for has come to pass."

"And yet... I have never been filled by so much sorrow and regret." Tears fell freely down her face, like water over a broken dam.

"Too late," the knight whispered. But still, even now, he was gentle and kind. He took Morgana's hand to comfort her.

"Do you think it ever could have been... a land of equals?"

Sir Bedivere shook his head. "It is not for me to say... but I think for time, it was."

Morgana buried her head in her hands and sobbed. Bedivere stroked her hair to comfort her.

"May I please take the body of my son and my brother, my King?" she finally asked the Enchanter Knight, after her tears ran dry.

Bedivere nodded kindly, and helped Morgana take their bodies to Avalon. Arthur's body was carried away toward the enchanted shores of Avalon. And with that... the age of Camelot ended... in tears and infinite regret.

Bards later sang of the Three Enchanter Knights of Britain: Sir Kay, the Fire Knight, Sir Gawain, the Sun Knight, and Sir Bedivere, the Rune Knight Three magical warriors who stood beside their king until the final battle. And though Camelot fell...their legends would never die...and the dream of a land of equals, respect, truth, and justice, lives on in the hearts of all those who can see the vision, and are willing to fight for it...

Silence fell over Camlann. The field was covered with the bodies of knights who had once sat together in brotherhood. The Round Table was no more.

For the age of Camelot had come to its end. And the once-great kingdom that had promised justice and glory for all Britain now faded into legend.

~ ~ ~

Arthur wheeled his horse back toward his men. "Form ranks!" he shouted.

But the valley was already chaos. Knights of the Round Table charged into Mordred's rebels, their banners whipping through the mist as swords flashed in every direction.

Arthur cut his way through the melee, Excalibur blazing in his hand. Men fell before him as he forced his path across the field. Through the swirling battle he saw Mordred's banner—the black dragon—rising above the fighting.

Arthur spurred his horse forward. "Mordred!" he shouted.

The rebel king turned. Seeing Arthur, he lowered his spear and charged.

The two leaders collided in the center of the battlefield. Mordred thrust first, his spear slamming into Arthur's shield.

Arthur knocked it aside and struck back with Excalibur, the blade carving across Mordred's armor. But Mordred was relentless. He swung his sword in a savage arc, striking Arthur's helm and staggering the king.

Arthur recovered instantly. With a roar he drove his spear forward with all his strength. The weapon pierced Mordred's chest. The rebel gasped, impaled upon the shaft.

For a moment it seemed finished. But even as he died, Mordred struck back.

With his last strength he lifted his sword and smashed it downward against Arthur's head. The blow split Arthur's helmet and sent him collapsing to his knees. Mordred fell dead at his feet.

The battle slowly faded around them as word spread. Both kings had fallen.

~ ~ ~

Later, as the sun sank red beyond the hills, only a few knights remained alive beside their wounded king. Among them were Bedivere and Lucan.

Arthur lay upon the blood-soaked ground, pale but still breathing. "The kingdom..." Arthur murmured weakly. Bedivere knelt beside him. "It still stands, my king."

Arthur's eyes drifted toward the distant horizon. "Then my work is done."

A small boat waited at the edge of a mist-covered lake. There, waiting beside the water, stood Morgan le Fay and the mysterious maidens of the enchanted isle. With great care, the surviving knights carried Arthur to the boat.

As the vessel drifted away across the dark water toward Avalon, the mist closed slowly behind it. And the age of Arthur passed into legend.

The battlefield of Battle of Camlann lay silent beneath a gray and sorrowful sky. The clash of swords had faded. The war cries were gone. Only the wind moved across the valley, whispering through broken banners and fallen armor.

Where once the knights of the Round Table had stood together in brotherhood, now the field was covered with their bodies. At the center of that ruin lay King Arthur, gravely wounded by the spear of his own son, Mordred.

Only one knight still stood beside the king. The loyal Bedivere.

Arthur leaned heavily upon him as they slowly walked away from the battlefield toward a quiet lake hidden among the hills. Each step left drops of blood upon the grass.

At last Arthur could walk no farther. He sank beside the water's edge.

When Bedivere returned and told Arthur what he had seen, the King nodded. "Then my time is truly finished."

Just then, across the lake, a dark barge appeared through the mist. Upon it stood three mysterious queens dressed in black robes.

Among them was the sorceress, Morgana. They guided the boat silently to the shore. Bedivere helped Arthur into the vessel.

As the king lay down among the queens, Morgana gently took his hand. "Brother," she said softly, "the wounds of this world will be healed where we take you."

Bedivere knelt in the water, watching helplessly. "My king... will you return?"

Arthur looked back at him one last time. "In the hour of Britain's greatest need," he said quietly, "I may come again."

The barge drifted away into the mist. Across the silent waters it carried the wounded king toward the mysterious isle of Avalon.

And there, according to legend, King Arthur did not die. He sleeps. Waiting. Until the day Britain calls for him once more.

~ *** ~

Chapter Twenty-Three
The Aftermath

"Go my love, go," King Arthur had ushered off his Queen. Even after her betrayal, all he could think about was saving her from the Kingdom that had turned on her.

They were demanding her beheading–and he would rather die himself than to allow his love, and best friend to die, even after they betrayed him. Even if it meant he would have to die himself.

"Where shall I go?" Guinevere cried.

"I've made arrangements. Just go with the nun. Her name is Teresa. She will take you there, and neither one of you shall return."

"My love–my King–my husband...I, I am so sorry."

"I know," Arthur took one last look at the face he would always love, and never forget. "I forgive you, both of you, and, I will always love you... goodbye my Guinevere. Now go, please, save yourself. I cannot bear to see your death."

His eyes filled with tears. And Guinevere's eyes were pouring with tears. The nun put her arms around her and half-carried her away from the King, from her Kingdom, and from her life as its Queen.

* * *

Teresa silently took her to the shore, where one boat lay. She helped Guinevere into it, and got in herself, rowing for what felt like hours and days. Then when they reached land once more, a carriage awaited them. It took them away. Further still.

For weeks, they traveled. It may have been months or years, for all Guinevere knew. Guinevere cared nothing for time. Her depression had fallen over her like a tomb.

Finally, they reached another shore. It was obscured by a fog. Another small boat awaited them.

At last, Guinevere broke her silence. "Where are you taking me?" she asked the nun.

"To an island off the coast of the West Pyrenees Mountains," the nun answered her.

"France," Guinevere sighed. Where Lancelot is from.

"You shall join my sisters and I there at the convent."

Guinevere just nodded, despondent. After all I've done, becoming a nun is just what I deserve. A penance for all I've cost Arthur, and his Kingdom.

It took a few months for Guinevere to settle into her new life. Of course, when Arthur had sent her away to save my life, he had no idea that was with child. Even she herself hadn't known.

The nuns were kind to Guinevere as she grew large with child. They could have been cruel, and they chose to be supportive. She was loved by the sisters. And she loved them too.

Many would find this hard to believe, after her sordid affair with Lancelot that cost Arthur the Kingdom, but she fit right in at the monastery.

Though there was no science to prove each child belonged to another father, she knew it was true in her heart. And just as she had loved both their fathers, she loved both her children, twins, a daughter and son.

Arthur's daughter, she named Ariana after him/ And for her son, whose father she believed to be Lancelot, she named Vance, for Lancelot, the Valiant.

Much time passed. She never stopped loving and missing both Arthur and Lancelot. News of King Arthur's death and the fall of Camelot took years to reach them at the monastery.

She stayed in the convent high in the remote mountains of the West Pyrenees in France, raising twins with the nuns.

Then one day, decades later, she felt compelled to go. Her children had grown up and left the monastery They spread the seeds of both men upon the earth, and the earth will likely be a better place for it.

Arianna and Vance... for her love of Arthur and Lancelot.

~ ~ ~

Find him...

Find him...

Lancelot lived in my dreams that haunted my soul. At last, I felt compelled to find him, if he even still lived.

I had suffered greatly for the loss of my beloved husband, my King, and the fall of Camelot. Nearly two decades had passed, and I felt I had done my penance. Maybe there was hope for a bit of happiness for me, after all.

I don't know how I found him. Some magic of Vivienne or Merlin, perhaps, sent me a bit of magic in the afterlife.

I found him living near remote lake in France; most did not know of. I knew of it, because once he told me where he'd come from.

To his own lost Kingdom, he had returned.

I found the ruins of a castle. Some parts of it still held the relics of its once proud beauty. I knew he was there before I saw him. I sensed his energy, his soul. I sensed that he still loved me and was alone.

Now that I was there, I felt suddenly overcome with nervousness to knock his door. Then I saw him leave his home. I watched and followed him from a distance.

He wandered into the woods. He walked for a while until he sat at the edge of the lake that had once brought him to Camelot. The lake where his mother, Vivienne, had rescued him as an orphan, so similar to how Merlin had taught Arthur, who had never met his real parents.

Lancelot sat there in silence. He'd brought a journal, and was writing in it.

Poetry, I guessed. He'd written me such beautiful poetry when we were together. He wrote me romantic verse for years before we consummated our passion in the physical.

I watched him for a while–overcome by the same feelings I'd had for him when I was young. Though he'd aged, by the same token, he looked the same. His spirit was the same, only tempered by wisdom, and regret.

His hair fell across his face as it once did, in the way that had melted my heart so long ago. I didn't know what to do, or how to handle the situation.

Then he looked up.

He looked right at me.

And truly it felt as if not a single day had passed.

He stood up, not noticing or caring that his discarded notebook fell into the autumn leaves.

In a few mere strides he was before me. Without words, he swept up in his arms.

"Guinevere," he whispered. "Guinevere... I never thought I'd see you again."

He bent his face down and kissed me, and it was as if we had never been apart. As if all the world was now righted, or at least, our piece in it.

"I've missed you so much," I told him.

"As have I," he murmured. "I've never stopped loving you."

"Nor I," I agreed. And it was if our youth was restored as our old love took flame once more.

Somehow, it was even better than before. Because so many years had gone by without any touch at all, when we made love, it was filled with that yearning, and aching, that fulfilled as we came together, so that as we become One, we brought heaven down to earth, or perhaps our souls with elevated up to heaven.

"Marry me," Lancelot passionately beseeched me, holding me in his arms in his bed the first night we were back together. He stroked my hair, clung to my naked body as he had so long ago... when our restless souls could only find rest being with each other.

"Become MY Queen... the Queen of this lost Kingdom in France, and let me be your King, the King of that was lost. Restore my heart, and make it whole, by being mine for the rest of our lives."

I drew closer to him and kissed him. That was all the answer he needed.

As the days passed, I told him about his son, and Arthur's daughter, twins with the seeds of two different men in my womb. I sent for them, and he met them. They accepted him as their father. He accepted both of them as his own.

I'd married Arthur in the winter. It was a Christmas wedding the whole Kingdom celebrated and was a part of.

Lancelot and I married in the spring, so that I would always be his bride. It was a small ceremony, just us and our children. And after so many years of isolation, I finally found love, family, and happiness again.

Making love to Lancelot after all these years, felt as if not a single day had passed. All the years of loneliness and regret felt like a distant memory every time he touched me.

There was an electrical current between us. A magnetic pull drew us into each other. It was just like before. Seeing him, it was impossible not to be with him.

We made love like we once had, like starving teenagers who hadn't eaten in days. We made love all day and all night, taking cat naps in between lovemaking.

Our bodies felt as strong and desirous as they had once been. It was as if our youth was restored a little more every time that we made love. It was as if not a day had passed since we'd been together.

But in reality, a lifetime had passed. And we both realized how fortunate we were to have found our way to one another once more.

God bless whatever magic lead us back to one another, believing I had paid my penance.

There were many who had wanted Lancelot and I to be beheaded, or at the very least, imprisoned for the length of our lives for our act of treason. It is very hard on the souls when love is an act of treason. And I believed in my heart, we had suffered enough.

I felt in my heart, that Lancelot and I being together was something Arthur would have wanted, and blessed. I believe he was watching over us like a guardian angel. And the last years of my life, were the best years of my life. Even better than as the Queen during the Age of Camelot...

END OF THE AGE OF CAMELOT

Epilogue

Long after Camelot had fallen, Vivienne returned to the lake. The world had changed. It always did. But the water remained.

She stood at its edge, looking out across its endless surface. "They remember him," she said.

"They always will," came the distant reply.

She nodded. Beneath the water, something stirred–something ancient, something waiting.

A sword.

Not lost. Not forgotten.

Waiting.

"For the next one?" the voice asked.

Vivienne's gaze lingered on the horizon.

"Perhaps," she said. "Or perhaps the world will not be ready again for a very long time."

She stepped into the lake, dissolving into its depths. And the surface closed behind her–smooth, silent, and full of secrets.

The Lady of the Lake did not rule Kingdoms. She shaped them. Quietly. Inevitably. Like water itself. A force of patience and persistence that shaped mountains, and boulders, and altered the shapes of countries and continents... throughout time.

~ ~ ~

King Arthur line's continued through the ages, as well as Guinevere's line with Sir Lancelot.

The wind moved softly through the ruins of a once beautiful castle. Where once banners had snapped proudly above white stone towers, there were now only broken arches and creeping ivy.

The great hall of Camelot stood open to the sky, its roof long since fallen, its round stone table dusty and gray with age. Time had not destroyed it in anger, but in quiet patience—like a tide that never ceased.

A lone figure walked among the remains. She moved slowly, as though each step carried memory with it. Her long cloak brushed the grass that had grown where knights once stood in shining armor.

She paused at the place where the Round Table had been, her fingers hovering over the worn stone as if she could still feel the echo of voices—laughter, oaths, the clash of ideals too bright for the world that held them.

"They believed it would last forever," she said softly. No one answered. Only the wind, threading through broken columns.

In the distance, the lake shimmered—unchanged, eternal. It reflected the sky just as it had in those golden years, when hope seemed not only possible, but certain.

She turned toward it.

"They were wrong," she continued, though there was no bitterness in her voice. "But they were not fools."

A raven called from somewhere among the ruins. Black, with red on its tail.

Camelot had not fallen in a single moment. It had unraveled—thread by thread. Love twisted into betrayal. Loyalty tested beyond its limits. The weight of human hearts proved heavier than any crown. And yet, for a time... for a brilliant, fleeting time... it had worked.

Knights had ridden not for glory, but for justice.

A King had tried to be more than a ruler—had tried to be worthy of his crown, a servant to his people.

For a while, the dream had lived.

She reached the edge of the lake and looked down into its still surface. For a moment, it seemed as though the past stirred there—faint shapes, like reflections of another world layered beneath this one.

A golden hall. A circle of sworn brothers. A King with tired eyes and an unyielding will.

Gone.

But not erased.

"They will tell our stories," she said quietly. "They already do. What once was fact shall become legend."

Stories of valor. Of tragedy. Of love that should never have been and loyalty that could not be broken. The truth would blur, as it always did, shaped by the people telling their tales. Some would call it myth. Others, a lesson.

She knelt and touched the water. "It was real," she whispered.

The lake rippled outward, carrying her words into its silent depth. Behind her, the ruins of Camelot stood not as a monument to failure, but as a testament to something rarer—the attempt. Imperfect, fragile, doomed perhaps from the start... but no less extraordinary for it.

The wind shifted.

For a fleeting instant, it almost sounded like distant voices—like echoes of knights calling to one another, of a

King giving quiet command, of a court alive with purpose.

Then it was gone.

The woman rose. The woman who had caused its fall by her use, or rather, misuse of magic. And at last, she understood what her mother had been trying to teach her all along.

If only she had listened—perhaps she could have used her magic to make the way smoother for the glorious age of Camelot.

Without looking back, she stepped into the mist that had begun to gather at the water's edge. It curled around her, soft and pale, until she was no longer visible—only the lake remained, and the ruins, and the quiet.

Camelot was gone.

But the idea of it—of what it had tried to be—lingered still, carried forward in memory, in story, in the stubborn hope that somewhere, someday, such a place might rise again. And for as long as that hope endured, Camelot lived on.

About the Author

Crystal Wolfe attended college at Purdue University. Wolfe has been published in newspapers across the country and is an award-winning writer.

Wolfe has put her time and resources into serving the homeless by founding her own nonprofit, The Solution to Hunger, Inc., to feed the homeless and families in need with the food excess from catering companies, schools, and restaurants—serving millions of meals and raising hundreds of thousands of toiletries and clothing for the poor. Her goal is to serve billions of meals across the nation, and perhaps one day, around the world. A portion of all book proceeds goes towards this mission.

You can keep up-to-date with Crystal Wolfe's nonprofit work serving the homeless, or purchase her novels, by checking out her website:

www.thesolutiontohunger.org

If you enjoyed reading *Age of Camelot: The Legend Comes to Life*, please kindly consider taking a few minutes to write a positive review for this novel on Amazon and/or Goodreads!

Other Novels by Crystal Wolfe

Devotional: *You Shall Know Them by Their Fruit: A 365 Daily Devotional for Cultivating the Fruits and Gifts of the Holy Trinity*

Poetry: *The Resurrected Dream: A Book of Poetry & Prose from an Awakened Soul*

Non-Fiction: *Our Invisible Neighbors: Accounts, Causes, & Solutions to the Epidemic of Homelessness*

Positive Thinking: *The 9 Principles of Positivity*

Children's Book: *Different*

Children's Book: *With Teddy Forever*

Fantasy/Sci-Fi: The Creation Series–

Volume One: *Where the Shadows Meet the Light*
Volume Two: *Within the Genesis of Time*
Volume Three: *While the Ashes Rise to Life*
Volume Four: *When the Lines of Lilith Unite*

Fantasy Romance Spin-Off of The Creation Series: *Age of Camelot: The Legend Comes to Life*

The Jimmy Hardwin Mystery Series—

Volume One: *Killer of the Voiceless*
Volume Two: *Murder of the Jewel of NYC*

www.ingramcontent.com/pod-product-compliance
Lightning Source LLC
LaVergne TN
LVHW091028080826
845145LV00002B/391

* 9 7 8 1 9 5 4 2 5 8 1 3 6 *